Tale of Rouen

Caterina Novelliere

Caterina Novelliere & Connections Across Time, LLC

www.caterinanovelliere.com

Book Layout © 2017 BookDesignTemplates.com
Cover Design: Bespokebookcovers.com

Tale of Rouen/ Caterina Novelliere. -- 1st ed.
ISBN 978-1732332737

Author's Note:

I would like to thank the Williamsburg Writers Group, the Silver Quill Writers Group, Kasey Steffek, Adam Haviaras, and Glenn DesOrmeaux for helping me to bring this work to fruition. I would also like to extend a thank you to Peter with BespokeBookCovers for another beautiful cover.

I want to remind folks that while you encounter historical figures, events, laws, and policies in this book, I am presenting them in a fictionalized portrayal or manner that works for my novel's storyline. That means I may have deviated from actual history or rendered a potential characterization based off historical sources I've read. Please do not use my book as a source for historical debates unless you have verified the information via primary source or other academic sources. I will be blogging about some of the events, policies, and people as a resource for readers to learn the accurate information about them.

Lastly, as a writer and historian, I feel it is important to give attribution to those whose works we build upon or that become popular sayings. In the first line of my book description, there is a popular misquote derived from George Santayana's "those who do not remember the past are condemned to repeat it." I chose to use the misquotation with the inaccuracies in brackets as it more powerfully delivers the emotional hook I wanted, and I could not find who started the misquotation in that form to give them credit as well. Unfortunately, foot notes don't go well in fictional works nor is it usually good practice to attribute an inaccurate quote to an author, but this one is well-known enough I felt it warranted I do so. I normally slide citation and attribution into dialogue or narrative on the very rare occasion I use someone else's words in a fiction work, but that won't work in the case of a book description. While the theme of "history repeating itself" is all too common, I couldn't in good conscience not give an authorly nod to Santayana.

Thank you for purchasing my book and I hope you enjoy it!

"From the example of the past, the man of the present acts prudently so as not to imperil the future."

–TIZIANO "TITIAN" VECELLI

The bus wound its way through the twisting and curving roads leading into Urbino. Its engine would rotate between a steady hum to noisily decelerating as it came around one curve then growling loudly as the bus climbed upward, navigating hillside roads. Recognizing the complementary mix of beige and maple-brown brick buildings topped with tiles ranging from russet to bronze, a sense of returning home and a promise of discovery roused a tired Jillian. After departing from Rome four hours earlier, she finally reached the city that would become her foreign refuge for the next couple of months. She had indulged in an hour-long nap, but did not allow herself any longer than that to minimize the drowsy plague of jetlag that always hit after a time change. There was no way she'd waste a minute of the limited time she had in Italy lounging in bed.

Time in Urbino helped Jillian find her calling in life as a researcher and historian when she studied at the local university as a graduate student several years ago. She hoped the magical, small town could help her find her way again.

Off the beaten tourist path, Urbino is a place where past and present converge in a fairy-tale like environment.

Jillian loved that tourism had yet to overwhelm the community. The *citta* maintains its historical roots as a haven for learning and the arts. Italian, French, and other foreign tongues frequently fill the air, forcing one to learn Italian if they wished to shop or eat out. Language is just one of the many ways life in Urbino sharply contrasted against the English-speaking tourism hubs of Florence and Rome. Weekend markets and seasonal festivals promised artisan goods and culinary delights paired with live music or theatre productions, immersing one fully into rural Italian life.

Jillian's suitcase clamored behind her, making a loud rumbling sound; the rubber and plastic wheels clashing against the gray cobblestones, alerting the inhabitants of the surrounding earthen-toned buildings of another outsider's arrival. She crossed under the large red bricked arch of the Porta Santa Lucia, strolled down the hill to Piazza Republica, the main town square, then up a long and gently sloping hill to her apartment rental on Via Saffi.

She stopped in front of two large, dark wood doors framed by ornately carved stone and rang the buzzer.

A few minutes later an Italian gentleman with black hair and equally dark eyes greeted her with a warm smile.

"Jillian, it is nice to finally meet you in person." He gave her a hug and a friendly air kiss on either cheek. They had exchanged emails for the past couple of months in preparation for Jillian's stay.

"Piacere mio, Mirko." Jillian politely expressed it was a pleasure to meet him as well. The warmth and hospitality always displayed by those she met in Urbino brought on a nostalgic sense of welcome missing in modern metropolises.

With a smile, Mirko took her bag, then led her up a set of stairs to the apartment. He gave her a brief tour and turned on the heat, so the place could warm up. While he tended to the thermostat, Jillian looked upward to admire the faded frescoed living room ceiling featuring red, green, and blue scroll work, flowers of some type, and a cherub in each corner. She had forgotten how lovely and ornate Italian ceilings could be.

The combination of medieval, Renaissance, and modern construction captured her attention as she followed Mirko through the cozy rental.

"And this is the bedroom." Mirko pushed open a white and gold painted door that almost served as a portal to stepping back in time.

In contrast to the colorful living room ceiling, her bedroom ceiling was a mix of white and wide, dark timber beams further sharing the building's age. A large hooded and stone fireplace projected from the wall separating the sleeping quarters from the kitchen. The queen-size bed sat towards the middle of the room with a desk across from it. A recently updated bathroom just off the bedroom featured an almost out-of-place shower, sink, toilet, and towel warmer.

Two large windows covered with white sheers allowed sunlight to enter the room. Mirko showed her how to operate the mechanical shade that clamored down to cover the window at night or anytime she needed privacy.

"I trust everything is satisfactory for you."

Jillian couldn't believe Mirko even asked. The apartment was more enchanting in real life than she imagined it to be after seeing the pictures of it online.

"It's perfect, Mirko."

"Good to hear." Mirko gestured towards the door.

The two walked together to the dining room table.

"If you would be kind enough to sign the paper copy of the lease for me, the keys are yours." Mirko handed Jillian a pen then opened a manilla folder holding the rental contract.

Jillian signed her name where he pointed and excitedly took the set of keys he handed her.

"Again, my cell phone number is in your renter's packet if you need anything. Enjoy your time in Urbino, Jillian." He hugged her once more then left her to unpack.

***

After putting her clothes and toiletries away, Jillian sighed, sitting down on the bed in the chilly apartment.

What should I do next?

It would take a couple of hours before the place fully warmed up. She could go out and get groceries to stock the fridge or wander the shops that would open once more for the afternoon in another hour. Grocery shopping didn't really appeal to her at the moment.

She walked to the living room and stared out a window at the countryside just beyond the walled historic center. Rolling green hills that transformed into blue-hued mountains surrounded the city. White snow crowned their distant peaks. The apartment offered spectacular views, but even they didn't stop the pang of loss tugging at Jillian's subconscious.

Nathan. The frown on her face deepened thinking of her now ex-husband. *Ten years down the drain. Ten long years putting her career on hold to support his.*

They drifted apart long before he handed her divorce papers on that sweltering summer afternoon. Texas heat oppressed worse than that of the summer she spent as a child in the deserts of Tunisia. In some ways, she felt she owed Nathan a thank you for finally getting her out of the state she never really adopted as home and for ending a marriage that deteriorated into friends living as roommates. They both deserved more, but neither could quite let go of what once was.

Stop thinking of what is over and start figuring out what new journey is beginning! That's why I came here. She scolded herself then chuckled. *That and my budget stretches further in Marche than other areas of Italy. Now, how to begin this new journey of single womanhood in the place that brought my younger self a sense of vision?*

Deciding *aperitivo*, Italian style happy hour, at her favorite cafe in Piazza Republica would be a pleasant way to end a long day, Jillian pulled her jacket back on and headed to the town center.

Finding an outdoor table near a gas heater strategically placed to prevent the evening chill from being too overbearing, Jillian set her bag down; enjoying the buzz of those passing by or gathering in the piazza's cafes at the end of day. A friendly server brought her a glass of Rosso Conero along with a few goodies to munch on. She watched locals and students alike in the square as the sun descended in the winter sky.

Across the piazza, a gentleman dressed in Renaissance clothing stood under an arched arcade, taking in the same scene she did. Individuals passed without giving him a second glance, almost as if it were perfectly normal for someone to be hanging out in period costume. He and Jillian's eyes briefly met before he turned and walked down the side street towards the old watchtower overlooking the Borgo Mercatale. Today, the Mercatale consisted of a few small businesses and a large parking lot that visitors and residents utilized due to the traffic restrictions placed on the historic town center.

Knowing she could get some breathtaking views of the setting sun from the city walls, Jillian wandered down the same street the Renaissance man had after she finished her wine.

Mother nature didn't disappoint. The sky changed to a spectacular display of color. Breaking her promise to herself to simply enjoy moments like these, she pulled the lens cap off her camera. She captured images of the flame-orange and red sky gingerly kissing snowcapped mountains fading from green and brown to purple and blue as darkness blanketed the landscape.

After the sun disappeared, Jillian turned to take pictures of the illuminated trademark dual towers of the palace behind her. The same man from the piazza stood on a white balcony staring out into the night. Jillian smiled, thinking he added some character to the renowned structure. Costumed guides or reenactors rarely graced the halls of the palace. She couldn't recall seeing anyone in costume during her previous visits to Urbino. The seasonal celebrations for the holidays had already passed. Summer would bring the next occasion where costumed revealers danced and paraded through cobblestone alleyways.

Shick! The shutter snapped, capturing a frame of the building and man. The sound of the shutter engaging again echoed in the night air.

Jillian zoomed in a little closer to better catch the reenactor and changed the setting on the camera to slightly blur the palace behind him.

A bright burst of light illuminated the dim corner, drawing the man's gaze in her direction.

The flash going off startled Jillian almost as much as it did her subject. *There was enough light for the nighttime setting. Flash wasn't needed. It shouldn't have gone off.*

Curiosity gave way to annoyance on the man's face. The stern look he gave her couldn't be missed from three stories below in the streetlight. He moved from the balcony railing, disappearing into the castle.

Jillian heard the warning chirp that the camera batteries died. With the man gone, she looked back down at her camera.

"Those were new batteries." She wondered if the camera turned on during her flight or the bus ride for them to drain so quickly.

No more pics for tonight.

Jillian went back to her apartment, swapped out the dead batteries for new ones, and loaded the pictures from the day onto her laptop. She edited her favorite of the sunset images to share on social media with family and friends. Satisfied with her edits and caption, she posted it online, then sorted through the photographs she had taken of the palace.

She thought her eyes deceived her as she stared at the first picture. No one stood on the white balcony.

She quickly pulled up the second shot. As with the first, the balcony appeared empty. Though there was a blurred outline and a visible shadow where he should have been.

What in the world was wrong with her camera? Maybe something got into the lens? That happened to her once before, but even that wouldn't erase a person or object within a photograph.

As the third picture opened, the gentleman stared at her from the 15" screen with eyes that were a shade of light gray or pale blue. She cleaned up the image to get a better look at him.

He certainly is a handsome figure.

Jillian scrolled back through her pictures, trying to figure out what happened for her camera to glitch when taking the two earlier shots. She copied the third image onto a thumb drive to print out at the camera shop down the street.

The next morning Jillian visited the ducal palace to see if she could learn more about the man from the night before. The cashier chuckled at her inquiry about any special tours or events after she claimed to have seen a Renaissance gentleman. He advised that there were no special events scheduled or folks dressed as a person from the Renaissance as far as he knew. She showed him the photograph of the costumed man. He shook his head no and restated his earlier answers.

Frustrated, Jillian bought an admission to the palace. Since she was there, she might as well explore it. She hadn't seen the works of art gracing the palace walls or marveled at the duke's private chapel in several years. This would also be the first opportunity to walk around the building on her own. All of her prior trips to the palace had been as a student. Each of those visits consisted of a themed tour and class work analyzing the architecture or a painting versus just enjoying the site and the artwork it housed at her leisure.

Coming out of the museum shop, Jillian saw her Renaissance man standing in the courtyard. He leaned against one of the white marble pillars, watching a tour group stop before the main staircase leading up into the sweeping galleries and halls. The re-enactor could have stepped out of a fresco or one of the paintings hung on the palace walls.

Was he real or a shadowy glimpse of the building's famous past?

Jillian walked towards him. He straightened, moving off the column. Those light eyes of his held hers. Realization that she sought him out caused the originally relaxed features of his face to tense.

Jillian stopped a few feet before him. She wasn't sure how to greet the gentleman. *You are in Italy, Jilli. Try your rusty Italian.*

"Boungiorno."

He didn't return the good morning. He merely stared back at her with a disturbed expression. His black leather boots seemed glued to the red and tan tiles beneath them. She noted the refinement of his costume. Someone had taken a great deal of time to align the brown and black velvet and leather in the jacket and doublet the man wore. The matching cloak hanging from his shoulders was fur trimmed. A gold collar festooned with topaz and onyx draped across his chest, indicating the man was a noble of the period. Long black leather gloves covered his hands. On his head sat a black velvet cap with matching ostrich plumes held in place by a jeweled hatpin. By his dark brows and sideburns, Jillian knew she'd discover brown hair hidden under the hat. His hand settled on the ornate hilt of the rapier hanging from his waist.

The light gray eyes resting on her only added to the haunting countenance of the man before her. *Where did such pale eyes come from in this part of Italy?*

The man's jaw ticked as he swallowed.

Not intimidated by his defensive posturing, Jillian took another step closer. She noted the medallion hanging from a gold chain around his neck. The distinctively shaped flower appearing in the collar surprised her.

"You are an English ambassador?"

Maybe he couldn't understand her.

"Parli englese, signore?"

The man continued to silently stare at her.

Jillian shrugged. "Maybe you are a figment of my imagination."

After another second of awkward quiet, Jillian turned to walk away.

He hurriedly stepped in front of her. Blocking her way so that she couldn't leave. "How did you know I am from England? Can you actually see me?"

The intense blend of suspicion and surprise on his face made Jillian let out a nervous laugh. "Well, you are a little hard to miss dressed like that."

His brows rose at her statement. "Is there something wrong with my attire?"

This guy is really into his role. Jillian kind of admired his dedication to whatever historical figure he portrayed.

Deciding to play along, she relaxed and smiled. "Oh, not at all, my good sir. The ensemble suits you. As to how I knew you are English, the Tudor rose in your collar is a dead giveaway to your identity."

It had been almost a century since anyone noticed his presence. No one ever walked up to him the way this woman had. "My god! You can see me!"

"We already established that. I can hear you very well too, just in case you are wondering if I am deaf." Jillian noted the grin that appeared before his formal and composed demeanor returned. "Are you giving tours or something?"

"What? Why would you think such a thing?"

Jillian gestured to his clothing. "It would explain the outfit and you wandering around town last night."

"I am not a tour guide."

"An actor promoting a play or film then?" Jillian had seen the community theater group promote upcoming productions or lectures.

He shook his head as if annoyed by her statement. "No, I am not an actor. I am... I am a merchant. I am here negotiating trade agreements with the duke."

"The duke?"

"Yes." He reaffirmed his earlier statement.

"Which duke would that be?" Jillian tried not to laugh.

The man seemed irritated again. "Is there more than one living Duke of Urbino?"

"There hasn't been a Duke of Urbino for almost five hundred years. Have fun playing merchant." Jillian headed for the steps leading into the main hall.

Why do I always manage to attract the crazy ones?

She heard the sound of his footsteps behind her on the marble treads.

"Wait! Please, wait!"

Jillian glared at him from halfway up the staircase. "Stop following me! *Lascia me* (leave me alone)."

"I do not mean you any harm, signora. I only wish to speak with you another moment." The Englishman wasn't going to just walk away now that he knew she could reach out to him when no one else could. "Please, what year is it?"

"Will you go away if I answer your question?"

"If that is what you truly wish me to do." He agreed, not wanting to further scare the woman. He would be feeling the same anxiety if their roles were reversed.

"It is 2018." She waited for another crazy question to come out of his mouth.

"2018? Have five hundred years truly passed since I last..."

Jillian ran up the rest of the steps, not waiting to hear the last of his inquiry. She glanced over her shoulder, hurrying through the first few rooms; wanting to place some distance between herself and the strange man. She stopped to admire a painting before moving into the rooftop gardens.

The cool late-morning breeze against her skin made her laugh and shake her head.

Thank god! He didn't follow me. What was his deal with asking about the year?

Sitting down, she pulled the picture of him on the balcony from her purse. He seemed as real as she was in the photograph. How could the gift shop worker not know about a costumed interpreter on site? He was definitely there.

Maybe he's a ghost. She joked with herself. *That can't be the answer either. It wasn't possible to capture such a lifelike picture of a ghost. At least I don't think it is.*

Jillian tucked the picture back into her bag, voicing the only reasonable conclusion she could arrive at if no one else could see the guy. "I've finally snapped after everything. That must be it. I am having a breakdown or midlife crisis. I am seeing and talking to people who don't exist."

"You have not 'snapped,' whatever that may reference. I exist. No one else can see me or speak with me. You are the only person I have encountered in almost a century that senses I am here, and the only one I am able to converse with in five hundred years. I was hoping only a century or two had passed since the witch revived the curse." The Englishman sat beside her, empathizing with how the situation confused her.

"Witches and curses? I've been reading too many paranormal romance novels at night." Jillian reached out to touch the man. Her hand went right through him, sending a jolt of fear from her head to her toes. "You're telling the truth!"

"Why would I lie about such a matter?"

Giving in to the urge to run back inside and find a docent, Jillian's upper body instinctively twisted towards the door.

The ghost changed the side of her he sat on. "Please, do

not leave! There is no need to be frightened. As I stated earlier, I mean you no harm. I only wished to speak with another person again." He reached to set his hand on her knee. She shivered when his hand came in contact with her before passing through her lower thigh and the bench. Disappointed by what just occurred, he shook his head. "No comfort at all from another living being."

"What?" The word popped out of Jillian's mouth before she could stop it. The utter dejection in the man's voice resonated within her subconscious, quieting her instinct to flee, and drawing out her inquisitive side.

"The curse. The witch damned me to never find comfort or compassion again from another living being for a thousand years. My punishment for protecting the weak and not taking up arms against my king."

"How can you end up cursed for doing something noble like protecting the weak? Curses are used to punish wrong doings."

He let out a bitter laugh. "One would think that is how they work. From the witch's point of view, I betrayed the family bloodline and wronged her. I would do the same again if the situation repeated itself."

"Betrayed the family bloodline? What were you? The heir to the throne and you did not feel like challenging the Tudors for your birthright?"

The idea of ancient men and curses intrigued Jillian. *Maybe the superstitions of the age leading to the passing of multiple heresy acts had some actual grounding in fact? Wouldn't that be the historical find of the century!*

"I would rather not say, my lady. As I told you, I am a merchant, not a noble."

The two stared at one another, silent once more.

Even though Jillian's heart finally stopped thumping, the whole scenario unnerved her. She wasn't up to coping with being the sole companion of a man from five centuries earlier, no matter how interesting his claim sounded.

"I'm going back inside. Where there are other people around. No offense."

"None taken. I understand this is overwhelming for you." The stoic expression returned to his face.

The man never spoke another word as he walked behind her.

Jillian did her best to ignore him. She stopped before a large painting on temporary exhibit.

The ghost frowned, staring at the gothic painting featuring the Archangels Michael and Gabriel. *Why did this one capture the woman's attention?* He almost asked her, but decided not to with how she turned her head in the opposite direction anytime he stepped into her peripheral vision.

Having nothing else to do over the centuries, he spent endless hours admiring the art around the city. There wasn't a brush stroke or single crack in the aged plaster walls of the palace or town that he didn't know. As he appreciated and analyzed each carefully created fresco, portrait, and sculpture, he had prayed for the Lord to send him someone who he could speak with or to end his curse. It appeared God heard his pleas and sent the woman.

Jillian leaned slightly towards him, drawing his attention away from the painting.

"Well, Mr. Ghost, Sir Cursed, or whatever your name is, it's been fascinating meeting you, but I... um... have an appointment I need to keep."

"I see. Will you return here anytime soon?"

"Maybe. If you are lucky." Jillian planned on bringing holy water and a crucifix to keep her new acquaintance away the next time she decided to tour the ducal palace.

The ghost watched the woman disappear into the crowded street before returning to his usual spot in the duke's study.

CHAPTER TWO

Jillian sat at her kitchen table trying to write. Her mind kept wandering back to the English ghost. *Had he even been real?* She frowned, looking at her watch. *It's only 7:30!* Winter days in Italy were short. The sun disappeared from the horizon before five.

She reviewed the opening of her article draft.

Urbino, a forgotten cultural icon, sits preserved in the hilltops of Marche. This small university town was the birthplace of Raffaello Sanzo, the inspiration for the *La Citta Ideale,* the Ideal City, and home to one of the most unique palaces constructed in Europe.

Federico Montefeltro, a powerful mercenary and duke, turned this small mountain top *commune* into one of the most prosperous commercial and creative hubs of the Italian Renaissance. Montefeltro put Urbino on the historical map through his sponsorship of the Arts, his creation of a renowned library that attracted scholars from across Europe, and his founding of an early academic institution, the College dei Dottore. As Montefeltro's wealth grew, so did Urbino. The duke commissioned new churches and buildings, then expanded the original footprint of the tall, brick walls to protect his thriving city.

Once one of the grandest courts with a sphere of influence from England to Persia, the town dissolved from historic memory and political fame. The Church took over management of the province, sending the area into an unrecoverable state of economic decline. Sadly, this once magnificent city featured in Castiglione's *Book of the Courtier* is now only a place few readily know.

Writer's block and indecision set in as Jillian debated what point she wanted to discuss next. Her mind drifted back to the man in the palace for the hundredth time that day.

Was he real? Of course, he's real. You photographed and talked to him; he's just cursed so no one else can see him.

Jillian laughed at her thoughts. "Did I really just justify my own delusions? Not that talking to myself is any better."

She picked up the photograph lying next to her laptop to stare at him once again. As much as she hated to admit it, there was only one way to solve this dilemma interfering with her writing.

Closing her laptop, she decided to walk over to the palace. As she laced up her hiking boots, Jillian tried to talk herself into staying in her nice, warm apartment. Too bad Sir Cursed and she hadn't met years ago. She would have made one of her classmates come with her. Unfortunately, this time around she was alone in Urbino.

The palace closed at five. You should go back in the morning. Do you really want to go ghost hunting at night in a town centuries older than the US?

Jillian ignored the fear within and zipped up her jacket. The lock on the apartment door seemed louder, almost ominous as the bolt slid into place.

You are just being paranoid! Jillian refused to let herself overdramatize the situation.

Oddly, no one walked this end of the city. Via Saffi transitioned into the Piazza Rinascimento as she strolled the center of the empty gray cobblestone street. Darkened university buildings built during the Middle Ages and Renaissance lined the road on either side of her.

Nearing the palace and duomo, Jillian could make out the silhouettes of the three statues on the bright white face of the city's basilica. Dim lamps under the church's arcade cast a yellow glow over the square and ducal palace entrance. The soft light paired with the dark, silent street could almost fool one into believing they stepped back in time.

As expected, the brown doors leading into the palace were closed, forming a large wooden wall; forbidding any entrance as they once did long ago to late comers that may stand outside the duke's door.

Now, what? Should I knock and see if he comes out?

She shoved her hands in her pockets as a gust of winter wind made its way up the hill. The cold gale danced and churned between the three walls trapping it within the bricked courtyard.

"You should not be unescorted at this hour, signora. The roads and countryside of Italy can be very dangerous at night when one does not know them." A baritone voice tinged with a light English accent chided.

Booted footsteps approached from her right. As the footsteps came closer, the outline of the ghost became more visible. Only when he stopped beside her did he appear entirely human like herself. A long black fur jacket with a brown collar and decorative trim covered the clothing he wore earlier.

"I know the streets of Urbino well. This isn't my first time in the city. If I recall correctly, no major crimes have been reported here for the last five hundred years or so. I also didn't know who to ask to get an 'escort' as you put it. People would think I was crazy if I randomly walked up to them and asked, 'Hey! Do you mind walking back to the palazzo with me as I want to see if there really is a ghost haunting the place?'" Jillian still doubted her vision as he listened to her with a quizzical look on his face.

"I understand your dilemma. You would be burned at the stake for speaking such heresy in my day. It appears I am luckier than I initially believed. I did not think you would return considering how quickly you departed this afternoon. I must admit, I am relieved and pleased that you sought me out."

Wow, he is tall! She hadn't noticed how she had to look up at him earlier. She guessed he stood over six feet. She wouldn't want to run into him in a dark alley in the six-teenth century.

"Do you have a name or do I just call you ghost?" Jillian tried to make the man smile versus having such a serious expression on his face.

"Rouen. My name is Rouen."

"French, with an English accent?"

"No, madam. I am English. The name is of Norman origin. It is a family name." He corrected her initial as-sumption.

"Norman? Then you are descended from one of William the Conqueror's men?"

"You know your history well, my lady." He curtly com-plimented her.

Jillian sensed heredity and genealogy were not the ghost's favorite topics.

Rouen noticed how the winter night air tinged her cheeks red. Her breath formed small clouds whenever she spoke. The periodic moving of her feet and shifting of her shoulders shared she tried to stay warm in the almost freezing temps. Unlike her, he no longer felt much of anything physically or emotionally between the curse and the isolation he lived in.

"With the chill in the air, you must be cold. It is not much warmer inside, but you will be out of the wind. I can open the door for you." Rouen politely offered, not wanting the woman to be uncomfortable.

"While I appreciate the offer, I don't think that is a good idea. The last thing I need is to try to explain to the police why I am standing in the duke's home after hours. I thought I saw you outside in Piazza Republica. Can you wander?"

By the way his brow slightly raised, she startled him with sharing that she saw him before he noticed her taking his picture.

"I can walk the city."

"Good. Let's go back to my apartment, and you can fill me in on how you ended up like this."

"I hardly think that is an appropriate invitation. Perhaps there is another establishment we can meet in?" Rouen objected to spending time alone with her in her quarters.

"A gentleman and a ghost?" Jillian earned another one of those stern, reprimanding looks that routinely covered his face. "Isn't an invite back to a lady's chambers what all men want at night?"

Unable to resist the lady's sense of humor, for the first time in centuries, Rouen genuinely grinned and chuckled.

"Ah! He does laugh and smile. I was beginning to think you weren't allowed to have any fun in the afterlife." Jillian delighted in the fact that the man had a personality hiding underneath his formal and somber exterior.

Rouen shook his head. "I have had little to laugh or

smile about in centuries."

"We need to fix that, Rouen. Life is too short not to en-joy. Or I guess in your case, half a millennium is too long to spend being miserable. The invite back to my place is total-ly appropriate this day and age. Not everyone retires to a private residence for an evening's pleasure in the twenty-first century. Besides, if you misbehave, I will pull out my crucifix then exorcise your butt out the door."

Rouen gave into the foreign urge to jest with her. "I can assure you, madam, there will be no cause given for you to do so. I am more concerned about my reputation and standing with the way you modern women behave."

"Ouch! I give you my word that I won't get too out of line. Regretfully, I cannot promise to be on my best behav-ior. I think we have two very different definitions of what that would be. Now, kindly escort me back to my residence, my chivalrous specter."

Instinctively, Rouen placed one hand on the woman's back and gestured with the other for her to lead the way. The palm he rested on the small of her back went through the jacket and into the winter air. Jillian did not seem to notice what occurred. He resisted the urge to offer his arm, knowing she could not take it.

Neither spoke, not wanting the three people they passed to question Jillian's sanity.

Reaching her apartment, Jillian unlocked her door and stepped inside. "Home sweet home. Come on in, Rouen."

Rouen looked around the front room while Jillian hung up her jacket.

"Simple lodgings for modern day."

Jillian laughed. "Yes, it is. My apartment back home is much larger. Though none of the ceilings are frescoed. At least it's warm in here."

She noted how curious he was. His pale eyes studied everything around him.

"Can I get you something to drink?" Jillian politely offered, not sure if he could even eat or drink.

"No, thank you." Rouen inclined his head towards her before noticing the two books sitting on the table.

Jillian walked over to the kettle sitting on the kitchen counter. Finding that it was still warm from her earlier use of it, she made a cup of hot tea for herself. "Care to share any more about this curse of yours?"

"Not particularly." He picked up the copy of *The Memoirs of the Dukes of Urbino* she had left out.

Jillian noted the title of the book he flipped through. "Do you like history, Rouen?"

"I am very fond of our past and origins. Many prominent historians have written about Classical Culture."

Jillian grinned. "Classical Culture? I enjoy Thucydides and Cassius Dio a great deal myself." That got the man's attention.

"You have read *The Peloponnesian Wars*?" He had never met a woman who had before tonight.

"I have. I am a big fan of Pericles and Nicias. I've also read Homer, Herodotus, and many others. I've even read Petrarch." She threw out a few more names of individuals that men of the Renaissance studied as she sat down on the couch.

"All great men and writers." Rouen cautiously sat beside her, almost as if he tested the couch cushions. Whatever troubled the ghost seemed to have vanished when he made eye contact with her once more. "I like Boccaccio and Dante myself. My tutor and mother read them to me."

"They were read to you? Can you not read?" She knew it wasn't unusual for the lower and middle classes of the period not to be able to read. However, with the way Rouen carried himself, she figured he was a learned man.

Rouen shook his head no. "Not very well. I can read some, Lady... I do not know your name."

"I am sorry, Rouen. I didn't realize I hadn't introduced myself. I'm Jillian, Jillian Mon... Fitzalan."

Rouen heard how she hesitated speaking her surname. "Lady Mon Fitzalan?"

"Just Fitzalan. Call me Jillian. It sounds strange to hear someone address me as Lady Fitzalan."

"As you wish, Jillian." Rouen smiled, enjoying being able to call her by her first name rather than addressing her formally.

"I bought a copy of Boccaccio's *De Cameron* to read this trip. It's been on the reading list forever. I haven't read much of Dante either. Tell me what you like about them." Jillian took a sip of the warm tea.

Literature and history provided a safe foundation to build some trust upon. An hour later, the two spoke as if they were old friends instead of strangers separated by centuries.

"Where in England are you from?" Jillian changed subjects wanting to know more about the man.

"Stafford. However, I have briefly lived in Hastings and London. I have also spent some time in Calais and Avignon. My father and the men in my family traveled between England and the Continent. I have even been to Turkey and Egypt."

"I take it you are a seafaring merchant of some type with all the traveling you do. Trading along the old Silk

Road?" Jillian brought a grin to his face.

"The Silk Road? If you mean trading in silks and spices from China, I do trade with the East at times. My family engages in sea commerce and exploration. I travel as needed and for pleasure."

They started as someone knocked on her door.

"Excuse me just a minute." Jillian wondered who it could be. Maybe Mirko?

She opened the door to reveal a short, smiling, gray-haired Italian woman.

"My husband and I did not see you at Basilli tonight. We wanted to make sure you had eaten and were settling in. Mirko told us about an American, which we figured out was you, temporarily being our neighbor."

"Oh. I am settling in just fine and ate an early dinner. It's nice to meet you, Signora?" Jillian waited for her to give her name.

"Corsi. Antonella Corsi. Please call me Antonella. Signora Corsi sounds so formal."

"Antonella it is. I hate to cut our conversation short, but I am getting ready to get on a conference call for work."

"Non preoccuparti. I do not want to hold you up from your call. My husband's name is Luigi. Should you need anything, please just knock on our door. Apartment 301."

"Grazie, Antonella. Buona serata."

Rouen chuckled. "They will know your routine within a week. There is no better look out than an Italian nonna."

Double checking that the door was shut and locked, Jillian laughed. "The downside to being a stranger in a small town. The same thing happens in a rural enough area in the US. Truthfully, the fact that your neighbors care about you is one of the things I love about Urbino."

A little bit hungry, she grabbed a small plate and pulled a mandarin from a bowl on the table. Rejoining Rouen on the couch, she offered him a piece of the fruit she just peeled.

Rouen politely held his hand up, signaling her to pull back the plate she held out. "I would love to indulge in an orange, but regretfully, I cannot partake."

"I am sorry. I'll finish this later." Jillian set her snack on the coffee table.

"If you are hungry, please eat, Jillian." Rouen assured her he didn't mind if she enjoyed the sweet little orange. "Mandarins used to be one of my favorite fruits whenever I found myself on the warm coasts of the Mediterranean. We would bring crates of them shipboard to take back to England."

"It still amazes me how far food travels. We are spoiled in modern times with being able to find many fruits year-round at grocery stores. Out of curiosity, how did you learn English, Rouen?"

"English is my native tongue." Rouen's brows came together. He didn't understand why she posed the question.

She realized she would have to more thoughtfully phrase her questions when engaging the ghost. "My apologies for not being clear, I meant more modern English than what you probably spoke in the sixteenth century."

"Ah, yes, that makes much more sense. I model my speech based on my observations of the English and American students I overhear. I assumed we could communicate more effectively with that style of speaking. Am I not using the words correctly or is my diction poorly?"

"I didn't mean to make you self-conscious." Jillian smiled at how Rouen thoughtfully changed his natural manner of speaking to better accommodate her. "You speak very well and your diction is perfect. I appreciate you using the more modern form of English as I left my Shakespearian dictionary at home. I'd have trouble understanding you."

"Shakespeare does not write his first play until I am well into in my eighties." Rouen's lips twitched, hinting that he stifled a chuckle. "I believe you would need a Middle English dictionary instead."

Jillian laughed at the wink Rouen gave her after speaking so matter-of-factly. "I guess I need to study up on linguistical history and my sixteenth-century writers."

Rouen stayed about another half hour. He decided it was time to depart when he noticed Jillian trying to hide a yawn.

Jillian walked him over to the door as she would any other guest.

"Thank you for the lively discussion and pleasant evening, Lady Fitzalan."

"I enjoyed it, Rouen. I guess we'll see each other around town." Jillian wasn't sure what to say to him.

"Hopefully. I look forward to our paths crossing again. Until then, good night, Jillian."

"Good ni..."

Rouen passing through the door halted the words coming out of Jillian's mouth.

Witnessing him do that freaked her out. She hoped he was as friendly and harmless as he seemed.

CHAPTER THREE

The next two days passed with no sign of Rouen. Jillian wondered what happened to him. Maybe he was one of those chance encounters meant for only a day that life periodically presents.

Seeing the normally closed doorway of one of the local churches open, she peeked inside it. Floor to ceiling vibrantly painted scenes filled her line of vision as she scanned the interior. To her delight, a sign set in the doorway welcomed visitors to explore the chapel.

Urbino had more churches within its walls than any American town she could think of that was equivalent in size.

The rich colors in near perfect condition drew her further into the church. Even with studying history all of these years, places like this never ceased to amaze her. A talented artist created the images well over six hundred years ago, yet the hues looked as if someone applied them just that morning. She slowly walked halfway down the wall then stopped to enjoy the more intricate details the artist incorporated in the scenes they painted.

"Beautiful piece, isn't it? I prefer the chapels in the Palazzo Ducale myself, but San Giovanni is still amazing." A male voice tinged with a British accent drew her out of her thoughts.

Jillian smiled as she saw who the voice belonged to. "I was beginning to think I had dreamt speaking with you the other night."

"Are you implying you missed my company, Jillian?" Rouen flashed her a playful grin.

She enjoyed the teasing in his tone. "Maybe just a little bit. Un po, signore. Nothing more."

"No appointments or plans for today?"

"None. Care to go adventuring around Urbino with me or do you have other plans?"

"What other plans do you think I would have?"

"I don't know what ghosts do in their free time. Maybe playing pranks on people visiting the palace or terrifying kids and old ladies." Jillian laughed at the cynical expression that splayed itself across his face.

"I terrify children and old ladies late at night. I am free at the moment. How do you propose we spend the afternoon together in the open without folks thinking you suffer from bouts of insanity talking to yourself?" Rouen dryly returned the jest.

"Viva la technologia! People will think I am on the phone." Jillian put her wireless headphones in her ears before heading towards the door.

Rouen enjoyed strolling the city streets with her. The two walked up Via Raffaello to the fort on the far side of the city. He watched Jillian snap pictures from the hilltop.

"This is such an amazing view! I can only imagine what it must have been like to ride into Urbino during the sixteenth century. Was it as awe-inspiring as it is today?" Jillian lowered her camera and looked over at the ghost patiently waiting for her to take her hundredth photo of the day.

"The town and palace were marvels in my time as well. They were a welcome sight after a long ride from Rome." Rouen thought back to the first time the walled city and towers of the palace appeared on the horizon as he rode towards the city with the guide he hired. While he preferred his home in England, he always enjoyed visiting the Italian countryside.

"It must have been difficult to watch the city decline."

A loud hmmm was the only response he offered to her inquiry. Rouen seemed transfixed as mist drifted down from the mountains to the hilltops of Urbino.

Did his eyes see something hers couldn't at that moment?

The midmorning mist reminded Jillian of billowy waves of white silk rolling across the lower portion of the city. They stood together watching a blend of white and gray blanket the town and palace below them, briefly hiding the structures from view, and then revealing them once more as the fog slowly dissipated. It was such a bizarre phenomenon to observe on a perfectly sunny day. She remembered eating a picnic lunch up at the park with two of her classmates one crisp, fall afternoon and observing the same type of occurrence. The three of them thought it was weird, but enjoyed watching the earthbound white streams of cloud nonetheless.

The moment made her mind drift over what she learned about the rise and fall of Urbino. Nature seemed to beautifully retell how seats of power cycle over the course of time; reconnecting her to her days as a graduate student studying history and cultural heritage.

Had Rouen observed her and her classmates at the park, stopping for an afternoon coffee at Mama's in the Borgo Mercatale, or laughing over a glass of wine at Basilli in the evenings? Why could she see him now and not back then? It seemed so strange that he was there all along, but they just met this trip.

For whatever reason, her thoughts caused a flashback to reading about how Della Rovere moved the Duchy Court to Pesaro in the 1520s. Wrapped up in the strange magic Urbino always created for her, she had forgotten that fact until just now. It didn't make sense that Rouen would meet with the duke here.

"Speaking of Urbino's decline, why did you and Della Rovere meet at the Urbino palace, instead of in Pesaro?"

Rouen turned his head in her direction as she drew him out of his thoughts. His half grin and raised brow conveyed that her inquiry impressed him. "Urbino offered a more private location to meet. Francesco still had duties to attend to here."

"I've always wanted to see the Villa Imperiale in Pesaro, but it was always closed to the public when I studied here. The pictures I've seen of the frescoes are incredible."

"Dissi and Genga's work is stunning to stand before."

Jillian laughed. "I am envious of you, Rouen. The wondrous things you have seen that I can only dream of ever viewing. To be able to walk in your shoes for just a day."

"There is nothing about my life to envy. I can assure you incurring the wrath of a witch is not something you ever wish to experience."

Jillian couldn't understand why anyone would curse a merchant, who more than likely kept to himself most of the time based on her interactions with him. "The whole curse thing still baffles me. You seem like such a nice guy. How did you end up like this?"

"It was a complicated situation."

"I can only imagine what events could lead to a witch cursing a man to live as a shade for a thousand years."

A bewildering upwelling of frustration and anger erupted within Rouen. He could not ever share what led to his current state. *The consequences of doing so…* He shuddered thinking of the potentially disastrous outcome should he utter even a hint of what sealed his fate. *I will remain damned before allowing someone else to ever experience even the smallest inkling of my sentence.*

Rouen scowled, finally meeting Jillian's gaze. Curious hazel eyes reminded him of the humanity stolen from him, along with the warmth and kindness one person could extend to another in times of need. The innocence and patience intermingled in her expression halted the harsh words he almost spoke. *Jillian was not his tormentor. The woman was only being inquisitive. She did not deserve his animosity.*

"Whatever you may imagine, I promise you, it is nowhere close to factual events. I can tell no one the truth of my circumstances, Jillian. No matter how much I may want too."

"Rouen, I didn't mean to upset you. I only want to understand…"

"There is nothing for you to understand. This curse is mine alone to bear. I will not see another harmed by my deeds."

"Harmed by your deeds? There is nothing anyone could do that deserves what you endure." Jillian wished the ghost would share more.

"You breach the boundaries of friendly discourse, Lady Fitzalan. Abandon this topic, or I will be forced to end our acquaintance."

"I only want to help you, Rouen. Maybe there is something I can do or something that I can find that will allow you to live a normal life once more." Jillian hoped her words would reach through the wall the man built around himself.

"Good day, Jillian."

Rouen vanished from the hilltop.

Had she really just offended a specter? His story didn't make any sense at all. How did one anger a witch by protecting the weak and their king?

Rouen seemed so quiet and reserved. She couldn't picture him inciting any sort of violence against anyone. A merchant wouldn't have a duty to take up arms like the nobility or knighted gentry of the period. She briefly thought about the rapier hanging from his side. Many sixteenth-century gentlemen carried them for self-defense and as a status symbol. With as polished as the hilt was, she doubted he regularly wielded the weapon in duels or battles.

***

Jillian put her camera away and walked down the hill back into town. She stopped at a bakery to buy some fresh bread, then in the regional wine and food shop to buy cacciotta cheese and salami to go with the bread and salad she planned for her lunch. After dropping the groceries off at her apartment, Jillian wandered over to the duomo, hoping to see Rouen. If he was there, he did not reveal his presence.

"Rouen. Please come back." Jillian whispered, sitting in a pew near the rear of the church.

"He likes the side chapel." A little boy joined her in the pew.

Jillian started, wondering if she heard the four or five-year-old, who climbed up to sit beside her, correctly. "What?"

"I've seen him too. He sits in the chapel with the sacrament."

The boy's mother called him back over to her.

Jillian walked to the side chapel on her left. Rouen didn't appear to be there. After sitting alone for about ten minutes, Jillian admired the paintings on the wall along with the gilded gold decorations on the ceiling.

Still no Rouen. Giving up on finding him, she walked outside to the main square.

* * *

A small festival featuring local artisans and goods brought the historic center to life. Jillian stopped before a gentleman selling flowers.

Roses in the middle of winter?

She bought a single white one with a gold ribbon tied around its stem.

When she passed a stationery shop, the shop owner greeted her from the doorway with a smile. Jillian browsed the paper and card lined shelves. She purchased a small image of the ducal palace drawn onto parchment paper then scribbled: *'I am sorry. I only wanted to help.'* on the back. Remembering that Rouen couldn't read at more than an elementary level, Jillian kept the apology simple. If a modern-day kindergartner could read her words, a sixteenth-century merchant should be able to figure them out.

Smiling as she slipped it in its accompanying envelope, she headed back to the church.

A few tourists explored the main chapel, but the side chapel Rouen seemed to enjoy remained empty. Jillian set the rose and card on the altar where she figured Rouen would most likely find it. If he didn't, one of the priests would eventually discard the flower and note.

CHAPTER FOUR

Rouen kept to the shadows, observing Jillian. He crossed the chapel, curious to see what she left behind. He recognized his name on the envelop lying next to the white flower. Puzzled, he pulled the card from the envelope. The eight words written in purple brought a scowl to his face.

"Why make the one person who can see me a woman asking endless questions about the past? Do you so enjoy tormenting me?" Rouen muttered under his breath, feeling as if fate enjoyed testing him with difficult circumstances.

"Have you an admirer, Rouen?" A smiling Eleonora Gonzaga, the Duchess of Urbino, approached him. She wore the same black velvet and gold decorated gown Titian immortalized her in. Her auburn hair concealed under a jeweled cap as the conservative standards of dress dictated for a married woman.

"My lady." Rouen quickly bowed, surprised the Duchess joined him. He had encountered her spirit a handful of times prior to today. *What brought her to the chapel at that moment?*

She extended her hand for the card Rouen held. Rouen placed it in her palm.

One of her dark brows raised as she read the English writing. "*I am sorry. I only wanted to help.* Interesting words. Whatever offense the woman caused you, she seems repentant for it. She prayed for you earlier. Two visits to a chapel in one afternoon, trying to amend a wrong. Perhaps, you should forgive her."

"There is nothing to forgive, Duchess. The woman has done no wrong. I merely wish to protect her from the curse."

Rouen reclaimed the card after Eleonora offered it back to him.

She smiled, staring at the rose in his hand. "Allora, she is the first living human to speak with you in five centuries. Mayhap, she does not need protecting. The curse does not seem to affect her. Do you truly wish to spend the next five hundred years alone when you are offered a temporary reprieve?"

Eleonora vanished as quickly as she appeared.

Rouen looked up from the rose in his hand to Barocci's vision of the Last Supper. The angels in the painting held his attention. While he may not live righteously all the time, he held great faith. Perhaps heaven sought to reward him for staying the course all of these years.

***

Finding Rouen standing behind her in her kitchen, Jillian almost dropped her glass of tea.

"You scared the crap out of me!" Jillian took a deep breath to calm her racing heart. She quickly put the ceramic mug down with how her hands still shook.

"I did not mean to frighten you."

"I know you didn't. What brings you back out of hiding, Rouen?"

Rouen laid the rose and note on the table beside Jillian's mug.

"I... I have not had a friend in a long time. I should not have reacted the way I did to your inquiry. Your intentions behind the question are innocent. I fear, if I answer it, some ill will may befall you. Or selfishly, I fear losing the rare gift of company fate suddenly blesses me with."

"Apology accepted. I won't ask again. You can decide if and when you will tell me what happened. I wouldn't want to lose this bizarre friendship either."

Rouen appreciated the woman's understanding. He noted the open book on the table along with the pen and paper. "What are you reading?"

"Francesco's memoirs. I am also translating some of the letters published in the appendix that the author refer-ences, but doesn't translate for the reader."

Her answer mystified Rouen. "Why would the duke's correspondence interest a modern woman?"

"I was hoping they might provide some insight into you. In case the note and rose didn't work."

"May I suggest leaving a red rose next time? The House of Tudor rules England, and I would not want to explain to Henry why I carry a white rose as a favor from a woman I met in Italy."

Jillian couldn't stifle the laugh his remark brought out.

Rouen enjoyed the sound of her laughter. It brought a smile to his own lips anytime he heard it.

Jillian picked up her mug, still giggling. "Henry is too busy dealing with establishing a new church and which woman to wed next to notice a merchant in his court wearing the wrong color rose."

"You would be surprised by what things draw the king's attention, even if other matters preoccupy him."

"Sounds as if you know the king well."

"I am fortunate to be in the king's good graces. He has called on my family a few times to assist with procuring various materials or items for the royal household." Rouen flipped through the pages of the book. He stopped on a page containing a black and white print of Titian's *Duchess of Urbino*. "Lady Eleonora. What does the text say about her?"

Jillian turned the book in her direction. "It describes her wedding day and the week that followed. She is a pretty woman."

"Yes. She is also very wise considering her age." Rouen settled his hand on top of Jillian's. *How he wished he could hold her fingers.* "You two would make good company for one another with your interests."

"An old soul in a young body?"

"Very much so." Rouen once again found himself intrigued by hazel eyes.

"Are there any other ghosts walking around the palace and duomo? Or is it just you and Eleanora?"

"Only myself and Eleanora as far as I am aware. It is possible that other spirits inhabit the town, and I have not made their acquaintance."

Jillian found it odd that Rouen couldn't interact with any other ghosts rumored to haunt Urbino. "How is it Eleanora can see you, but you can't communicate with other ghosts?"

"Are there that many specters present in Urbino?" Rouen wondered who else Jillian might have seen.

"None that I can confirm besides Eleanora and yourself, but there are plenty of tales about ghosts throughout Urbino. Quit avoiding my question, Rouen. Why can the duchess visit with you?"

"I... I am not certain. I believe..." Rouen stopped himself from sharing his theory on why he and the duchess could engage with one another.

Jillian heard the hesitation in his tone and noticed how the ghost fidgeted again. "You can trust me, Rouen."

Rouen glanced at her apartment door.

Jillian knew by Rouen's expression the ghost debated bolting out of the apartment. "Please don't disappear on me again. I won't ask any further questions about Eleanora."

"Do you truly wish me to stay?" Rouen struggled with the idea of anyone enjoying his company. Those sensitive to him in the past ran from whatever room they felt his presence in. After almost five hundred years of that reaction and living a mostly solitary existence, he found interacting with another person challenging. Needing to balance guarding his words with his desire for companionship made him morose company at best.

"Yes." Jillian smiled up at the ghost working through whatever emotions churned inside his head.

Rouen noticed the jeweled band on her ring finger. "Did your husband not accompany you to Urbino?"

His inquiry caught Jillian by surprise. "I don't have a husband, Rouen."

"But you wear a ring on the same hand a wife does?"

Jillian exhaled loudly, staring down at the channel set emerald and diamond ring she wore. "This isn't a wedding band. I bought for myself as I thought it was pretty. In modern day, women, single or married, wear rings on any hand they choose."

"I sense there is more to your marital status than you are disclosing."

"When you decide to trust me with your story, I will trust you with the more personal portions of mine." Jillian didn't mean to snap at Rouen, but the ghost pricked a sensitive nerve.

Rouen sat down in the chair beside Jillian. He noted the way her eyes closed as she turned the band on her left hand. "You are right, Jillian. It is impolite of me to make inquiries of you without being willing to share the details of my situation. My sincerest apologies for making inappropriate queries of a personal nature."

"It's okay, Rouen. I guess I now understand how you feel when I ask you about the curse." Jillian shook her head, wondering how long it would smart anytime anyone asked her if she was married.

Rouen debated what was worse, the tense silence they sat in or the wounded expression on the woman's face. Whatever secret she harbored couldn't be half as destructive as Giselle's curse. He briefly pondered Eleonora's remark about the curse not affecting Jillian. "I suppose... I suppose no harm could befall a modern woman if I disclose the events that led to my current state."

Jillian waited to see if he would say more.

Rouen heavily exhaled; a trouble expression darkened his features. "Do not say I did not warn you, if what I share causes you further distress, Jillian. A witch named Giselle cursed me after I refused to destroy a neighboring town and to assassinate the noble ruling it. The noble committed no wrong and his people, his people loved him. I could not harm any of them. The first cycle of this curse alienated me from my family. The second cycle began when Giselle and I encountered one another in the duke's court. Imagine her surprise to find the merchant who disobeyed her earlier wishes, in Urbino, as a guest of the duke and emissary of the king. Henry sent me here to ensure trade continued between Della Rovere and Henry after Francesco's nomination as a Knight of the Garter failed to muster enough votes. Henry's decision to leave the Church and a general feeling of unease towards our Italian friends caused his nomination to fail.

"Giselle threatened Eleonora's life if I refused her wishes a second time. To protect Eleanora, I attempted to murder the witch. My assault failed. Her black magic healed her, and in retaliation, she added a thousand years of invisibly inhabiting Urbino with no comfort or compassion from another living being. Eleonora entered the courtyard as Giselle and my's encounter ended. I faded from almost all human sight as the duchess walked towards me. Eleonora called for the guards and bishop to capture the witch, but Giselle fled. Since that day, I have lived as an apparition in the shadows. I believe Eleanora can interact with me as she witnessed everything that occurred. Her presence in the courtyard excluded her from the conditions of the curse."

"Wow." Jillian struggled to frame a response to what he shared. *Logically, nothing he said made any sense; yet, he sat before her as evidence that he told the truth.* "Why you, Rouen? Why ask a merchant to do such an awful thing? This Giselle could have approached a political rival or mercenary to do her bidding."

"The noble held me in high esteem. I could enter his residence without causing alarm. I also had the financial resources to hire the necessary mercenaries to decimate the town. My conscience would never allow me to do such a thing."

"Did she offer you anything in return for killing him?"

"His title and lands." Rouen glowered, vividly recalling the conversation, or rather argument, between Giselle and himself.

"I hope the nobleman appreciated your friendship. Land and titles would be enough for many others to do exactly what this Giselle wanted."

"I will never know if the duke appreciated my fidelity."

The title caught Jillian's attention. "The duke? Did she order you to assassinate Francesco?"

"No, the duke Giselle wanted me to kill is an English noble." Rouen expected Jillian to send him away now that she knew the truth. To desert him as everyone else had in the past. Even Eleonora ignored him until she died, the situation frightened the Duchess so badly.

Instead, Jillian sadly smiled at him. "You certainly have some bad luck to run into Giselle in two countries. Is there a way to break this curse of yours?"

Rouen shook his head. "No. It must run its course."

How tragic. Jillian kept her thoughts to herself.

Hoping to lighten the heaviness that hung over the two of them, she thought about what activities they could easily do together without drawing unwanted attention. Looking over at the black screen across the room, the perfect solution hit her. "Do you like movies, Rouen?"

"Movies? I am not sure what you reference." The change in subjects puzzled Rouen.

"Stories told through actors, but watched on television or a big screen. They are like plays, but not live. I was going to watch a film called *Kingdom of Heaven* before you showed up. It's about the Crusades. Some of it is accurate, other parts are fictionalized. I think you would enjoy it if you would like to stay and watch it with me."

"It would be an honor to see this Crusader movie with you." Rouen's mood seemed to brighten some with the invitation.

He followed her to the living room then observed her sliding a round disc into a box attached to the big square like thing the Italians referred to as a television. While he had noticed humans watching films before, he never really watched one himself before this evening.

Part way through the film, Jillian looked over at the man sitting beside her. He seemed mesmerized by the movie. His facial expressions and shifting at different points shared his reaction to each character and issue the film attempted to address. When the movie ended, he stared thoughtfully at the words rolling upwards on the screen.

"So, what do you think about your first official movie?" Jillian half wondered if Rouen was in some weird state of shock with how he started to open his mouth then closed it.

"The story it told was intriguing," Rouen's expression grew serious. "However, the battle scenes are not true to form. A siege like the one depicted would be much more brutal, with graver injuries."

"And how would a merchant know that?"

"Merchants frequently find themselves caught in the crossfire, particularly when they are at sea or delivering goods. It is not a pleasant experience. Why does the past interest you so much, Jillian?"

"I am a historian at heart, Rouen. Humanity's journey intrigues me, and I think those of us in the modern world benefit a great deal by studying our past. Understanding other cultures and times helps us better relate to one another and enjoy the world in which we live."

"Both those statements are debatable, and with all of the comforts the modern world offers an individual, you are much better off living in the present." Rouen stood. "As it once again grows late, I believe it best I take my leave. Other than our earlier disagreements, it was pleasurable spending the day with you, Jillian."

"I enjoyed today as well. Have a good night." Jillian smiled at how he politely bowed his head to her.

"Jillian?" Rouen halted, reaching the door.

She wondered what stopped his exit. "Yes?"

"May I continue to call on you? I have missed being able to speak with someone else a great deal."

Jillian couldn't imagine the hell it must be to live in complete isolation; to be an invisible element in a world full of life.

"Come by anytime you like. Just no creepy stuff or watching me in the shower."

Rouen chuckled. "I can happily honor those terms. Good night."

Jillian shook her head at how he effortlessly passed through the wooden door a second time. There is no way she would ever get used to seeing the man who seemed more human than spirit walk through walls.

CHAPTER FIVE

Over the next two weeks, Jillian got used to Rouen's random appearances around town. He still maintained a polite emotional distance from her whenever they spoke. With such polished manners and a dignified air to him, he had to be more than a merchant.

She went to the archives to see if she could learn anything about him. Unsurprisingly, her search turned up nothing. Maybe she was looking at the wrong sources.

Seeing the Director of the Archives returned from his morning meeting, Jillian knocked on the door and introduced herself.

"Hi, my name is Jillian Fitzalan. I am researching visitors and artisans to the Della Rovere Court." Jillian used English knowing the Director spoke it. He had taken her class on a tour of the archives years ago.

"Francesco Gracchi. How may I be of assistance to you, Miss Fitzalan?"

"I am trying to locate one particular visitor. A merchant who came to Urbino around 1535."

"Commercial contacts weren't consistently tracked, unless supplies were purchased specifically for the ducal household. You most likely won't find anything if the merchant didn't provide goods to the Della Roveres."

"This merchant wasn't here to provide supplies to the duke. He was enlisting the duke's aid with brokering a trade agreement between Urbino and the Tudor Court."

The Archival Director cocked his head, giving her a skeptical look. "That kind of negotiating couldn't have occurred. On the off chance it did, a merchant wouldn't be the one representing England's interest to the duke."

"Why couldn't it have?" Jillian initially thought similarly herself, but Rouen's existence said otherwise.

"The Dukes of Urbino were fiercely loyal to the Pope, Miss Fitzalan. Della Rovere would never have engaged in unsanctioned trade agreements with Henry. The relationship between the Tudors and Della Roveres soured shortly before that time."

"No disrespect intended, Signore Gracchi, I am not certain that is an accurate depiction of the diplomacy or commerce between both courts. Della Rovere was a candidate for the Knights of the Garter. There were Italian diplomats at the Tudor Court, even with Henry's excommunication. Goods from Italy made their way to England and vice versa. Is there any place other than the database that I could look to try and track down my merchant?"

"I am sorry, Miss Fitzalan, but if the merchant you seek is not in the database, then your search is at an end. Only those with credentials and a letter of introduction confirming legitimate research projects are permitted to search the original ducal records."

Knowing she didn't have either at the moment, Jillian

thanked him for his time.

Frustrated, she walked back to her apartment empty handed. It was almost as if Rouen never existed. Maybe her suspicions about Rouen's social status were wrong. Certainly, a visiting English noble would be logged in the palace records somewhere, especially if trade agreements between the two states were being negotiated.

***

Rouen looked over Jillian's shoulder as she sat at the dining room table reworking the rough draft of her article. While he didn't entirely grasp her love of writing, he respected her discipline to practice her craft and how excited she became about whatever new thing she discovered. Her intelligence and ability to understand the politics and laws of the Renaissance and Antiquity never failed to impress him. He had not met many women with her education in his day.

She read what she had written aloud to see if it made sense.

"I am missing something. I know I am. What is it?" She reopened one of her books and read the two pages she flagged over again.

"Are you talking to yourself or to me?" Rouen made her laugh as she continued skimming the pages before her.

"In most people's eyes, talking to you is just like talking to myself. No doubt my neighbors think I am a loon when they walk by the door at night. This phrase isn't Italian, it's Latin! That's why this isn't making sense. I need to retranslate it." Jillian reached for her iPad to pull up her translator app.

"You do not need that device." Rouen read the passage aloud in perfect Latin, then translated it to English for her, forgetting he played illiterate with her just a few weeks before.

"You are so busted! You can read more than you claim to. And you read Latin at that." Jillian knew that literacy and knowledge of Latin was limited even in the aristocracy of the period.

Rouen realized his error in translating the passage. Unable to deny his actions, he decided to be honest with her. "Yes, I can."

"Why did you lie to me, Rouen? I hate to be lied to."

"I apologize, Jillian. I never meant to deceive you. I, I do not know why I was not honest with you."

"Anything else I should know about you, Rouen? Can you write as well?" Jillian wondered why the ghost hid his literacy. *Was there a stigma in his day with education for him to act as he did?*

"Yes. My father felt it was important that I read, write, and speak French and Latin in addition to English." Rouen further surprised Jillian.

"You are not just any old merchant to have that type of education." Now, Jillian really doubted the ghost's initial claim of what he did for a living.

"One needs to be educated to transact trade agreements and contracts or he finds himself at the mercy of potentially dishonest men." Rouen downplayed what he told her.

"So your family wanted to protect profits and your father invested in your education. How many languages do you speak again?" Jillian knew better.

"Four fluently."

"How about just conversationally?" Jillian dug a little deeper.

"Three others."

"Three others? Is Greek or Arabic one of those three?"

He raised a brow, suspicious of her question. "I speak a minor amount of both those languages."

"Hmm. Have you ever read Plato?"

"I have. I do not care a great deal for Plato." Rouen wondered what caused the onslaught of questions.

"Was England using cannons in your day?" Jillian went back to her book.

"How did we move from philosophy and language to cannons? Yes. We fortified castles, manor houses, and our towns with cannons, among other things."

"Did you attend Oxford or Cambridge?" Jillian looked up from her book to watch the ghost's reaction. He frowned and his brow creased. Rouen really hated when she inquired about his past.

"Well, Rouen, which is it? I know you have a college education with what we just discussed." Jillian sat her book down and patiently waited for an answer.

After a moment of silence, Rouen grudgingly answered her. "Oxford."

"Excellent school."

"Yes." Rouen stared out her living room window, not wanting to converse any further about his education.

Seeing the irritation on Rouen's face, Jillian changed subjects. "Do you have any hobbies?"

"Hobbies?" Rouen relaxed with her no longer inquiring about his past.

Jillian wondered if he wasn't familiar with the word. "Things you like to do in your spare time."

"I know what a hobby is, Jillian. I like to go riding or hunting. I enjoy archery and occasionally, going to the theater."

As long as Jillian kept the conversation centered on his interests and nothing educational or politically related, Rouen remained unperturbed. Jillian found him to be rather charming whenever he spoke about something that meant a lot to him. She was very curious to find out more about the specter who visited her.

***

Drinking her morning coffee and thinking about her and Rouen's discussions the past couple of days, Jillian became even more determined to find a way to end his supposed curse. So far, her efforts to learn more about Rouen or the curse turned up nothing. If internet searches and a trip to the archives proved useless, there had to be someplace else to start gathering the information she needed. Maybe she was looking for the wrong thing.

After writing a list of alternate topics that might lead to Rouen or Renaissance era curses and places to potentially visit, she asked herself how she overcame prior project failures. She laughed, remembering how she would bounce her ideas or problems off a mentor. Who did she still know in Urbino that could assist with a historical research project? Manuela! They met in graduate school. Manuela was now a professor teaching art history at the University of Urbino.

She called Manuela and invited her to lunch. Conveniently, Manuela could meet her at a local restaurant known for its food and lovely frescoes aptly named the Osteria of the Artists today.

***

Once they finished catching up, Jillian posed the question that prompted her to call her old friend. "If you wanted to research a dignitary who visited the duke and duchess in the 1500s, where would you look?"

"The archives then I would speak with the Palazzo Ducale Director." Manuela wondered why Jillian asked that question. As an experienced researcher, she should know exactly where to begin her search.

"I tried that. I couldn't find anything. This particular individual was not of high standing, so I am thinking any information about him may be buried in old *college dei dottore* records or maybe in the histories of Paltroni. I don't have any sort of letter of introduction to support official research. Would you know someone who might be willing to help me gain access to the older archives?"

Manuela took a sip of her wine, contemplating who she knew that could best assist Jillian. "I can introduce you to one of my peers in the History Department. Perhaps Francesca can assist you with a letter of introduction. If that doesn't work, I can try drafting a letter on your behalf. Why are you researching such an obscure person here in Urbino when there are other more well-known individuals that interacted with the dukes?"

"I am thinking about writing a book on this gentleman as there isn't much published on him or his family. I just recently learned he came to Urbino as a trade negotiator on behalf of Henry Tudor." Jillian hated to make up such an answer. But who knows, she might draft an article or manuscript, depending on how much information she could find.

Manuela smiled. "Give me a day or two to arrange for introductions."

***

Three days later, Jillian sat in the archives, wearing gloves and carefully reviewing documents from the

Renaissance, looking for any mention of Rouen. She jotted down notes from what she could translate on her own, and asked the archival assistant, Simonetta, for help with translating sections that were beyond her abilities. The day flew by.

Simonetta opened the door to the private office, startling Jillian. "We are closing up. You can leave everything here as I can lock the office door to secure the documents."

"Thanks, Simonetta. I appreciate all of your help today."

Jillian closed her portfolio, put on her jacket, then headed to her apartment. She didn't find anything exciting, but it felt good to be doing historical research again. Being an analyst and consultant allowed her to keep her research skills up, but online searches and modern-day documents were never as fun to review as historical ones.

***

The scent of something delightful wafted over Jillian as her door swung open.

Dinner awaited her on the small table.

Was she in the wrong apartment?

Rouen noticed Jillian standing in the doorway. "I wondered when you would return."

"You cook?" Jillian closed the door, stunned that Rouen made her dinner.

Rouen pulled out a chair for her. "A man has to eat."

"I thought you didn't eat."

Jillian sat, curious to see what Rouen prepared.

"I do not, but you do. I wanted to do something in exchange for the kindness you show me."

Jillian smiled, a bit hesitant to sample the dish Rouen prepared, but the aroma rising from the bowl in front of her made her stomach growl. She warily picked up the spoon and gave it a try. The passatelli in brodo pleasantly warmed her chilled self. The hints of nutmeg and lemon mixed into the soft finger like noodles made from Parmigiano-Reggiano and bread crumbs enraptured her taste buds, reminding her of the first time she tried this simple, but tasty soup.

"This is delicious. Did you really make this?"

"Yes. And it is just the first course, my lady." Rouen grinned, pleased that she enjoyed his first culinary creation in centuries. "I was beginning to worry you might not return home by your normal dinner time."

"I was in the archives and lost track of time."

Rouen's brow immediately shot up. "The archives?"

"Yes. I have decided to write a book about local traditions and visitors to the courts of the Dukes of Urbino." Jillian ignored the momentary jab of guilt for not telling Rouen the full truth about her latest book project.

"Mayhap, I can assist you with your research."

"We will have to get creative for you to do that. I would love to document your thoughts and observations in the book, but I will need to have some sort of text or letters from the sixteenth century to support them. How do you propose we find those if you haven't written any?"

The widening smile on Rouen's face followed by a mischievous chuckle revealed the ghost knew how to solve that problem. "If one knows where to look for said items, she will have any resource she needs. And if I haven't left behind the items she needs, I can create them to be miraculously discovered."

"How has anything you may have drafted not been discovered over the past five hundred years?" Jillian wondered what Rouen hid away.

"The Lady Leonora and I may have moved certain items from one location to another if anyone stumbled across them or came close to discovering them."

Rouen's comment intrigued Jillian. "What is the Duchess hiding from the world?"

"Nothing for you to concern yourself with, Jillian. I believe you would consider the items boring correspondence about managing her husband's affairs whenever he was away."

Jillian laughed, having never considered some of the dead ends researchers experienced being caused by anything other than lost documents over the passage of time. "The two of you are going to make some researcher or archeologist very excited one day when they discover whatever it is you all keep moving. I can only imagine how many academics and historians you have frustrated over the years."

"They weren't the right parties to surface the information. You, on the other hand, are an excellent storyteller and would do great justice with the information should you choose to publish it. Are you ready for your second course?"

"I believe I am." Jillian wondered what main dish Rouen cooked. She hoped the larger meal would allow her to investigate the statement he made.

Rouen pulled a pan from the oven. Some sort of roast surrounded by potatoes rested in the confines of the dish.

Jillian walked over to get a closer look. "Porchetta e potati (pork roast and potatoes)?"

Rouen sliced open the roast with a grin on his face. "Non è solo porchetta. È conglio in porchetta, signora. (Not just pork roast. It is rabbit in pork roast.) Now, go sit down and I will bring your plate to you. I am taking care of you this evening."

"I won't have to cook for the rest of the week with all the food you've made." Jillian reached for the wine bottle on the counter to refill her glass.

A quick, light tap of a wooden spoon against her fingers thwarted her attempt to obtain the bottle.

"Sit." Rouen scolded the woman ignoring his earlier request.

Jillian pulled her hand back, not quite believing he hit her with the utensil. "Fine, grumpy. You shouldn't hit people by the way. It isn't nice."

"Nor is being disrespectful to someone who is attempting to be benevolent to you."

"Can't argue with that." Jillian made her way back to the table with her empty wine glass.

Rouen brought her plate to her then refilled her glass. He sat down across from her as she ate her second course. With how much he enjoyed her company, he found it odd that some man hadn't claimed her as a wife years ago.

"Why aren't you married, Jillian? Surely a modern man finds you a worthy partner."

For a brief second, a bitter taste filled Jillian's mouth, sharply contrasting with the pleasant flavor of the roasted rosemary potato she just ate. She could understand Rouen's curiosity about why she wasn't married. Being single in your late thirties went against the cultural norms of his day.

"Apparently not. I am divorced. Nathan, my ex-husband, and I drifted apart over the years. Our marriage finally reached a point neither one of us wanted to continue it."

Rouen noted the hurt in her expression. "Your divorce

happened recently."

"Yes. It's why I am in Italy. I need to regroup and find my way again." Jillian sipped her wine, unsure of what else to tell him. She didn't like discussing the divorce with her own family, much less a newly made acquaintance.

"Your ex-husband wounded you with the dissolution of your marriage."

"No, not exactly." Jillian shook her head, making eye contact with Rouen once more. "It's hard to explain. Losing what Nathan and I had years ago along with the failure of a long-term relationship is more what hurts than the divorce itself. In all honesty, we should have divorced well before the ten-year mark as we knew we didn't make one another happy way before that point. I was ready to end things and move on when we finally signed the papers. Neither one of us wanted to continue living as distant roommates. I guess it's a combination of losing the romance we had early on, regretting the time lost to supporting something that we both accepted had failed, and wondering if one is too old to find that kind of passionate love again. This time with the right guy. If the right guy even exists."

"This Nathan, he is a fool to not value a woman such as yourself."

Jillian forced a smile. "Thank you. What about you, Rouen? Are you married?"

"No." Rouen's gaze dropped.

Jillian wondered what caused him to break eye contact with her. Gray eyes seemed stormy when they met hers once more.

"I too am divorced. My wife petitioned the Church for an annulment after three years of marriage since I could not get her with child."

"I am sorry, Rouen. Marriage should be more about love and partnership than kids or giving up one's identity constantly."

Jillian didn't know what else to say. Divorce in the sixteenth century would have been scandalous for someone like Rouen. As a member of the middle-class, he was extremely lucky to have the Church approve his divorce. She found it almost ironic a merchant succeeded in obtaining something that the Pope denied the king Rouen served.

Rouen shrugged. "It is in the past. We must learn to leave our woes behind us and to live in the present."

"You are a wise advisor in addition to a fantastic chef." Jillian enjoyed the way Rouen laughed at her compliment.

***

The next morning Jillian continued scouring the duke and duchess's papers along with the old colleghi records for any hint of Rouen. Disappointed at finding nothing, she skimmed the last two documents in the stack on the table.

How could there be no record of him? Surely, an Italian court loyal to the Pope would want to carefully document any contact with an English representative.

A brief line about an English ambassador sent on behalf of Henry Tudor at the bottom of the next page caught her eye. There was an odd handwritten number beside the sentence.

Jillian carried the document over to Simonetta's desk. "Simonetta, what does this number mean?"

"It references another palace record. I will see if I can find it for you." Simonetta disappeared into the restricted back storage area of the archives while Jillian scribbled down a reminder to ask about any numbers found in the margins of a record. The archivist returned with another book and two loose pieces of paper. "Here you are."

Jillian smiled in disbelief. "A trade agreement. We may have found exactly what I have been searching for!"

Simonetta laughed, sharing in Jillian's excitement that something may have finally surfaced about her research subject. "I hope you have indeed found your English ambassador."

***

Overhearing the two women, Simonetta's boss frowned. He went into his office and picked up the phone.

"There is an American woman here researching English and Italian trade relations. She is particularly interested in an ambassador named Rouen." The Director of the Archives looked out his window to see the smile on Jillian's face growing. "And it appears she found something linking him with Della Rovere."

***

Jillian couldn't stop smiling. It wasn't much of a discovery, but there was Rouen's name and signature on the bottom of a trade agreement next to the Duke of Urbino's, guaranteeing the exchange of wine, grain, and pottery between the Marche region and England. She wished Rouen had neater handwriting, so she could make out his last name. Rouen carried a letter from Henry calling Francesco and Eleonora dear friends to himself and regretting that the duke was not confirmed as a Knight of the Garter.

Jillian asked to take a photograph of the document. Simonetta said she could as long as she didn't use her cell phone's flash.

"Are there any other documents from around this date that mention the ambassador or England?"

"I am not sure. I can pull what we have for you tonight

and have them ready for your review in the morning." Simonetta wrote down the timeframe Jillian needed. "It is amazing how we keep learning more and more about the Della Rovere and Urbino's relationship with Henry Tudor centuries later."

"That is why I love history!" Jillian gathered up her notes, feeling like she finally made some progress in her mission to help Rouen get free of his curse. "See you tomorrow, Simonetta."

CHAPTER SIX

Rouen found himself standing outside Jillian's apartment again. The halls of the building were silent. No light shone from under her door. He knew Jillian would be sound asleep at this hour. The large, empty palace now bothered him. He shouldn't be here, but he longed for someone to be near him. The past month with the woman reminded him of what it was like to live again. He enjoyed their odd conversations; the way she simply accepted him when she could run him off at any time. No one would know he existed if she did.

He decided no harm could come from checking in on her. Rouen stepped through the door, then made his way to her bedside. She slept so peacefully, curled up under the heavy comforter. He stared down at his hands again, struggling with why he was there, why he craved the woman's company as much as he did.

"Rouen." She whispered his name in her sleep.

He looked back over at her. She smiled and laughed to herself. The smile disappeared as she retreated deeper into her dreams.

"Do you dream of me, Jillian?" He wondered what caused her to say his name. "Or perhaps I should inquire, what do you dream about me to smile as you did, maid?"

After another minute or two of watching her, Rouen departed then meandered the streets of the sleeping city.

***

Visiting Jillian for just a few minutes as he took his midnight strolls became a routine practice. A week into his nightly stops, Rouen felt drowsy for the first time that he could recall in years. He let his eyelids close as weariness overtook him.

The sandman worked his magic on the apparition. Rouen drifted off into dreams of home.

Images flashed of him riding across the countryside. They transitioned to him standing on the deck of one of his family's ships. After a day of sailing, he journeyed home. Brian, his steward and a longtime friend, greeted him at the door. A dinner with family and friends awaited him next. He laughed and enjoyed each course brought out to celebrate his return home. Finally, it was time to retire for the evening. He lay in his bed reading a book that reminded him of Jillian. She was the only thing missing from his life. He looked up from his book as she appeared giggling in his doorway. He smiled at the sound of her laughter. As he set down the book, she crossed the room to him. Her lips met his when he pulled her onto the bed. Just as he started to explore the woman in his arms a screeching sound interrupted the dream.

***

Jillian yawned and slapped the snooze button on her alarm clock. She rubbed the sleep from her eyes and debated staying under the covers for a few more minutes.

A shadow in the shape of a man sitting at the small desk at the foot of her bed caused her to quickly sit up and turn on the light.

"Rouen?" She recognized the shadow now that the light was on. He looked as if he had been sleeping in the chair.

"What was that infernal racket?" Rouen fought back a yawn, his eyes adjusting to the light.

"An alarm clock. What are you doing here?"

"I am trying to figure that out myself. I stopped by to see if you were still awake and next thing I know, I am dreaming of home until that damn clock of yours went off." Rouen couldn't believe he had fallen asleep.

"I didn't know ghosts slept."

"Neither did I until just now."

"Are you becoming human again on me, Briton?" Jillian teased.

"You have no idea how much I wish that were true." Rouen joined her on the bed. After the dream he had, he ached to slip under the covers and further tussle the long, coppery-brown hair that was already a mess from her sleeping. He couldn't remember the last time he made love to a woman.

"Only 493 years to go until you are." Jillian made him smile.

"I do not know why I am smiling. That really is not very amusing." Rouen almost groaned at the reminder that he still had half a millennia before he could really enjoy a night with the fairer sex. In times gone by, he would have tasted the lips just a short distance from his. He found himself back in the frustrating early days of the curse where he mourned for the loss of companionship.

Jillian reached for the gold, diamond, and honey topaz

pendant that hung from his neck as he leaned in her direction. The sensation of cold metal against her skin sent a shiver through her. She heard the chain jingle. Startled, Jillian slid her hand behind the large pendant. The jewel rested solidly her palm.

"Rouen, I can hold your crest or whatever this is."

His nerves on edge and his hand trembling, the ghost reached for Jillian. *Was he mortal once again?*

Disappointment filled him as his fingers found nothing when they reached her cheek.

Jillian wasn't sure what words of encouragement or comfort she could offer him after the hope that briefly flickered in his eyes disappeared.

"You will be human again one day. Maybe the medallion is the first step towards that."

"Maybe." He unclasped the chain. *What called the ancient amulet to the woman?*

Jillian admired the gem as Rouen brushed aside the dark locks of her hair that his fingers could not truly feel, and secured the chain around her neck.

He gave the jewel to the new owner it desired. It frustrated him to no end that the stone and metal settled itself against her collarbone as if the necklace belonged in the twenty-first century with her.

"I can't accept this." Jillian started to remove the elaborate gift.

Rouen shook his head. "You can and will, Jillian. It's the least I can offer you for the kindness you've shown me recently."

"You owe me nothing. I have learned a great deal from you since we've met. Your friendship is payment enough. This is way too much, Rouen. A pendant like this must be worth a small fortune."

"It could buy you a castle." Rouen joked, causing her to reach to remove it. "I jest, Jillian. It might get you a manor house or a cottage at most. It looks lovely on you. Keep it and think of the poor soul having to wander Urbino alone for the next 493 years after you leave."

"That is a depressing memory to bring home from Italy. I would much rather remember a grumpy ghost, who was occasionally charming, either at rest or returned to his time instead. Are you certain there isn't a way to break this curse of yours?"

"I am sure there is, but no one has ever shared it with me."

"Really? The witch who gris grised you, didn't share the way to break the curse?"

"Gris grised?" Rouen wasn't familiar with the word.

"It's Cajun for cursed." Jillian smiled, playing with the pendant.

"What is a Cajun?"

Jillian laughed, grabbing her clothes off the dresser. "Never mind. I don't have time to give you a lesson on North American history and ethnicities this morning. Why don't you see if there are any clues out there on how to free your immortal soul from whatever mess it is in?"

"How do you propose I do that, maid? I cannot speak to anyone but you." Rouen followed her to the bathroom.

"You can touch objects. You read Latin and Italian. Maybe you should try visiting a library and reading up on witches. Or go find a gypsy. Aren't they supposed to be all over Italy?" Jillian turned on the shower water, so it could get warm. "Now, if you don't mind, I need some privacy."

She closed the bathroom door then remembered Rouen

could walk through walls. When she cracked the bathroom door open again, he sat at her desk.

"It might be better for you to wait in the living room, in case I need to get something I may have forgotten to bring in here with me. I wouldn't want things to get awkward between us."

"How would they become awkward?" Rouen smirked as he asked the question.

Jillian laughed. "By that grin on your face, I don't need to answer that. We had a deal, ghost. No creepy stuff and no watching me in the shower. Now, kindly wait in the living room and close the bedroom door behind you."

"As you wish." Rouen muttered. "You act like I am not a man of my word."

Jillian resisted the urge to respond to his last remark. She heard the door click shut, confirming he did as requested.

Bored, Rouen flipped through one of her history books. He noticed her iPad laying on the table. Curiosity got the better of him and he went through the photos on it. He stopped scrolling through them after finding pictures of her and who he guessed was her mother in England. He smiled at her standing on one of the walls of the Tower. London in his day was so different from the London in her photos.

Jillian walked out of the bedroom, towel drying her hair. She peered over Rouen's shoulder to see him looking at pictures from her trip to London the previous summer. "Is it possible the solution to your dilemma is in England?"

"Anything is possible. Unfortunately, I cannot leave Urbino." Rouen studied one of the photos. "Where is this?"

Jillian looked at the coat of arms in the photograph.

"Hampton Court, I believe. I don't think it was Windsor."

"I will let you get on with your day, Jillian." Rouen vanished.

Jillian googled the coat of arms and found it associated to the Hurrey family. *What was the connection between Rouen and the Hurreys?*

She made a quick note to lookup the Hurrey family.

Eager to see what new discoveries she would make today, Jillian headed over to the archives.

Simonetta greeted her with a smile and a "Buongiorno."

A few extra-file folders and a new ledger lay on the table Jillian utilized. Wanting to review the trade agreement before delving into anything new, Jillian reached for the folder it was in to find the document missing. In its place was general correspondence between Della Rovere and the Tudor Court.

"Simonetta, did you move the trade agreement to another file?"

"No. It should be in the document folder." Simonetta helped Jillian go through the files on the table, searching for it. Neither woman could find it with the other papers in the file. "Strange. Perhaps Francesco moved it last night. He helped me pull the files for you. I will ask him at lunch."

Jillian frowned, but got to work reviewing the new paperwork Simonetta pulled for her.

No references to Rouen, a trade agreement, or any international affairs between the duke and England.

The letter and trade agreement couldn't just vanish.

Rouen's earlier offer to help with her research sounded in Jillian's head as she stared down at the folder.

Or could they? Had he removed them from the archives now that he knew she researched the Court of Urbino?

CHAPTER SEVEN

Needing to give her eyes a break after a couple hours of reviewing a new set of papers, Jillian ate lunch at her favorite cafe off Piazza Republica. The small, front dining room buzzed with voices as locals and college students stood at the counter drinking coffee. Only two of the other circular tables had people sitting around them.

She stared down at the pictures of the trade agreement and letter on her phone. She would ask Rouen about both documents the next time she saw him.

Rouen's pendant stood out against the gold turtleneck she wore. It caught the eye of one of the visiting faculty checking in on the British students studying there.

"Scusi, signora. La tua collana e molto interessante. Dove l'hai presa?" (Excuse me, ma'am. Your necklace is very interesting. Where did you get it?)

"Mi dispiace, non parlo italiano molto bene. Come sei dice gift?" (I am sorry. I don't speak Italian very well. How do you say gift?) Jillian didn't recall how to say present or gift in Italian.

The gentleman smiled. "Regalo is the word for gift."

"Thank you. My Italian is rusty. I haven't used it in a few years."

"It will come back to you with practice. May I join you? I would really like to know a bit more about your pendant."

"Sure. I am Jillian." She gestured to the man to sit down.

"Kieran Moreland. Nice to meet you, Jillian." He pulled out the chair next to her and sat his satchel down on the table beside her books.

Jillian noted Kieran was definitely British by his accent. She hadn't seen him around town previously. New faces stood out in Urbino. "Are you an Erasmus student here?"

Kieran smiled, surfacing a pair of dimples and some of the most perfectly white teeth Jillian had seen. "No, I am an archaeology professor at Cambridge University. I am guest lecturing this week on Roman Britain."

Dimples, dark hair, archaeology professor with a specialty in ancient Rome; had the universe just brought her dream man into her life? Jillian grinned. "I am a fan of Roman history, and would love to hear your lecture. Is it open to everyone?"

"It is a closed lecture, but I will see what I can do for you in exchange for a chance to ask you a few questions about the piece you are wearing. May I see it?"

"You have a deal, Dr. Moreland. Nothing personal, but you are going to have to study it while it is on my person. I am very fond of it and never take it off."

Rouen's chain was long enough that the professor could inspect it without her unclasping it.

"Exquisite piece! From the late Middle Ages or early Renaissance, if my eyes aren't deceiving me. You said it was a gift?"

"Yes. I am impressed, professor, as its design is based

on a piece from the sixteenth century." Jillian watched the way the man continued his evaluation of the jewel.

"This is older than the sixteenth century. You can tell by the jeweler's stamp and the craftsmanship. Look at this." Kieran flipped the pendant over and showed her a tiny imprint on the backside. "This is the mark of the royal jeweler. I would guess the piece is actually fourteenth or fifteenth century, definitely not sixteenth. We both know this is not a reproduction of any sort. May I ask who your friend is?"

Jillian thought about how to answer him. He studied her with some of the most inviting warm brown eyes she had ever seen.

"My friend is a very private individual. He is a businessman. I will need to ask his permission to say anything more. You are certain the piece is older than the sixteenth century?"

"Jillian, let me put it this way, your necklace should be in a museum or a safe, not around your neck. It would be a great loss if it were stolen. You are wearing one of the finest pieces of jewelry from the late Middle Ages that I have laid eyes on."

"You wouldn't know about pagan practices in the fifteenth and sixteenth centuries, would you?" Jillian wondered if Kieran might be a resource to help Rouen.

"My specialty is Roman Britain, but I know enough about England in the Middle Ages and Renaissance to be dangerous. What exactly do you want to know about?"

"Curses, witchcraft, and sorcery of the time." Jillian could tell she surprised Kieran with her answer.

"Didn't expect that. Odd areas of interest."

Jillian laughed. "Yes, they are. I am just curious to learn about the medieval perspective on curses. Were they used, why they were used, and if there is any documentation about how one breaks them? I recently heard a story about a man being cursed in the fifteen-hundreds. It struck me as odd that the tale existed, as so many legends throughout the Dark Ages and early Renaissance are more Christian themed."

"Jillian, I hate to dispel your perception of medieval literature, but it is not all Christian themed. Look at the legend of Arthur or Beowulf. Both are filled with magic and mythical creatures." Kieran looked down at the crest in his hands again before releasing it.

"Both still have Christian themes woven in. Beowulf and Arthur worshipped one god, and Grendel was a child of Cain's curse for murdering Abel. The tale I learned about did not have any religious themes. The hero was cursed by a witch for a noble deed, of all things. He was damned to wander one city for a thousand years alone, never to find compassion or comfort from the living or the dead."

Kieran straightened hearing the story claimed someone was cursed for doing something good. "Harsh punishment for a noble deed. What did the poor man do?"

"I am not exactly sure. My understanding is he was cursed trying to protect the meek and for refusing to turn on a nobleman as others did."

Intrigued, Kieran raised a brow. "Never heard a story like that one before today. Is it Italian or English?"

"English like yourself, Dr. Moreland."

"Give me a few days, and I will see what I can find out for you. My lecture is in studio four of the Colle building at three. Don't be late! I will start at three pm sharp. There will be a reserved seat for you in the back of the room." Kieran offered her his hand.

Jillian shook it. "Thank you, Dr. Moreland. I will be there at 2:55 to ensure I am on time. Your help with finding out more about the strange parable I recently learned is appreciated."

"Delighted to be of assistance with your literary search, and, umm, call me Kieran, not Dr. Moreland. You aren't one of my students."

Jillian watched the charming archeology professor leave the cafe. Strange to meet him when she did. Luckily, her afternoon was clear.

***

As promised, she sat down in the chair reserved for her at exactly five minutes to three. Kieran smiled as she pulled out her iPad to take notes on the lecture.

Damn, those dimples! She was such a sucker for them. Fascinated by his presentation and not wanting to miss anything, Jillian closed the cover of her iPad.

When the lecture finished, Jillian tried to quietly slip out the door as Kieran spoke with a few students.

Kieran saw her leaving out of the corner of his eye. "Jillian, please wait a moment. I would like to finish our discussion after I wrap up with the class here."

"Sure, professor." Jillian took the nearest empty seat to wait for him.

Once all the students left, Kieran joined her. They sat in the classroom for another hour discussing what Jillian referred to as the Tale of Rouen and the necklace she wore.

Changing subjects, Jillian picked his brain on the Roman occupation of Britain.

"You have to be a historian to ask the questions you do." Kieran laughed at one of her comments.

"I was, once upon a time." She confessed with a smile.

"I get the feeling you still are."

Kieran walked her back to her apartment after she looked at her watch and told him she needed to get going.

"Would you be interested in having dinner with me tomorrow night?"

Jillian couldn't believe the man invited her to dinner. "Sure. We can discuss some more of Hadrian's policies."

Kieran grinned. "I suppose we could. Not exactly the ideal dinner conversation for a date, but if it makes you happy."

"A date? I thought the invite was a professional one..."

"Yes, a date, if that is okay with you. If it's not, I understand."

"No. I mean yes. It's perfectly fine." With how warm her cheeks became, Jillian knew she blushed. "I am sorry. You just caught me off guard. I would love to have dinner with you, Kieran."

"Good. I'll meet you here at seven." Kieran kissed her on the cheek before leaving.

***

Jillian reminded herself to keep it together as she turned to open her apartment door.

I just scored a date with a real-life Indiana Jones!

"Who was that? And what is a date?" Rouen revealed himself as Jillian unlocked the door and turned the knob.

Not expecting him to be standing there, she jumped at the ghost's curt tone. "His name is Kieran Moreland. He is a professor at Cambridge. And a date, well, a date is a date."

Jillian took off her jacket and gloves after shutting the door.

"We do not have dates beyond those of the calendar in fifteen-thirty-five. Explain what it is to me."

"I guess dating is like courting. One person invites another on an outing and they get to know each other."

"He is seeking your hand?" Rouen's brows rose at the idea of this dark-haired teacher courting Jillian.

A discomforting anger developed in Rouen's chest. The ghost unconsciously clenched his fist. *This reprobate professor arrives in Urbino just that morning and is suddenly infatuated with Jillian enough to want to marry her! Was she truly entertaining such a farcical thing?*

Jillian grinned at the perplexed expression on Rouen's face. "No, this is more casual than that. People date when they think they like each other. It doesn't necessarily lead to marriage. Sometimes it does, and other times, it leads to friendship or learning you don't like the person after all."

"Do you have a chaperone for this 'date' as you call it tomorrow?"

"No. We don't use chaperones anymore."

The idea of Jillian out alone with Kieran riled Rouen further.

"It is absurd that modern day disregards practices designed to protect individuals! You need a proper attendant. You do not know that man and should not be alone with him."

"It is just dinner, Rouen. We will be in a public place. What are you, my father now?"

"Hardly! I am concerned for your welfare. Being unmarried and upstanding as you are, I am fretful about your virtue. Not all men are gentlemen, Jillian."

"Maybe it is the professor that needs to worry about his virtue. You know how beguiling women can be. Maybe I want a man to seduce me. It has been awhile." Jillian looked back at the ghost behind her. He stared at her with his mouth partway open as if unsure what to say. She enjoyed that for a change, it was she who disconcerted the Renaissance man. "I have a feeling you were the rake you want to protect me from in your day."

Snapping out of the momentary state of shock he found himself in, Rouen chuckled. "I freely admit, I did not always behave as a gentleman should."

"You still don't behave like an upper-class merchant should. You are grumpy and impulsive. Not to mention you peep on ladies as they sleep." Jillian ignored the feigned look of indignation on the ghost's face.

"You wound me with such a defamatory statement. I do not peep! I merely stopped by to ensure you were well, maid."

Jillian gave Rouen a doubtful expression

The ghost sighed. "All right. I will add I was lonely and missed your company, but I never spied on you."

"You missed my company? That is very flattering, Rouen. We really are becoming friends, aren't we?"

The word 'friends' and the smile on Jillian's face brought on a pang of longing in Rouen. He almost felt human again, bantering and staring down into eyes filled with laughter. His hand extended towards her. Her eyes closed as his thumb traveled the curve of her cheek.

"Can you feel my touch?"

"No." Jillian shook her head, her eyes reopening, and her lips curving into another warm smile. "I was imaging what your fingers might feel like against my skin. I wonder if you'd smell like the leather of your jacket or something else."

The spontaneous statement caused Rouen's brows to raise once more. The throbbing ache returned, prompting him to step forward; closing the distance between them. "How often do you ponder what a man may smell like, Jillian?"

The deepened tone of his voice sent a delightful tingle of desire from her heart down her belly. She couldn't recall the last time a man did such a thing to her with merely the sound of his voice. She nervously laughed and broke eye contact with him.

"You are the first Renaissance man I've ever met. The historian in me is curious about the hygiene standards of the day. While you make a striking figure, maybe you would reek to high heaven in real life."

Jillian walked towards the small kitchen to make dinner.

Rouen followed her, delighted that the woman described him as striking. "Does the lady fancy her ghost more than the living professor who takes her on a, what was the term, date tomorrow?"

"No." Jillian turned on the burner and set a pot of water on the stove to boil. "But, I will admit that I think you are a good-looking and rather charming guy when you aren't being all grumpy and moody. Can you hand me the pasta over there?"

Jillian noticed the flattered grin on Rouen's face as she took the homemade pasta from him. "It confuses me that you can pick up and touch so many things, but can't make any sort of contact with another human being."

"Objects can't offer comfort or kindness. I cannot touch animals either."

Rouen pulled a knife out to help Jillian prepare her dinner. He sliced up the fresh vegetables she washed as she warmed the tomato sauce leftover from the night before.

"For someone who can't enjoy the things you prepare,

you create some wonderfully delicious dishes, my noble sir."

"In my day, referring to me as a noble or sir would get you into trouble. There are laws against addressing one with a title they do not truly bear."

"Out of curiosity, where'd you learn to cook?" Jillian watched him sauté the vegetables he just cut up.

"With nothing else to do, I observed many people preparing meals over the centuries. I loved local cuisine when I was alive. Mayhap, part of me hoped if I ever found myself human again, that I could prepare some of my favorite meals. The winters do get cold and lonely in England just as they can here." Rouen shrugged, taking over preparing dinner. This would be the second time the ghost made her evening meal.

"It sounds almost as if you don't like England. Why return there if you enjoy Italy more?"

"I have an obligation to my family that requires I return home. If this wretched curse is ever broken."

Jillian poured herself a glass of Piklr, knowing it would pair nicely with the meal. "It will be broken. You will see England once more."

Rouen smiled. "I am afraid it will more than likely have to run its course. Your dinner, my lady."

"Maybe Kieran will know something that can help you." Jillian twirled the long ribbon of pasta around her fork before tipping the utensil with a slice of zucchini.

"Most professors believe in logic and books, not magic and fairytales."

"He might surprise you, Rouen. Kieran recognized your medallion wasn't a reproduction as I claimed. He even mentioned knowing the family the crest represented."

Rouen shrugged, doubting the professor did. "He was more than likely trying to impress you, so he could win your confidence and you would permit him to court you."

"Do you not like Kieran?" Jillian found the ghost's reaction to the professor strange.

"I do not know the man; therefore, I cannot determine if I like him or not. I am only concerned about my new friend's safety and well-being."

Knowing Rouen had no interest in discussing the professor, Jillian dropped the subject.

"I found two documents related to your visit to Urbino."

Rouen seemed startled by her statement.

"I was not aware any documentation of my visit existed."

"You signed a trade agreement and brought the duke or Eleonora a letter from the king." Jillian pulled up the photographs of each document on the phone before handing it to Rouen.

"I had forgotten about the trade agreement." Rouen half smiled, reading the record. He swiped to the picture of the letter he carried on Henry's behalf. He had never seen the contents of it before today. "Typical diplomatic correspondence between courts. Did you intentionally look for these or did you find them researching the court for your book?"

Jillian swallowed her mouthful of pasta, breaking eye contact with Rouen. He would be mad if she revealed she looked further into him and his curse. "The letter and agreement vanished between last night and this morning."

"Vanished?" The puzzlement on the ghost's face shared he knew nothing about the mysterious disappearance of the records.

"Simonetta, the archivist, and I searched through all the folders and records for the period and neither document could be found. It's like they never existed or someone destroyed them. The reference number for them was even removed from the master ledger."

Rouen frowned, not liking what she described. *Who would take such harmless works?* "I will see if there is something I may do to assist in locating them once more."

"Leonora wouldn't have moved them, would she?"

"No. She only hides her personal correspondence."

"Are you aware of anything in the letter or agreement that someone might not want surfaced?" Jillian still doubted that Rouen didn't have a hand in the documents vanishing.

"Neither of those items contain anything concerning other than their possible link to me."

Jillian sat back in her chair. "Why would that link be concerning?"

"I am in the dark as you are, Jillian. Perhaps, someone is troubled about revealing the diplomacy between Henry and Della Rovere. Or, another researcher is worried you may publish the documents before they release their work, so they stole them. You know how historians can be about such matters."

Jillian studied Rouen, wondering about his deflection. The ghost watched her take another sip of wine from her glass. "What if I was researching you and your curse, Rouen?"

"Jillian, do you honestly think I would not have looked for answers in the duke's library at some point in the past five hundred years? I found nothing about Giselle or any indication of a way to end the curse. Do not walk a path that ends with you frustrated and empty-handed. Forget me and focus on this book you want to write."

Rouen spent the evening with Jillian, watching her write another piece for her blog about her extended stay in Italy. He enjoyed their long conversations. He covered her with a blanket after she fell asleep on the couch and turned off the TV. He left the foyer light on, so she could find her way around the apartment if she woke up, then slipped out into the frigid night.

* * *

The vibrating sensation of movement and a soft rumble woke Jillian from a dead sleep. The muted, strange sound grew louder. A wine bottle fell from the table, shattering on the floor. The screaming of other tenants in the old building and the sound of footsteps fleeing down the hall snapped Jillian the rest of the way awake.

An earthquake rattled the Renaissance city.

Grasping that the building swayed, she frantically put on her shoes. With heart racing, she ran down the stairs then into the street with the other residents. Thankfully, the trembling and groaning of the earth ceased without the buildings tumbling down.

Jillian looked upward to see the moon and stars above. The sky was still dark with no signs of dawn. *What time was it?*

"Jillian!"

Hearing someone calling her name, she turned toward the street.

Rouen ran through the throng of people towards her.

She instinctively reached for him when he reached her. The realization of what just happened set in as she embraced the ghost. Adrenalin and fear caused tears to flow down her face.

Holding her tightly against him, Rouen gently rocked her. "You are safe, Jillian. It is all right."

She felt his fingers in her hair as he soothed her back. The warmth and security she found in strong arms eased the panic seizing control of her. She clutched his shoulders, drawing him closer.

"Calm yourself, sweetheart. I won't let anything harm you as long as you are in Urbino." Rouen felt her trembling start to slow as Jillian began to compose herself. He thanked God for the earthquake being a relatively minor one that didn't hurt anyone or cause major damage. The thought of having to dig Jillian out from under the rubble of her apartment building mortified him.

"Singora Fitzalan!" The landlord shouted as he and another man hurried in their direction.

Jillian hated that the cold bite of the night wind now whipped against her face. The feeling of warmth and masculine scent of leather, clove, and cinnamon mixed with frankincense from the small chapel Rouen frequently sat in vanished. "Rouen?"

"I am still here." He looked down at his hands, wondering how he could have held her. *Was the curse weakening?*

Kieran wrapped his jacket around Jillian's shoulders. "Thank goodness the quake wasn't worse!"

"Kieran? What are you doing here?"

"I am staying in the building next to yours. You scared Mr. Rosetti as he didn't see you at first. Whatever are you doing over here in the alleyway?"

"I am not sure. I just ran away from the building." Jillian stared over at Rouen before looking at her surroundings.

How did they end up here when she exited the front of the

structure?

"It will be an hour or so before we can go back inside. The *vigile* are inspecting the historic center. The cafe around the corner is opening up for all of us. May I buy you a cup of coffee?"

Jillian only partially heard what Kieran said due to fully grasping that Rouen was able to physically touch her for a few minutes. *Did his curse and the quake have something to do with one another? Was he okay with all that happened tonight?*

Kieran glanced back at the empty alleyway wondering what held the woman's attention. Nothing was there.

Rouen smiled, noting the worry on her face. "Go, Jillian. I will call on you later."

Jillian snapped out of whatever thoughts she was lost in as she looked back at Kieran.

"Sure, Kieran. A cup of coffee sounds great after this. Maybe they will have something stronger available."

"I need to check on the other tenants now that we found you. You two enjoy your caffe." Mirko patted Jillian on the back then walked over to a group of people just a short distance away.

Rouen watched Kieran and Jillian from the window. They talked while drinking coffee at a table perfectly sized for a party of two. Jillian smiled at something the professor said. For a fleeting second, he wished to be able to sit with them, sipping a warm cup of espresso. He envied Kieran's ability to completely enjoy Jillian's company.

The professor's arm rested across the top of the chair behind her, almost claiming the woman as his own.

There was something about Kieran that bothered Rouen. The ghost wished he knew what it was about Jillian's new friend that perturbed him so much.

CHAPTER EIGHT

Jillian called the archives to see if they would be open. Simonetta advised they were closed to the general public, but with the compressed timeline Jillian worked under, she could make an exception for Jillian to come in for the day. The authorities had cleared the building for operation earlier that morning.

Jillian picked up the two folders that slid off the desk during the earthquake. Her research notes and the other documents she translated only shifted on the table in the wee hours of morning.

"Out of curiosity, did Francesco know where the trade agreement and letter went?" Jillian asked Simonetta.

"No. He seemed confused when I inquired about them. Maybe another staff member misplaced them."

Or a ghost. Jillian thought to herself, opening the ledger she started to read the afternoon prior.

***

Rouen followed Kieran from the faculty dorm to Café Basilli. The professor ordered a cup of coffee, then sat down at a table outside the shop. A few minutes later, an

Italian man joined him. Rouen recognized Francesco, the archival director. *How did the two know one another?*

"You are certain she is researching an English diplomat named Rouen? She claimed to be writing a book on artist patronage by the Dukes of Urbino when we spoke." Kieran sipped his coffee, half-wondering if Francesco overreacted to the brief discussion Jillian had with Simonetta.

Francesco leaned forward and slammed a hand down on the table. "I wouldn't have called you and William over nothing. With the emblem she wears, you believe her when she states she is researching artists and their funding in the Urbino court?"

Kieran set his cup down, giving Francesco a cynical stare. "Why would she lie to me? She has no idea who I am."

"Perhaps, she does." Francesco disagreed. "Maybe someone or something warned her."

"Francesco, I think the dust in the archives must have something in it that is getting to you."

Francesco laughed. "You nor William are taking this seriously. If your new American friend isn't being guided by someone, how did she randomly stumble across these?"

Kieran took the folder Francesco slid across the table and opened it. The archaeologist let out a long, loud, annoyed breath, skimming the letter from Henry VIII and seeing the signature of the English representative on the trade agreement.

Rouen caught a glimpse of the portfolio's contents before Kieran closed it. *The documents Jillian inquired about the evening prior hadn't disappeared, Francesco removed them from the archive! Why would he do that?*

Kieran stared at the archival director, contemplating whether or not there was cause for alarm or to alert their bosses. "Odd coincidence or sheer, dumb luck maybe? I need more than these to take any action."

"She has to have seen or spoken with him. No one else has even remotely blinked an eye at his name. She actively looks for references to him."

"Francesco, multiple agents have searched Urbino, and Rome for that matter, many times over the years. Nothing has ever turned up. I sincerely doubt some random woman would discover our lost merchant in the exact place where more experienced individuals have thoroughly searched after all this time."

"Maybe, he didn't want to be found. Or Giselle's magic..."

"Giselle's magic." Kieran scoffed, tucking the documents into his briefcase. "The witch isn't that powerful. I have a dinner date with Jillian this evening. I will see if she shares anything that warrants further investigation. I really do think you are overreacting to all of this."

Rouen went to Jillian's apartment hoping to talk her out of any further meetings with Kieran. He knocked on her door, but she didn't answer. Concerned about her welfare, he slipped inside.

There was no sign of her. Her laptop and notebook were also missing. She must have gone to the archives again.

**

Jillian racked her brain trying to find other links to Rouen. "Who else was at court on the fifteenth of March?"

Simonetta looked through the digital copies of the archival records on her computer. "This can't be right. There is a reference to Baldassare."

"Baldassare? As in Castiglione and *The Book of the Courtier*?" Jillian leaned down to look at Simonetta's screen.

"One in the same."

The name Castiglione scribbled across the scanned parchment puzzled Jillian as much as it did Simonetta. "Are Baldassare's papers here or somewhere else?"

"We have some of them. I will see if I have anything that links March 1535 and Castiglione."

Simonetta disappeared into the archival vaults.

Jillian searched the internet for any connections she might be able to make between Castiglione and Henry Tudor. The name Giovanni Battista Castiglione surfaced in the list of results. Jillian skimmed a couple articles on the man who was a mercenary for Henry VIII.

"We do have a journal entry from the duchess confirming Castiglione was indeed here in March. We also have two letters he wrote to Eleonora and Federico." Simonetta opened the Eleonora's diary and set the other documents on the table for Jillian to review.

Jillian blinked to ensure her eyes read the journal entry correctly. Eleonora confirmed Rouen's presence at dinner and a social event on the evening of March fifteenth. Jillian yanked on her gloves, and carefully opened Castiglione's letters. She almost dropped one letter reading Francesco agreed to provide England with fifty mercenaries from the duke's ranks and would contact one of the Venetian Doges to arrange for three warships to protect English mercantile vessels.

Mercenaries? Were they to protect trade between the two states or something else?

Jillian continued reading: Furthermore, sixty cases of wine, ten soldiers, and two crates of Italian-made weapons would be escorted to Windsor by Giovanni Battista, since the English military ambassador suffered an assault resulting in the man's death the evening of March six-teenth.

"Military ambassador?" Jillian reread the words aloud. A merchant would never serve as a military liaison on behalf of a king. *Who else was in Urbino with Rouen? And who killed the other Brit?*

"Jillian!" Rouen entered the private office, interrupting her musings.

She noted the way his eyes traveled over all the items on the desk. The panic grew in his expression as he realized what each of them were.

"You are researching me."

Jillian felt her cheeks warm. Anger replaced the surprise she initially felt. "If you were honest with me, I wouldn't have to. Who else was in Urbino with you, and what were you really doing here?"

"I cannot answer those queries, Jillian."

"Did you murder Henry's military liaison provoking the witch that cursed you?" Jillian wanted to know what type of man her ghost once was.

Taken back by the tone she used, Rouen worried about what Jillian discovered in the archives. *Had Francesco and Kieran planted false documents vilifying him?*

"No. Why would you think I would do such a thing?"

"If Baldassare's account is accurate, the man died the same night you disappeared." Jillian held the letter out to Rouen.

The ghost frowned, taking it from her. "Gesu Criste." Rouen shook his head, reading what Castiglione docu-mented for posterity. "I did not kill anyone, Jillian. You must believe me, and you must stop researching anything to do with me or the negotiations between Urbino and

England that I participated in."

"What are you hiding that you don't want anyone to know?" Jillian intently studied the sixteenth-century man, wondering what he concealed now.

"Some things are better left unknown, Jillian."

Afraid he might destroy it, Jillian jerked the letter out of his hand. "Stay away from me."

Rouen frowned, watching her slide her notes and laptop into her bag.

"I don't know what I am uncovering here, Rouen. But you are crazy if you think I am going to walk away from it. I originally wanted to help break this curse of yours. Now, I wonder if you deserved what you got. I am also wondering if whatever you are covering up is something that would alter history."

Her words visibly troubled Rouen. Jillian noted how his hands began to shake; the way his adam's apple dipped as he swallowed, biting back whatever response he wanted to utter. He took a step towards her.

"What I am not sharing will not alter history, Jillian! You cannot change the events of the past."

"No, but I can change our understanding of it. You never said a word about military negotiations with Della Rovere, or that you and whoever your companion was hired fifty elite Italian mercenaries. Considering Francesco was the Pope's mightiest military leader, Henry needed specialized troops for something, and I doubt it was to put down the Pilgrimage of Grace."

"Pilgrimage of what?" The event she spoke of distracted Rouen from warning her away from further looking into his purpose in Urbino.

"It's an uprising against Henry and Cromwell for some

of their Reformation policies."

"I couldn't care less about Henry, Cromwell, and whatever uprising or pilgrimages occurred centuries ago. I am worried about you. You are drawing attention to more than me, Jillian. You must stop your research! Do not go anywhere near Kieran Moreland."

The intensity with which he spoke and the fear in his eyes flabbergasted Jillian.

"Let me guess. You can't tell me why you want me to avoid Kieran either."

Rouen's mouth opened then closed.

Jillian knew by the angry glare he shot her that he would deny her the truth once more.

"Please trust me, Jillian."

"I am sorry, Rouen. Until you are honest with me, I can't do that." Jillian zipped shut her laptop bag.

"You endanger yourself if you continue, woman!"

"Endanger myself?" Jillian shook her head, laughing in disbelief. "Who is my research upsetting besides you, Rouen? Giselle? Is the boogeyman or some other imaginary creature going to get me if I continue?"

Rouen snatched the journal and letters off the table. "Since you won't listen, I will be taking these along with anything in the archives from February and March of fifteen-thirty-five. If there are no sources, you can do no research."

A cold breeze wafted over the room. Rouen and the artifacts disappeared. Simonetta screamed in the vault. No one other than archival staff were allowed to enter, but Jillian sprinted to the vault anyway.

Three boxes of paintings, letters, books, and other documents vanished from the room. Jillian tried to calm a panicked Simonetta down.

"We will find where they went." Jillian set her hands on Simonetta's shoulders. "The closure to the general public buys us some time to do so."

***

Jillian gathered her belongings and headed to the church, hoping to find Rouen in the side chapel. With no sign of him there, she paid for admission to the ducal palace and walked the building searching for him. Reaching the rooftop garden, she felt as if someone watched her; however, no one else stood in the private courtyard.

"Rouen, I know you can most likely hear me. I sense someone is here, and my money is on you."

Jillian scanned the area once more, but the ghost didn't show himself.

"You are an asshole, Rouen! Simonetta could be fired due to you taking the papers and artifacts from the archives."

The buzz of people from the street next to the palazzo remained the only sound in her ears.

"Fine! You are on your own. Spend the remainder of your curse with no company. I want nothing to do with you. And if you let Simonetta get fired because of your antics, that tells me all I need to know about your supposed character. It also makes you look guilty as hell when it comes to being the prime suspect in the English ambassador's death."

Jillian paused as if waiting for a response.

"What have you done to anger your lady so?" Eleonora joined Rouen and Jillian in the garden.

"She is not my lady." Rouen felt a twinge of guilt with the way the Duchess of Urbino frowned at him. "It is better this way."

Eleonora snorted, but said nothing further.

Rouen raised an irritated brow at the female specter. "With all due respect, Duchess, my personal affairs are none of your concern."

"Everything that occurs within Urbino's walls is of concern to me." Eleonora rebuked the angry ghost.

Jillian looked down at her watch. "You had your one chance to explain yourself. And look at the time. I need to get ready for my dinner with the *evil* Dr. Kieran Moreland. Have a nice half a millennium alone!"

"A rival suitor?" Eleonora grinned at Rouen. "You are most likely correct in that the two of you part ways. Mayhap, this Moreland is a better fit for her as he is still living. Is there a particular reason she describes him as evil?"

"She is mocking my warning to be wary of him. I believe he is a member of the Order of Saint John."

The two ghosts watched Jillian re-enter the castle.

Eleonora stared at Rouen once more. "Why would a Hospitaller journey to Italy to do her harm, Rouen?"

"I am not certain of why."

"This whole situation is troubling. Does the lady have a chaperone for this evening in case your concerns are valid?"

Rouen shook his head no. "Modern-day courtship does not see the need for a chaperone."

"If that is the case, let us hope your fears are unfounded." Eleonora left Rouen standing alone in the garden.

The Duchess walked out onto the same balcony Rouen stood upon the night Jillian photographed him. She looked over the territory she and her husband once governed.

***

Angry and unsure of what to do about Rouen, Jillian walked down to the small coffee shop just off the palace walls. The early hints of dusk appeared in the sky as she ordered a glass of wine and sat at one of the outdoor tables overlooking the Borgo Mercatale and the valley off its far end.

Maybe sunset paired with a good vino would help Jillian figure out what to do about Rouen's shenanigans. *Did he not realize the harm he caused?*

Jillian took a deep gulp of the wine in her glass, still not believing he stole the archival materials.

The sound of a chair sliding out beside her caused her to turn her head. "Hey, you okay, beautiful? You look upset."

A smiling Kieran sat down beside her.

"I am okay. Where'd you come from?" Jillian found the timing of the archaeologist's appearance odd.

Kieran gestured to a large group of people with a tour guide standing across the street, looking up at the palace towers and balconies.

"I agreed to take over a class for the week, so their professor could present at a conference. They had a palace tour scheduled for today. I saw you over here and wanted to say hello. You sure you're okay?"

"Yeah, I just hit a dead end with my research today."

"What kind of dead end?"

Jillian shook her head, unsure of how to explain the issue. "I guess one could say, the disappearing documents kind."

"Disappearing documents? By that, do you mean documents that were lost over time or something else?" Kieran thought her choice of words was odd.

Jillian laughed. "Sure. We'll go with that."

Kieran watched her take another sip of wine. "Keep digging. I am sure you'll find something on whatever you were researching. We often do if we take a break and regroup."

Jillian's eyes left Kieran's to look out across the valley again.

"Something more than a bad day at the archives has to be troubling you, Jillian. I don't mean to brag, but I am a damn good problem solver. Talk to me." Kieran slid an arm around her shoulders and gave her a friendly squeeze.

"You wouldn't believe me if I told you."

"Tell me anyway."

"I have this friend." Jillian paused, thinking about how best to word things. "He's, he's very temperamental over minor matters, and I don't know how to take him at times. He's going through something very difficult no one would ever want to experience. At least I know I wouldn't want to go through what he is. I've been trying to help him out, and well, today, today he blew up on me about everything." Jillian heard the deep breath Kieran took in. She looked over to see a slightly disappointed look on his face.

"When one is going through troubles, they don't always appreciate the things others do for them. Give him a few days to cool off. He'll more than likely come around to seeing you only meant to help him. If he doesn't, well, he's an idiot." Kieran smiled, hearing the short laugh she let out. "Feeling any better now that you've got your troubles off your chest?"

"Yes. Thank you." Jillian returned the smile he gave her.

Kieran took her hand in his. "You are most welcome."

Jillian leaned closer to Kieran, allowing herself to get lost in the combination of warm brown eyes and the orange hues of twilight. "You are a very charming guy, Dr.

Moreland."

"You think so?" Kieran grinned, mirroring the way the woman's body leaned towards his.

"Absolutely." Jillian whispered, just before Kieran's lips met hers.

***

"Rouen," Eleanora heard the door close as Rouen came inside from the gardens. "I know you are angry with Jillian, but I think it best you not allow her to dine alone with this Hospitaller you said is here."

Rouen noted how the Duchess stared down at something from the balcony. "What causes you to say that?"

Eleonora glanced over at Rouen before returning her attention to the street below. "I worry your new friend may not realize the knight is taking advantage of her charitable nature."

"Taking advantage of?" Rouen crossed the room, not liking the Duchess' choice of words. He spotted the cause of Eleanora's concern. For the second time that day, a flood of betrayal and anger coursed through him. If he were human, he would call the bloody bastard out for daring to kiss Jillian.

***

"Get it, Dr. Moreland!" One of the students shouted, seeing the guest lecturer lip-locked with some woman across the street.

A few more of their classmates whistled and shouted, interrupting the kiss.

"College students." Kieran scoffed, enjoying the smile on Jillian's face.

Jillian loved the way Kieran so easily took things in stride. "With the way you kiss, you can get it anytime you like, Dr. Moreland."

Kieran chuckled. "Now, I am really looking forward to our date this evening. Let me get back to the unruly class I am temporarily supervising." He gave her a light kiss on the lips before standing up. "See you in two hours, Jillian."

"A presto." Jillian used the Italian phrase for see you soon, watching Kieran rejoin the tour group.

"Dr. M, the Urbino Casanova!" A second student teased Kieran once Kieran stood beside the tour guide.

"I hope you paid as much attention to the tour as you did your professor with the quiz you are all getting at the start of class tomorrow."

Hearing the collective groan from the group, Jillian laughed. *Well played, professor.*

CHAPTER NINE

Aloud knock sounded on Jillian's door exactly at seven.

"Right on time." Jillian smiled, impressed with Kieran keeping his word.

Rouen yanked her jacket from her hands.

"What are you doing here?" Jillian whispered before yelling to Kieran she would be right there.

"Chaperoning."

"Oh no, you are not! You can go back to the palace or wherever you prefer to hang out, but you are not coming with us." Jillian tried to tug her jacket out of Rouen's grip.

"I will not let you dine alone with him, Jillian."

"You are not ruining my date with any more of this secretive nonsense of yours! Go find some other tourist to harass tonight." Jillian freed her jacket from him then picked up her purse.

She wondered why Rouen still stood there staring at her. His eyes settled on the necklace she wore.

"My crest looks very nice with your choice of garments this evening."

"Thank you. At least I think that was a compliment. Now, go away!"

"I am not leaving." Rouen folded his arms over his chest to reaffirm that she would have to endure his company wherever she might go with Kieran.

Jillian debated ripping the crucifix off the wall and conducting an impromptu exorcism.

Rouen smirked as he realized what she looked at. "A cross won't keep me away. You really should open the door since you insist on dining with Kieran. The man will think you are having second thoughts if you leave him out there too long."

Both stared the other down in a test of wills that riled Jillian.

"Jillian, I only wish to keep you safe. You do not know Kieran well."

"After this morning's tirade, you expect me to believe Kieran is the one I should be worried about?"

Rouen's cheek twitched as his jaw tensed, showing Jillian struck a nerve, "I apologize for this morning. I should not have acted in the manner that I did. You must believe me when I tell you the professor's appearance in Urbino is not some random happening."

"What is it then?" Jillian doubted that Kieran heralded any omen of ill fate.

"I do not know. My instincts never lie to me. There is an ulterior motive behind Kieran's dinner invite." Rouen knew Jillian distrusted him by the cynical expression on her face. "What is the worst that happens if I accompany you? He will never know I am there."

The stupid ghost would more than likely follow us anyway! As Rouen stated, Kieran wouldn't be aware of the ghost's presence. On the off-chance Rouen's claim of Kieran being in Urbino was something darker than a guest lecture, it couldn't hurt to have an escort for the evening.

"Behave, Rouen, or I will call for a priest to send you back to the sixteenth century." Jillian glared at the ghost one last time before opening the apartment door.

"You look wonderful tonight. I see you are still wearing what is quickly becoming one of my favorite relics." Kieran greeted her with a dazzling smile.

"Thank you. Is the necklace truly that amazing a discovery, professor?" Jillian slid her arms into her jacket as he held it up for her. She really enjoyed the manners of European men over most of the Americans she had dated.

"It most certainly is. Not only is it priceless, the woman who adorns herself with it is a rare and exquisite find."

Noting the flattered smile on Jillian's face, Rouen rolled his eyes.

"I think I will need to conduct further study into the necklace and yourself, Jillian."

"Let's go. You can do your treasure hunting and research over dinner." Jillian locked her door, then the two walked to one of the cozy restaurants in town.

Jillian did her best to ignore Rouen and any side bar comments he muttered under his breath throughout dinner. She really liked Kieran. The man seemed genuinely interested in her.

"Did you by chance hear anything further from the friend you told me about?" Kieran casually inquired.

"No." Jillian guiltily glanced over at Rouen causing the ghost's brows to raise.

"I bet he gives you a call and apologizes tomorrow. As I said earlier, the man is an idiot if he doesn't realize you are trying to help him with whatever he is going through."

Rouen eyed Jillian after Kieran elaborated on his inquiry. "Who is this friend the professor speaks of?"

"No one important." Jillian whispered, picking up her water glass.

"What was that?" Kieran didn't catch what Jillian mumbled.

"I didn't say anything. I had a tickle in my throat." Jillian took another drink of water, hoping she sounded convincing. She resisted the urge to look over at Rouen again hearing him snort at her answer. "Kieran, I really appreciate you saying hello and letting me vent earlier. It was very sweet of you to do."

"My pleasure, Jillian. You know, I've been thinking about your research dilemma. With the wealth of sources just in Urbino, you can probably get around the road block of whatever these lost documents are by changing your approach. Who exactly are you researching again?"

Jillian ignored the "I told you so" expression now on Rouen's face. "My topic isn't exactly a who, it's more of a what. I guess a shift in focus could help, but I am not sure how to reframe my original idea. And you're right, there are so many records on artist patronage in the archives one could get lost in them. I think I am just feeling overwhelmed by the source material I am making my way through more than really dealing with lost sources. I haven't even looked at the actual works produced by the artisans yet."

"Maybe it would be helpful if you narrowed your scope from a general overview of patronage to specific case studies of one or two artists."

"As much as I hate to admit it, I think that is the

approach I may have to take." Jillian savored the mouthful of strozzapreti carciofi she ordered. The rich flavors sent a pleasant sensation across her palate. "How long do you have left in Urbino, Kieran?"

"A week, but I was thinking of extending my visit. Maybe lending a hand to a historian I met, so she can finish her project before she has to return stateside. Signore Rosetti advised that the apartment next to yours will be available in a few days. He's willing to do a short-term rental if you would like some help with your book research."

Kieran's unexpected offer and the flirtatious grin on his face sent a red warmth up Jillian's face.

"I am hoping the pink in your cheeks along with the way you are smiling at me means you are accepting my offer."

"Does artist patronage really interest you to the point you would want to spend hours at a time looking at dusty papers with me?"

"To be honest, anything that would allow me to spend large amounts of time getting to know you better interests me."

Rouen kicked the bottom of her chair, bouncing it and Jillian. "Please tell me you do not honestly believe this man's cleverly crafted statements."

Jillian couldn't help laughing at the disgusted look on Rouen's face.

"I have a confession to make, Kieran. I am not really researching artist patronage. As interesting a topic as that is, it's not one I want to write about." Jillian took a sip of her wine to watch his reaction. She noted how Rouen studied their companion as intently as she did.

"Hmmm." Kieran sat back in his seat as if troubled by what she said. "That is disappointing to learn. I can't express my dismay at not having to read numerous accounting ledgers documenting payment amounts to random artists. After all, forensic accounting is such a passion of mine."

Jillian giggled at his sarcastic tone.

Kieran grinned, pleased that he made her laugh once more. "So, what are you researching? And please, let it be much more intriguing than your initial topic."

"It absolutely is. I am hoping to discover new information on Baldassare Castiglione's fifteen-thirty-five visit to Urbino. I recently stumbled across a letter of his. It appears the mercenary may have been secretly negotiating some sort of military support agreement on behalf of Henry Tudor."

Kieran's brows immediately came together. He leaned forward, settling his hands on the table. "Now, that is much more interesting. A Papal state lending military support to an enemy of the Church. Whatever brought this unknown discovery to your attention? I don't think I've ever read a historical work referencing anything of the sort."

"I found the negotiations quite by accident doing general research on the period. I am not sure how much we will find on the matter as a few of the sources seemed to have disappeared." Jillian shot Rouen a glare before smiling at Kieran once more.

"You were serious about documents disappearing earlier, weren't you?" Kieran looked to his right, wondering why the lady glanced in that direction.

"Yes. One of the archivists think they were misplaced by another staff member."

"It sounds like you don't buy that excuse."

Jillian took Kieran's hand, drawing his gaze back to her.

She noted the tensing of Rouen's jaw as the ghost looked down at her and the professor's joined hands.

"I am not sure what to think; other than, it's weird that sixteenth-century documents randomly vanished without a trace."

Kieran affectionately squeezed the fingers he held. "Well, we will just have to hope they reappear or seek out alternate ones. I am up to the challenge."

Rouen frowned, sitting back down in the empty chair on the right side of the table. He didn't utter another word the remainder of the evening.

Jillian almost forgot he was present.

He quietly trailed behind them as Kieran walked Jillian back to her apartment.

"Good night, Jillian." Kieran almost whispered, angling his head closer to Jillian's.

"Sogni d'oro." Jillian closed her eyes, feeling the professor's nose brush hers.

Her door slamming open against the wall stopped the kiss about to take place.

If looks could kill, Kieran would be dead in the hallway. Jillian half wondered if Rouen would cause a full-on poltergeist moment, sending objects flying at her and Kieran.

"See you tomorrow." She kissed Kieran's cheek then stepped inside her apartment.

"You should probably get that door checked." Kieran glanced around her apartment as if looking for something.

"I'll mention it to Mirko the next time I see him."

Kieran turned to leave then stopped. "I just remembered we have a faculty meeting and field trip to Rome tomorrow. We won't be back until Thursday afternoon. Would you be open to dinner again Thursday night since I can't see you tomorrow?"

Hearing the invite, Rouen hmphed.

"Thursday it is." Jillian held the door to prevent Rouen from throwing it shut in Kieran's face.

"See you then." Kieran walked back down the hall.

Jillian almost laughed at the way Rouen continued to watch Kieran until the archaeologist rounded the corner of the staircase and disappeared from sight. "Jealous."

"I am not jealous at all. That man is deceiving you, and you are falling for his tricks."

With how dinner went and Kieran not once batting an eye about Castiglione or making any further inquiries into the topic, Rouen was mistaken about why Kieran was in Urbino.

Jillian locked the deadbolt. "He's harmless, Rouen."

"He is far from harmless." Rouen followed her over to the couch.

"Next, you will be telling me he is immortal or cursed like you." Jillian pulled off her shoes and curled her legs up underneath her. "Or that you two know one another."

"I have never encountered Kieran before nor is he cursed as far as I can tell. I do not trust him. He conceals something."

"Apparently, he isn't alone in that, Sir Cursed. Until you can share something more or Kieran turns into some sort of monster, the topic of Kieran being the devil is off the table. Are you going to bring back the archival materials you stole?" Jillian hoped Rouen would realize nothing endangered her.

"Are you agreeing to leave matters as they are?"

"Not at all. You are overdramatizing everything, Rouen." Jillian could tell her answer disappointed him by the way his eyes momentarily dropped to the floor.

Rouen scooted closer to her. "If I could find a way to prove that I am not overreacting, would you stop researching me?"

The worry in the ghost's eyes caused Jillian's heart to skip a beat.

What if he's telling the truth? Rouen hadn't harmed her, and he always remained calm until that morning. Hell, he even helped her when she initially told him she was writing a book on the Court of Urbino. Maybe she had too much wine that night to forgive him so quickly for his irrational behavior in the archives.

"All right, Rouen. You have through Thursday night to prove this conspiracy theory of yours about Kieran. I won't go back to the archives until Friday."

"Thank you for placing your faith in me once more, Jillian." Rouen smiled for the first time that day. "I would like to remain with you until Kieran departs in the morning."

Somehow Jillian knew he would ask to stay the night. "If it eases whatever brings out the crazy poltergeist in you, you are a welcomed guest. I am going to bed. If I get up in the morning and find my notes gone or any of the files on my laptop deleted, you're getting a holy water shower. Then I am sprinkling salt around my apartment, so you can't enter."

The ghost chuckled at the threat. "I will not touch any of your precious research. Have pleasant dreams."

"Good night, Rouen." Jillian headed to the bedroom. Reaching the door, she looked back at Rouen. "Out of curiosity, what are you going to do if Kieran breaks in here? You can't touch him."

"There are other things I can do to scare him off. I am

not out to hurt the man. I merely want to protect you."

The warm tone Rouen used as he walked towards her made her heartbeat faster. Since the night of the earthquake, Jillian found herself almost drawn to Rouen. She smiled, thinking of how amazing he smelled when he held her for those fleeting few moments. His presence created a strange sense of security and comfort when he appeared lately.

Those are the last things you should feel around a ghost, especially one that hid things as this one did! It is stupid to even let your thoughts stray in any sort of romantic direction. Nothing could ever happen between the two of you.

Jillian forced the negative, self-castigation from her head, so she could selfishly indulge in the way Rouen stared down at her. The intensity in his eyes clashed with the grin gently curving his lips upward.

"What are you thinking to smile as you are, Jillian?"

"I am thinking that I am very thankful to have met you, Rouen. And even though you are a bit overzealous at times, I appreciate your looking out for me."

"The pleasure of making your acquaintance will always be the highlight of my existence, my lady historian." Rouen admired the woman he couldn't touch.

Jillian went up on tiptoe, placing her lips where his cheek should be, then whispered 'goodnight' to him.

Rouen appreciated her gesture; his fingers lightly touched the side his face. Maybe one day he'd know what her lips would feel like against his skin.

CHAPTER TEN

J illian woke to find two red roses lying on her table. A cream-colored notecard was left beside them.

Thank you for forgiving me.

She picked up the note, wondering whose artful handwriting graced the paper. *Did Rouen write it or did he have Lady Eleonora draft it for him?*

Jillian put the roses in some water, chuckling at their color. *Were they red because they represented the House of Tudor and England? Or was Rouen sharing that he recognized the mutual affection between them?*

She opened the window curtains after making her morning coffee. With the sun shining and her promise to Rouen, a winter hike through the outskirts of Urbino seemed like a good plan for the day. Her phone rang, ending her perusal of the countryside.

"Jillian, all the boxes are back in the archives. Nothing is missing any longer." Simonetta sounded ecstatic on the other end of the phone.

Rouen returning everything impressed Jillian. "That is wonderful news."

"Will you be coming in today?"

"No. I am going to take a day off after all the excitement yesterday." Jillian couldn't break her promise to Rouen after his gestures that morning. He ensured Simonetta didn't lose her job, and he made every effort to apologize for his behavior.

"You didn't tell anyone what happened?" Simonetta worried Francesco might learn that things temporarily went missing.

"Not a soul. And I suddenly don't recall anything odd happening while visiting the archives."

"Grazie, Jillian. If there is anything you need from our facility, ask and I will get it for you."

"Have a good day, Simonetta."

***

Her phone rang a second time as Jillian finished her breakfast.

"Hello." Jillian propped the phone between her ear and shoulder. She tried to quietly set her dishes in the sink.

"Good morning, Jillian."

Recognizing the voice, Jillian smiled. "Kieran. I thought you were on your way to Rome."

"I am. I am calling you from the train. You mentioned that you found a letter from Baldassare written in 1535 when we spoke last night."

"It was signed B. Castiglione." Jillian wondered what about the letter caused Kieran to call her.

"You didn't take a picture of the letter by chance, did you?"

"Simonetta approved me taking a pic as long as I didn't use the flash and didn't publish the image anywhere."

"Can you send it to me? I'd like to take a look at it."

"Sure. Give me a second. I need to scroll through the pics on my phone. Do you want me to email it or text it to you?" Jillian switched the phone to speaker and thumbed through her pictures.

"Email it, so I can look at it on the laptop. I trust the train's WiFi more than I do my cell signal at the moment."

After finding the image and entering Kieran's email address in the "To" field, Jillian hit send. "It's en route to you. Why are you worried about a letter when you are on your way to one of the most fascinating cities on earth?"

Kieran laughed. "I was thinking of our date and my mind drifted to our conversation last night. I'll answer your question about the letter as soon as it finishes downloading. Do you have anything special planned today?"

"I was thinking of a hike then visiting Santa Chiara."

"Nice! If you haven't ever been for a massage at Hotel Mamani, you might want to see if they have any availability today or tomorrow."

"A massage sounds good."

"Give me a second to read this, Jillie."

Jillian smiled at how Kieran shortened her name. She pulled her shoes over to the couch.

"Jillian, you've definitely stumbled across a very unique letter, but it wasn't written by Baldassare."

"How do you know Baldassare wasn't the author?" Jillian stopped tying her laces, confused by Kieran's statement.

"Firstly, Baldassare died in 1529." Kieran's voice dropped to a muffled pitch once more.

By his mumbling, Jillian knew he was reading the letter. Forgetting about her shoe laces, Jillian turned her laptop on, wanting to confirm when Baldassare died. She groaned, seeing Kieran was right. She should have verified

Baldassare was the author before telling anyone about the document.

"Sorry, Jillian. I was rereading the closing of the letter. This is an incredible find! Giovanni Battista Castiglione wrote it. If you look closely, you will see a faint outline of a G before the B. The camera lens may pick it up better than your eye does with as faded as it is. There's been suspicion that Giovanni served as a secret liaison to Italy on Henry's behalf, but no one could prove it until now. He was even sent to the Tower for a period of time. The English ambassador mentioned in the note must have been the one who provided it to the duke. It doesn't sound like the ambassador traveled alone. Do you know who else was with him?"

"No idea." Jillian winced as she forced the lie out. "Would it be normal for Henry to dispatch a merchant to assist in negotiating trade agreements?"

"A merchant? I suppose anything is possible, considering how covertly the negotiations between the Duke of Urbino and Henry were conducted, but realistically, that would be highly unlikely. What makes you think Henry sent a merchant to represent him?"

"The court records document the presence of an English merchant in Urbino at the same time as the ambassador." Jillian prayed she sounded more confident than she felt about her answer.

"Tell you what, I will call a friend of mine who is a specialist on diplomacy during the Tudor period to see if a merchant negotiating on the king's behalf could have occurred. More than likely, the merchant you found was the one who transported and escorted the ambassador to Urbino. Did the records mention if the merchant disappeared like the ambassador?"

"No, nothing further is written beside the one entry."
Jillian's suspicions about Rouen and his part in the negotiations once again turned in an uncomfortable direction. *Did Rouen have a role in the ambassador's death?*

She heard a ding followed by a loud, muffled announcement through the phone along with the sounds of people pulling down their luggage.

"We are coming into Bologna and need to change trains. I'll call you as soon as I hear back from my colleague at the University of London."

"Thanks, Kieran. Safe travels to Rome." Jillian hung up and finished tying her shoes.

A long hike would calm her nerves once more. Rouen couldn't have harmed anyone. Other than the occasional outburst, the ghost didn't exhibit any behaviors that suggested he was capable of killing.

***

After her hike, Jillian stopped at Santa Chiara. The High Institute for Art Industries claimed the old monastery building. Jillian wondered what Francesco di Giorgio Martini and Federico Montefeltro might think of their religious institution being transformed for secular use.

Francesco Della Rovere and Eleonora, Lady Leonora as Rouen referred to her, rested within the church along with several other important figures of Urbino's past.

Jillian stood in front of the tomb believed to hold Battista Sforza's remains. Battista was Federico Montefeltro's second wife. Federico, arguably the most well-known Duke of Urbino, declared her to be the love of his life in his writings. He commissioned multiple paintings of her shortly after she died. She birthed seven of the duke's heirs at a young age. She died ten years earlier than Federico. When he passed away in 1482, he couldn't be buried with her as the church was still part of an active convent. The duke had a special funerary chapel constructed for himself on the adjacent hill facing the convent so that he may see his wife every day from his resting place.

"What draws you to visit Battista?" Rouen's voice interrupted her musings.

"I am not sure. I swear I once heard a tale of Federico riding out here daily to visit his wife after she died. Is it true?"

"It is. Federico made those trips to pay tribute to his wife and to visit with those here at the monastery. He was the principal patron for Santa Chiara while he lived."

"Do you believe the stories of Battista and Federico being madly in love with one another?" Jillian watched an amused smile spread across Rouen's face.

"Federico never remarried after she died. Others described them as 'two souls in one body.' I think that description bears testimony to what Battista and Federico felt toward one another."

Jillian maintained direct eye contact with the ghost. She wanted to know what those storm-colored eyes witnessed over the expanse of time; to discover whatever secret he tried to keep buried in the hills of Urbino.

"So you believe it is possible for two people to fall that deeply in love with one another? Even in a situation like an arranged marriage?"

"I believe I am living proof that anything we may imagine, good or bad, is possible, Jillian. What preoccupies your thoughts for you to ask such questions?"

"I am contemplating whether what we know of the world we live in and what we call history is fact oriented or more myth based on what those before us want us to remember."

Rouen looked away from her. "All stories contain bias of some kind. No matter who holds the pen, there is always a reason the author inscribes words on paper."

"What would an author share about your life?"

"I would hope historians would write that I was a man who tried to live with integrity and to honor my commitments."

"How can anyone write that with the secrets you keep?" Jillian noted the sideways glance he gave her.

At that moment, she understood Rouen would more than likely never share the answers to the questions she had. It hurt a bit to realize she would never fully know who he was.

"Would love be somewhere in your story, Rouen?"

The question captured his attention with how quickly his gaze turned back to hers.

"I hope one day it will be. That poets and writers will describe my relationship with whatever woman finds her way into my life in a similar fashion to Battista and Federico."

His response surprised Jillian. She half expected him to declare love was not a consideration in his life. That he was a man married only to whatever tasking the king assigned him. "Sounds like you are a romantic at heart underneath that reserved exterior."

"Does it truly surprise you to learn I desire to share my days with someone?"

"Yes, actually, it does. You seem to be a man of logic and reason. Love like you describe is neither rational nor logical. May you find what you long for, Rouen. In the meantime, I guess the two of us will have to tolerate one another's company. Have you found any evidence of what-ever Kieran may be plotting? I assume that is what you've been up to today."

"Nothing damning that would convince you to heed my warnings. Even so, I have not given up my search yet. I am also more than happy to have you as my lone companion, Jillian. You are a brilliant woman, albeit troublesome at times."

Jillian noted how Rouen once again smiled before staring at one of the frescoes on the ceiling. "Thank you for returning everything to the archives. Doing so ensures Simonetta keeps her job."

"As I have told you numerous times before, I have no desire to harm anyone. I merely need to protect them from my circumstances."

"Care to elaborate on that?"

After standing beside him in silence, Jillian shrugged. "All right, ghost. Have it your way. With the sources back, I will figure it out on my own."

Jillian picked up her backpack then walked out the door.

"Jillian! Where are you going?" Rouen followed her outside. He didn't want to fight with her again. *Damn, the woman was stubborn if she headed to the archives after promising not to.*

"Basilli, for a glass of wine then the apartment. You coming or are you communing with Leonora to dig up dirt on Kieran? You've only got about twenty-six hours left to prove your theory of Kieran being evil."

"I am not wrong, Jillian."

Her laughter as she continued her trek towards the historic center further irritated him.

"Well, I guess one assassin would recognize another."

Jillian tested the ghost more than she should have.

"Assassin?" Rouen caught up with her, not liking her associating him with such a profession.

"Ever heard the name Giovanni Battista Castiglione?" Jillian turned to face him once more.

"The young teacher from Gassino?"

"We both know Castiglione was also a mercenary for hire. He fought for Charles the Fifth and for Henry, if I recall correctly. He wrote the letter I found in the archives. Did you or the ambassador carry it to Urbino?"

Rouen looked away from her, debating how to answer. He needed her to believe him. No harm could come from telling her the truth about the letter.

"I carried it. We risked the letter being discovered if anyone else transported it. Neither Cromwell nor the Pope's men would search me for it, as they wouldn't suspect me to be an agent of the king."

"You carried it? Explain to me what you were doing here with the ambassador again."

"Is there a reason for this newfound mistrust of me, Jillian?" Rouen kept his eyes level with hers.

"I am awaiting a call from an expert on Tudor diplomacy. You better hope to God that he confirms it is possible that a merchant could conduct negotiations on a king's behalf."

Rouen laughed. "Kieran Moreland is hardly an expert in Tudor diplomacy. What lies is the Hospitaller spinning now?"

"Hospitaller? As in a member of the Knights of Saint John or the Order of Malta?" Jillian recognized the name, but didn't see how Kieran connected to the order.

"Ask your dear professor about the Order of Saint John.

There is an ancient sect that broke off from the Order of Malta. I suspect Dr. Moreland is a member of that group with the emblem sewn into his jacket and his meetings with Francesco."

"Wait. What meetings?" Rouen's claims further puzzled Jillian.

"The Director of the Archives and Kieran met about you and your research over coffee at Basilli. Francesco contacted Kieran and someone else about the papers you found."

"I don't believe you, Rouen. Kieran was surprised when I shared what I was really researching. He's been nothing but helpful."

"No doubt he has been. Please share his colleague's name from London once you learn it. If it has Jordan or William in it, be on your guard, Jillian. I will see you tomorrow." Rouen walked back towards the Art Institute.

"Tomorrow? Where are you going?"

"To find the evidence to prove Dr. Moreland is not here to lecture, but instead, to investigate you. That way you will steer clear of the professor going forward." Rouen vanished from sight.

I hate it when he does that! Jillian wasn't sure which of the two men to trust now.

Kieran sent her a text later that evening to check her email. She opened it to find a forwarded message stating that merchants could serve as envoys in an ambassadorial party, but held no authority to negotiate on behalf of the king or anyone else in the Tudor Court. The author of the forwarded email was a Jordan D'Abernon.

Jillian did a quick internet search on Jordan D'Abernon. She almost dropped her glass of wine after finding a picture of *Sir* Jordan D'Abernon, lecturer at the University of

London, and knight of the Order of Saint John.

CHAPTER ELEVEN

Yesterday had been chilly, but beautiful. Today's weather contrasted that. Miserable was the only word Jillian could think of to describe the darkened skies over the normally colorful countryside. She sat on the couch enjoying a lazy afternoon curled up under a blanket with a cup of hot tea. She listened to the rain striking against her windows.

Rouen hadn't paid his daily visit yet. She wondered what he might be doing with as intent as he was on proving Kieran's villainous motives for being in Urbino. She chuckled to herself thinking Rouen imagined things or was jealous that he now had to share her attention with someone else.

Her phone buzzed as a text came in.

Jillian smiled, seeing Kieran's name above the text. *Well, think of the devil...*

> We should be back in Urbino between six and six thirty. Does meeting at Trattoria Leone around seven work for dinner?

The man had good taste. Trattoria Leone was one of her favorite restaurants in town.

Works perfectly! See you then. She typed back then hit send.

"Why do you insist on associating with Kieran after I have warned you about him?" Rouen announced his arrival, reading the text over her shoulder.

"Because I like Kieran, and you haven't produced any proof that the professor has dishonorable intentions."

"Did you ever learn the professor's name who is a supposed expert on Tudor diplomacy?"

"Oddly enough, the man's name is Jordan D'Abernon. Sir Jordan D'Abernon, a Knight in the Order of Saint John." Jillian set her phone down seeing a bag in Rouen's hands.

Rouen extended it to Jillian. "The evidence into Kieran's character you requested, my lady."

"Did you steal this from his room?"

"Look inside it."

"Rouen, you should not take other people's things if you want historians to say you are a man with integrity."

"Open the bag, Jillian." Rouen scowled, not appreciating her rebuking him.

Jillian muttered under her breath, but pulled the flap aside and unzipped the main compartment. She withdrew a brown document portfolio from the soft leather case.

"I can't believe I am letting you drag me down to your level, Rouen." She undid the band around the portfolio to discover the missing trade agreement and Henry's letter. "What in the...? How did he get these?"

"I told you not to trust him."

"How do I know you didn't put them in Kieran's bag?" Jillian tested the ghost. It was possible he concocted such a scheme with as much as he disliked Kieran. The way

Rouen's nose wrinkled and brow furled at the accusation confirmed he hadn't. Indignation like what was in his expression couldn't be faked.

"Your accusation offends me, madam. This is almost as disgraceful as being accused of killing a fellow Englishman. You asked for proof. I delivered it to you. Now, I must endure being insulted for producing what you requested."

"I am sorry, Rouen. I don't know what to think about all of this. All it proves is he is verifying my research."

Jillian tucked the folder back into Kieran's bag.

"He is doing more than verifying what you shared with him."

Jillian closed up the portfolio, debating what to do about dinner. "Take this back to his room."

"Jillian, you must exercise more caution in any conversations with him. I will find a way to prove my accusation. Can you not give me the benefit with my knowing the other professor's name and tie to the Order of Saint John?"

Jillian groaned, still unsure of what to think about everything. She rubbed her temples, wondering what Rouen did that she was caught up in now.

"How are you and the Order of Saint John linked? At least tell me that."

"My father was a knight of the order."

Rouen sat down beside her.

"But you aren't landed gentry or a noble. You expect me to believe a merchant was a knight in a medieval order?"

"My father was a minor member of the order. And merchants could be made knights if they served the king in my time, just as they are today. They did not need to be landed gentry or nobles."

Jillian shook her head, wishing Rouen would tell her the

truth about everything. "Will you please just share what really happened five hundred years ago?"

"I already told you. I came to Urbino in a diplomatic capacity to negotiate trade agreements. Giselle and I crossed paths once more here. She extended my curse to a thousand years and limited my travels to Urbino alone."

"Do you think Kieran is an associate of Giselle's?" Jillian couldn't believe she actually uttered that question.

"No. There are no talismans in his room to suggest he is a warlock of any sort."

Jillian found how authoritatively Rouen spoke even more outlandish than his refusal to give her all the details about his time in Urbino.

"Witches, ghosts, trade agreements, and now evil archaeologists. I regret deciding to come back to Urbino. I should have just had a mid-life crisis back in Texas. It would have been easier to deal with."

The laughter that emanated from Rouen brought a smile to her face. She made the man genuinely laugh as she never had previously.

**

Rouen escorted Jillian to dinner. Tonight, she didn't argue with him about playing chaperone. She wanted him there.

She noticed the rapier gracing his hip once more. The weapon had been missing the last few times she saw him.

"Rouen, do I need to cancel dinner with Kieran?"

"I do not think that is necessary. If Kieran intended to physically harm you, he would have done so by now."

Jillian stepped out of the main road to allow others to pass them. "Then why are you armed?"

"I am always armed, Jillian. I conceal a dagger on my

person. I carry the rapier in the evenings and when traveling in unknown territory. Even in times of peace, one can never be too careful. Urbino was not as safe in 1535 as it is in modern day."

"That makes me feel a little better. I was worried that you wore it because of Kieran, not that you could do anything to him anyhow."

"Kieran does not display any traits of an assassin. If he did, I would have nailed your apartment door shut so that you could not leave it."

Jillian laughed at how Rouen tried to ease the tension she felt. "Does an assassin display tells to their profession?"

"Indeed, they do. And no, I will not share how I have such knowledge. Shall we continue on, Jillian, or have you changed your mind about another date with Kieran?"

Jillian started towards the restaurant once more. "Until you either come clean or provide something other than archival documents that support Kieran's alleged ill intent, I am willing to take my chances with the professor."

"But you are beginning to have doubts about the man's character to notice my sidearm and our discussion earlier."

"I am wondering about both your and Kieran's character to be honest. You know how to remedy that." Jillian turned down the street where the restaurant was located.

"I have shared all I can, Jillian."

Kieran met them outside the trattoria door. "You look lovely as always this evening."

"Thank you. How was Rome?" Jillian politely inquired as they followed the host over to their table.

"Much more tolerable than normal with this engaged group of students. While Rome is my favorite place to visit, it isn't always enjoyable if you have to death-march a group of undergrads from site to site."

Their conversation stayed centered on Rome as they ate. Rouen's relaxed demeanor lessened Jillian's anxiety about Kieran. Kieran's friendly manner and love of Rome managed to erase any doubts Jillian had about being safe with him.

Jillian cast a quick glance over at Rouen sitting beside her. The ghost's arms were folded over his chest, his head slightly angled down as if watching something on the table. He was probably bored out of his mind. While it was nice of him to want to protect her, it was unfair to ask him to continually supervise any interactions with Kieran. Not to mention, she didn't want him constantly around if the relationship between her and Kieran evolved into a more romantic nature. There was only one way to find out if Kieran was some villainous mastermind or the nice professor he seemed to be.

"Kieran, how do you and Jordan D'Aberon know one another?"

Rouen's head snapped up. The inquiry got both men's attention with the way Kieran stared at Jillian, puzzled.

"We met at a conference. We've also worked together on a couple of projects. He was the site historian, and I was the archaeologist overseeing the excavations. Why do you ask?"

Jillian toyed with what was left on her plate. "I noticed D'Aberon was a Knight of Malta when I looked him up. I wanted to know his background in case I needed help with any future research projects."

"He's an excellent contact to have. I would be happy to make introductions if you'd like." Kieran wondered where the conversation really headed.

"I know this is going to sound crazy, but do you work for someone other than Cambridge University?"

"I consult and freelance as an independent contractor at times. Jillian, if something about me is upsetting or concerning to you, just say it outright."

"Someone told me you had a meeting with Francesco about my research."

Kieran sat back in his chair. "I did."

"He freely admits it?" Rouen thought Kieran bold to so casually confirm he met with the archival director.

Other than a quick glance Rouen's way, Jillian stayed focused on Kieran.

"Why were the two of you discussing my work?"

"I wanted to help you out. Francesco and I have collaborated in the past on an archaeological seminar jointly offered by Cambridge and the University of Urbino. I hoped he might know where the documents were that went missing."

Jillian set her napkin down on the table louder than she meant to. "You told Francesco? I promised Simonetta no one would find out, and you tell her boss without asking me first. I told you all of that in confidence."

"Jillian, I am sorry." Kieran gently took her hand. "You never told me Francesco didn't know about the missing documents. And don't worry about Simonetta. Her job is safe. Next time, I will invite you to any meetings I have about your research."

Rouen glared at Kieran with how he spoke in half-truths.

Kieran's thumb soothingly traveled Jillian's knuckles. "I swear to you, Jillian, I never meant to betray your confidences or hurt you in anyway."

"I hate being lied to, Kieran. I also hate learning things about the men in my life through the grapevine. You asked me to be up front with you, please do the same for me. Nathan repeatedly lied to me about the affair he was having, instead of just ending things." More came out of her mouth than intended.

"Oh, Jillian." Kieran scooted his chair over and hugged her. "I am sorry you went through that."

Seeing Kieran lean to kiss her, Rouen flipped Kieran's full water glass.

Ice water cascaded down the front of the professor.

The freezing sensation on his chest and lap caused Kieran to jerk back. "Bloody hell! I don't even know how I managed to spill that."

"Freak accidents happen." Jillian handed Kieran her napkin, giving Rouen a stern stare. She knew exactly how the glass tipped over.

"Bid this lying, hedge-born churl a good night. He isn't worthy of your company. He is lucky I cannot do anything to him after that performance. Damn crooked-nose knave."

"Rouen!" Jillian tried not to laugh at the medieval insults the ghost rattled off.

"What did you just call me?" Kieran wondered about the name Jillian used.

"I am sorry. The past few days have been so crazy. I meant to say Kieran." Jillian noted how Rouen's eyes remained locked on Kieran. "We should probably call it a night. You are going to need to change, and I'm, I'm a bit tired after the long hike today. Aperitivo tomorrow?"

"I was hoping for breakfast instead, but beggars can't be choosers." Kieran winked at Jillian, making her smile again.

The loud scoff Rouen let out caused Jillian to look up at him. The ghost looked ready to slay the man.

"Disrespectful, ridiculous, yaldson! Urbino Casanova is exactly what this man is, Jillian. As if I would allow some impertinent ass to take you to his bed."

"I'll call you tomorrow, Kieran." Jillian kissed Kieran on the cheek to avoid inciting Rouen's temper any further.

She could barely contain her laughter with the barrage of insults and comments that spewed from Rouen's mouth until they reached the restaurant door.

Out of Kieran's earshot, Jillian burst into hysterics as they walked down the street. "Stop, Rouen! You are going to make me cry. I am laughing so much."

"I fail to see the humor in the events of this evening. Kieran lies to you, then implies he intended to bed you. That is no way for a man to converse with a lady. This sort of behavior is the exact reason I did not want you alone with him. You should cease seeing him."

"It's called flirting, Rouen."

"There was nothing flirtatious about his remark, Jillian. The man meant what he said. He desires you in a carnal manner."

"I can see this discussion is going nowhere." Jillian rolled her eyes then walked silently beside Rouen, so the ghost's temper could cool.

After Rouen seemed calm, Jillian decided to set some ground rules for future dates.

"You didn't need to throw the glass of water on him."

"I didn't throw it. I tipped it over." Rouen muttered, fighting the urge to snarl at her. "What else could I have done to cool the man's passions?"

"His passions? He really got under your skin tonight."

"He attempted to kiss you immediately after spewing falsehoods."

"Kieran admitted to meeting with Francesco and apologized for it. And he didn't know about Nathan." Jillian defended the archaeologist.

"He still did not disclose the entirety of he and Francesco's discussion."

"Rouen, I appreciate that you want to look out for me, but from my perspective, Kieran was honest with me tonight. I am willing to give him a second chance."

Rouen shook his head. "He is not worthy of one."

"Let me decide that. I am a big girl." Jillian unlocked the apartment building's front door since they reached it. "As my original date of the evening had to go change clothes, I don't suppose you'd want to take his place in watching a movie with me."

"Is that a sincere invitation, Jillian?" Rouen doubted she would want him hanging around.

"There's room for an archaeologist and a grumpy ghost in my life. Just try to be nicer to Kieran from now on."

"I cannot promise anything." Rouen looked away from Jillian before following her upstairs.

***

Halfway through the film, Jillian looked over at Rouen sitting in the dark next to her. Part of her was curious to know what he'd be like as a human. Maybe it was the movie's storyline or the fourth glass of wine she had when they got home, but the impulse to touch him caused her hand to reach out for his thigh.

The movement made him aware that she watched him. He enjoyed the way she now rested her head against her hand, her elbow propped against the back of the couch, openly admiring him.

"What are you contemplating, Jillian?"

"You." Jillian widened the smile on his face.

"What about me?"

"I am sure it's the wine talking. But, I am wondering, if you were real, could it work between us?" Jillian's pulse beat a little louder in her ears. She looked down at the cushion under her, not believing she was voicing her thoughts aloud.

"Could what work between us?" Rouen pretended not to understand the remark.

The deepening of his voice conveyed he knew what she meant. Jillian raised her eyes to his again.

"I guess I mean, could this crazy relationship between us be something more than friendship if you were human?"

"If I ever find myself human again, and no one claims you, I would more than happily court you." Rouen surprised himself by admitting that he would.

Jillian caught herself starting to lean closer to him. "I am definitely buzzed. I think it's bedtime."

She got up from the couch.

Not wanting her to leave him just yet, Rouen's fingers closed around her wrist. Without thinking, he gently pulled her downward once more.

Finding herself in his lap, Jillian laughed. One of her arms settled around his shoulders and neck. "If only you were real, Rouen."

Rouen swallowed hard, staring at the woman he held. Feeling the soft shirt she wore, the weight of her body against his, and her fingers brushing against the stubble dotting his jaw exhilarated and terrified him at the same time. A faint whiff of lavender subtly teased his nose; an aphrodisiacal thrill coursed through his being. The light floral scent wafting off Jillian's skin had never before seduced him as it did tonight. He closed his eyes; immersing himself in the intimate moment with Jillian. The way her fingers moved upward into his hair then followed the outline of his ear, drifting downwards until her hand found a comfortable resting place against his chest, lulled him into a deceiving state of blissful desire. He wanted Jillian more than he could ever recall wanting another woman. Tonight, fate presented him the opportunity for respite from centuries of seclusion. All he had to do was place his lips to hers.

Only Giselle creates such alluring moments! Rouen's conscience checked his emotions. *The witch trifles with me!* The last thing he wanted was for Jillian to somehow be caught up in his curse. She didn't deserve that kind of suffering.

He opened his eyes to find Jillian curiously staring up at him. The strengthening of his pulse warned he needed to end whatever was happening.

"Jillian?"

"Yes?" Jillian's eyes lowered to his lips.

He didn't need her to share that she wondered what it would be like to kiss him. Her body more than shouted her thoughts at him. She titled her face closer to his; further tempting Rouen to cross the line of polite decorum. Afraid he'd give in, he cleared his throat and forced himself to sit straighter against the back of the couch, creating a bit more physical distance between them.

"You've definitely imbibed too much wine this evening. Go to bed, love."

"Good night, Rouen." She whispered in his ear, then kissed his cheek.

The lingering kiss seared his skin. He fought the urge to

ever-so-slightly turn his face, so that his lips would meet her's. Her fingers trailed down his arm, then fell into thin air after they grazed the top of his hand.

Rouen shifted uncomfortably; watching Jillian close her bedroom door. He existed as a mere shade once more. But for a fleeting moment, Jillian made him flesh and blood. That brief encounter was all the incentive he needed to re-gain hope of eventual reprieve. After what happened tonight, he was willing to be damned a thousand times more before he would ever allow Kieran to freely romance Jillian. The professor was not worthy of a woman that could gift humanity to a lost soul.

CHAPTER TWELVE

Deciding to go back to the archives to see if she could find any further information on Rouen or the mysterious English ambassador, Jillian picked up her briefcase and grabbed her keys.

Her apartment door bouncing off the wall on its own made her drop her bag back onto the table.

"Knock instead of giving me a heart attack." Jillian knew Rouen must have been the invisible force that threw the door open.

Rouen shoved a green folder into her hands. "You need to see this, now."

"Why right now?" Jillian set the folder beside her brief case then checked to ensure she hadn't damaged her laptop when she dropped it.

"Kieran is on his way here. Forget about your computer and look at that folder. We only have a few minutes." Rouen picked up the folder and held it out to her once more.

"Fine." Jillian separated the two sections of the folder, expecting to see some random papers. Photographs of her and handwritten notes about her activities in Urbino rested inside the pockets. She pulled the notes out, not believing someone tracked her from her second day in town.

"That is not my hand. You cannot accuse me of forging those." Rouen half expected her to dismiss the notes as she did the archival documents.

"This is definitely Kieran's handwriting. I recognize it from his lecture notes and when he signed the bill. Why is Kieran on his way here?"

A knock on the open door announced Kieran's arrival. He stood in the open doorway with a puzzled expression on his face. "I am here to sign my lease on the apartment next door. Who are you talking to?"

"No one." Jillian glanced back down at the folder in her hand. "What is this, Kieran? Please tell me you aren't stalking me."

Kieran recognized the green folder she held. "How did you..."

"How I got it isn't important." Jillian cut off the question, giving him a glare.

"I... I can explain that. Give me a minute. I need to get something from next door." Kieran pulled the keys to his new place out of his jacket pocket. "I'll be right back."

The archaeologist disappeared from the doorway.

Jillian heard a wood door slab hit its stopper and hurried footsteps on the other side of the wall.

Rouen couldn't believe Jillian just stood there. "You aren't honestly going to listen to the man? He's lied to you from the moment he met you."

"You haven't exactly been honest yourself. I want to know what is going on and why someone is watching me."

Kieran returned and handed Jillian a small wrapped package. "You will want to sit down for this."

Jillian pulled a chair out at the table, then stared at the package she held.

"Open it." Kieran sat in the chair next to hers.

She carefully unwrapped the parcel. The worn leather cover of an old book surfaced from underneath the brown paper. It was a collection of folklore from England.

"Turn to the page I marked and read it."

Jillian couldn't believe what was written in the book. She re-read the short tale of a cursed knight who refused to give in to a witch tempting him to oppose William the First. At his refusal to do so, the witch burned the village he was lord of to the ground. The knight fought the witch and her minions as his men evacuated the village. For standing between her and her desire to see Normandy fall, the witch damned the man to spend eternity as a shade. No one could ever see or hear him. Nothing living would show him compassion or comfort of any kind.

"Rouen." Jillian muttered the ghost's name, catching his attention.

Rouen immediately tensed. *What had the professor given to her?*

Jillian stared at Kieran flabbergasted. "You found my tale of Rouen."

Kieran smiled. "I was surprised to find it myself when flipping through the book last night. I almost didn't bring it with me. I'm glad I changed my mind. While it's not the right time period and the man's name isn't Rouen, it's the closest story I could find to the one you shared. The next page has an illustration you need to see."

Jillian turned the page. She brought her fingers to her lips, trying to hide her surprise. Everything in the hand-drawn picture of the knight confronting the witch was in black and white except for the pendant around his neck. The citrine almost jumped off the page with its warm, honey-gold hue.

Kieran noted how Jillian looked up at the empty end of the table.

"There's a bit more I learned about this tale and the mystery surrounding a few families descended from William's knights." Kieran drew her attention back to him.

Rouen placed one hand on the back of her chair and his other on the table to see what was captured in the book. His face went whiter than normal, recognizing the illustration.

"Please turn the page back to the fairytale that this belongs to."

Jillian flipped the page, pretending to admire the calligraphy, so Rouen could read it.

Kieran thought Jillian's shifting of the book was a bit strange, but he continued saying what he needed to.

"The witch supposedly wandered through the Norman knights and tempted three others. Two of whom were found dead the morning after she confronted them. The third attempted to assassinate the king, but was stopped by an archangel who appeared at the exact moment the knight attacked William. The angel warned William of the witch's scheme. The king immediately ordered his bishops to find the witch and vanquish her. She used to be rumored to walk the Norman provinces every hundred years, trying to avenge her vanquishing, and to find a champion that would strike down William's descendants. The tale was told to little boys to teach them the importance of loyalty. It fell out of favor during the Enlightenment."

"Is it possible the witch returned in the early fifteen-hundreds?" Jillian asked, moved that Kieran actually looked into Rouen's situation for her.

"Very possible. If you believe in that sort of thing." Kieran noted how Jillian unconsciously touched the stone hanging from her neck, "Your friend's gift also has an interesting history. It is said that the stone was given to William by the archangel. William, in turn, gave it to who was rumored to be his favorite son."

Everything Kieran shared fascinated Jillian.

"Which one of his four? Was it William II if he inherited England?"

"No." Kieran shook his head,

"Robert? Henry? Richard?" Jillian named the king's other three sons.

"Those are the sons history wants the world to remember. Lore has it, that William fell in love with a woman before his marriage to Mathilda. That woman bore him a child raised with the king's legitimate sons. William changed his name to Reynard Durrant to hide the boy's birthright. The archangel stressed to the king that the eldest son's identity remain a secret until it was necessary that his true lineage be revealed as the witch searched for that particular son. William confessed the boy's existence to a monk on his deathbed. The Church erased the story from most documents to preserve Mathilda's reputation and to prevent any future conflicts between the sons. The pendant you are wearing was passed down the Durrant line. Whoever your friend is, he is the descendant of the son who rightfully should have inherited William's throne."

"Ask him if he has any evidence to legitimize this ludicrous story." Rouen almost growled behind her. Kieran slandered one of the most famous monarchs of all time with the fallacies he spoke.

Jillian noted the way Rouen clenched his jaw every so often, staring holes into Kieran.

"Kieran, that is an amazing account if it is true. It would be one hell of a historical find if it were ever more than just rumor. Where did you find out about all this? Are there any sources to substantiate everything you just told me?" Jillian was as curious as Rouen was defensive of the monarch.

"My father told me the story and his father told him. My great-grandfather told my grandfather, and so on. My ancestors include the monk the king confessed to and the brother of the second knight the witch tempted. My family has the monk's written account. We've watched over the Durrant line for centuries now. Well, that is until one of them disappeared in Urbino almost five centuries ago. You are the first person to successfully find any proof of his existence. Francesco alerted me and Jordan of your research. After Francesco emailed us a copy of the photograph you took of the 're-enactor' on the palazzo balcony, we had one of our local contacts look in to who you were."

Kieran laid a pendant similar to Jillian's on the table. The only difference was the stone in his was an amethyst.

"I am a member of the Order of Saint John, Jillian. If you've found Reynard's descendant, we need to know."

Rouen mumbled something, then shook his head, backing away from the table.

Jillian only caught a part of what the ghost mumbled. "What do you mean he'll bring her here?"

Rouen dissolved from Jillian's view.

Confusion painted itself across Kieran's face. "Bring who, where?"

"I am so sorry, Kieran. I have to go."

"Go?" Kieran grabbed her arm. "Where are you

going?"

"I'll explain later." Jillian kissed him then ran out the door.

Kieran stared down at the illustration, wondering about Jillian's exit. Revelation set in. A businessman gave her the pendant! A merchant was another name for a businessman. He now understood why Jillian periodically stared into empty corners and the reason she called him Rouen last night. Francesco was right about someone guiding Jillian!

He grabbed her keys off the table and shut the apartment door behind him.

Jillian was nowhere in sight by the time he made it down to the street. He asked several people walking by if they had seen her. After he described her, they pointed towards the ducal palace.

CHAPTER THIRTEEN

"Rouen! Rouen, please come out! I know you are here and I cannot come to you." Jillian called from outside the locked doors of the church. She grew more and more frustrated when the spirit didn't show himself. "Fine, be the stubborn pain in the ass that you are! I look like a crazy woman standing out here yelling. We also just left the one person who might be able to help you."

The doors to the church remained a sealed, looming barrier before her. Frustrated, she slapped her hand against them.

"You were right about Kieran, Rouen. I am sorry I didn't listen. I should have known better than to believe he had a sincere interest in me after you tried to warn me. Guys like that just don't notice women like me." She muttered the last sentence under her breath.

The door to the church swung open.

"I am certain that last statement is not at all true. You have caught the eye of more than one man over the past month."

Jillian smiled, relieved that Rouen answered her. Not seeing him in the doorway, she headed to the side chapel where she knew he regularly sat. The lights turned on as she neared it.

"Why did you leave so suddenly?"

"Kieran is not who I feared him to be." Rouen turned from the altar to look at her.

"You are a terrible liar, Rouen. I saw your face as you looked at the drawing and Kieran's medallion. I heard you say something about someone coming here. You left because something spooked you."

"I suffer one of the worst fates that a man can receive. Nonsense and children's stories are not about to frighten me."

"It sure doesn't look that way to me. If it wasn't the children's stories, it was the pendant. Are you Reynard Durrant's descendant?" Jillian believed the exposure of his true identity upset him more than anything.

Rouen stared at her, not saying a word. He seemed frozen in time.

"You are, aren't you? You're the surviving heir to William's throne." The weight of Rouen's heredity set in. "You could usurp Henry's right to rule with that lineage. Is Henry the noble Giselle wanted you to kill?"

Rouen grasped Jillian by the arms. "Swear to me, you will never repeat those words to anyone."

Jillian could feel the man's strong hands wrapped around her forearms. She could smell the leather in the jacket he wore.

He shook her, getting her attention again. "Promise me, Jillian. What you just spoke is treason, and in the wrong company, would threaten your life."

She saw the concern on his face and nodded yes. Finding her voice again, she softly swore to never repeat what she knew. Her fingertips brushed his cheek.

Rouen's features changed from troubled to stupefied.

"I can touch you, Rouen. I can feel the velvet and fur you wear. I smell the leather in your jacket. Either you are becoming mortal or I am joining you in your curse."

Rouen took her face in his hands, testing the truth of her words. Her skin was warm. His fingers could stroke the silky strands of her hair. *He could touch another living being!* He almost cried out in triumph at the feat as he clasped the woman fate brought into his life to his chest.

Jillian could feel his breath on her skin.

Rouen's cheek grazed hers as he loosened his hold and pulled back slightly to stare down at her once more. He was once again a living being subject to the unique desire only corporeality can spark. Lost in a torrent of craving brought on by the proximity of Jillian's body, his lips brushed hers; tentatively testing to see if she would welcome or rebuke his advances.

Jillian's fingers grasped the back of his shoulders, drawing him closer as a second kiss began. Her mouth yielded to the firm pressure of Rouen's against it. She welcomed him to taste her further, enjoying the pleasurable waves traveling through her. Rouen's hand drifting lower on her back to bring her tighter against him only intensified the need awakened within her.

Adrift in the intense magnetism filling the air; past and present converged into one time stopping paradox.

"Droyn Durrant? Can it really be you after all this time?" A male voice interrupted the intimate moment.

Jillian and Rouen turned their heads to see who invaded

the sanctuary the chapel provided them.

Kieran stood in the doorway, dumbfounded by who he now saw. The last direct descendant of Reynard Durrant couldn't be standing before him. The man had disappeared five centuries earlier.

The first-born male Moreland of every generation since the eleventh century was entrusted with protecting the story of the Durrants. Kieran painstakingly memorized every drawing, painting, and history of each family member growing up. There was no doubt in his mind that the last Durrant stood with Jillian.

"You can see Rouen?" The second miracle of the day thrilled Jillian.

"I can. I never imagined the story you told me was true, but the main character stands before me."

The mysterious, lost Durrant was Jillian's Rouen.

"You're free." Jillian whispered, tracing shapes with her finger on Rouen's chest before staring up at him. She loved the smile that spread across his face.

"I am afraid to hope that is the truth." Rouen would give anything to continue holding Jillian as he was.

Jillian laughed. "Find some faith, Rouen. Your days as a shade have ended."

Rouen glanced over his shoulder as if he heard something behind him.

"What is it?" Jillian wondered what caused the change in the man's demeanor. The fear in Rouen's expression when he looked back at her killed any joy she felt.

"Damn it! I hoped she wouldn't follow you here." Rouen's arms fell from Jillian. "Jillian, you must leave. We've endangered ourselves and Urbino."

"I don't understand, Rouen. How have we endangered

Urbino? I am not leaving until you explain everything."

"There's no time." Rouen led Jillian over to Kieran, "You carry the emblem of the order. If Michael and Jordan trusted you with it and the story of the Durrants, I can entrust you with the woman's safety."

"My safety? Why does Kieran need to worry about my safety?"

Rouen drew the weapon at his side for the second time since he came to Italy. He pulled Jillian behind him. His head turned as if he watched something slinking along the walls.

Jillian didn't like the way he acted. "What is it, Rouen?"

Kieran seemed to hear whatever Rouen did. The professor's eyes searched the ceiling above them then dropped to scan the small chapel.

"We're trapped in here." Kieran drew a dagger from his inner jacket pocket. "Their shadows are at the doors."

Jillian couldn't see any shadows. The chapel was silent other than the occasional muffled voice of passersby outside. "Whose shadows? There is nothing at the doors or in here."

The weird sound only Kieran and Rouen heard intensified.

Rouen cast a nervous glance at Kieran. "We must find a way to detain them. You know what she did in York and Dover. She could decimate Urbino in modern times."

Kieran nodded in agreement. "If we can't negotiate with her, I will ensure she doesn't harm Urbino."

"Who are you two talking about?" Jillian snapped louder than either man cared for.

Both shushed her.

"The witch returns." Rouen whispered to Jillian.

"Witches like Giselle don't exist this..." Jillian stopped mid-sentence as the chapel went black.

The candles around the entryway re-lit on their own, casting a dim glow over the small space. A woman came towards them. She reminded Jillian of a sinister supermodel. Tall and lithe with champagne-colored hair.

"Your sentence is not yet served, Rouen Durrant. Who calls you back to the world of the living?"

"Go with Kieran, Jillian. He knows what must be done."

The witch cackled, spotting Jillian behind the man absent from history. "This is the first time a woman makes you mortal, Rouen of Normandy. Has your father's last wish been granted?"

"His final wish was to ensure you could never harm another living soul. I bear this cycle of curses fulfilling his last request." Rouen maneuvered around Giselle, so he could get Jillian closer to the door.

The witch chanted and thrust her hand out at him to send him back to being a shade.

Nothing happened.

Rouen remained flesh and bone before her.

"No! This is not possible."

Rouen laughed at the troubled tone of her voice. "Your magic finally used up, witch?"

"I may not be able to send you back to being a shade, but I can still ensure you spend the rest of your days alone." The witch raised her hand again.

Jillian yanked the gold crucifix from the side altar. "You will not keep torturing him like this. Go back to whatever hell you came from."

She swung the crucifix as hard as she could into the witch's shoulder, knocking her sideways.

"Jillian, no!" Rouen's warning came too late.

Giselle found her feet again. "Perhaps you should take his place!"

Rouen stepped in front of Jillian to shield her from the witch's wrath. He would willingly bear the brunt of whatever attack the magician might launch in retaliation.

"Giselle, the woman only seeks to protect me." Rouen tried to redirect the witch's attention. He kept the tip of his raised weapon pointed at her. "You cannot harm her without releasing me. Saxony can never rise from its ashes if you curse her. I am the only one who can wear my father's crown because of the spell you cast. Your precious state will forever be lost if you punish another person not guilty of the crimes my father committed."

Jillian heard the well-disguised hints of desperation in Rouen's voice. If she hadn't spent so much time with him, she would have missed them. Rouen squared off with a mythical enemy like some gallant hero of old. As Jillian stared up at him, it dawned on her he was the champion of an age long gone. She clearly saw him as he stood in the book's illustration facing the witch for the first time.

"You're the archangel, the knight, and the king's son." Jillian pieced everything together. There was no Reynard Durrant. Whoever Kieran's family studied was the same person in different time periods.

"Keep my secrets. They are not for the world to ever know." Rouen cautioned Jillian to keep her insight to herself.

"If I cannot place you back between the realm of the living and the deceased, you will return to the last life you left, Durrant. Men shall fear you. They will whisper about a cursed man. You will be forced to serve the tyrant on the throne since you refuse to claim your birthright. You will be lord of an ungrateful lot who despise and fear you. No woman of the time will bring you happiness or heirs. Any marriage you pursue will end in betrayal. You will lead as lonely an existence as you did as a shade."

"Until love freely finds its way to him." Jillian said in French, knowing a Saxon would hate the Norman tongue being used in their presence.

"What are you doing?" Rouen thought she lost her senses to provoke Giselle again.

"All curses must have an out, Rouen. Don't you know how fairytales work?" Jillian repeated her earlier statement in French louder. "Do you understand what I am saying, witch? Or do you lack the capacity to speak a foreign tongue?"

"It is the barbarians that lack the competence to understand any language but their own." Giselle raised her hand again to finish the spell.

"What did I say if you understood me?" Jillian knew the witch needed to say the words.

"Do you really think that will save him, naïve woman? Love cannot find a way to a damned soul in the world I am sending him to."

"Then what harm can come from adding it? If you hold the upper hand, there is nothing to lose. Or are you a weak sorcerer easily overridden by something as rare as true love?"

"I am neither weak nor fearful. As the lady wishes, this new curse will be broken only when a love that supersedes time finds you, Durrant." Giselle added her own twist to Jillian's words.

Rouen shoved Jillian in Kieran's direction.

"Run!" was the last thing they heard from him.

Creatures that reminded Jillian of gothic gargoyles converged on Rouen.

They couldn't be real! None of this could be happening!

The moving hoard of wings and misshapen bodies collapsed inward; Rouen disappeared under the monstrous mass.

CHAPTER FOURTEEN

Jillian sprinted with Kieran from the duomo into the city streets.

"This way." Kieran tugged on Jillian's wrist, so they turned down a side street.

"Do you even know where you are going?" Jillian asked, out of breath.

"Unfortunately, yes." Kieran never thought he'd actually be playing the role of guardian as his ancestors did.

He knocked on the door of one of the older homes in the city. He showed his amethyst pendant to a man who answered.

The door swung open. An older gentleman ushered the two inside. They followed him down a hall to an open living room with a large couch. A little boy played contently with some toys in the center of the room.

"You are safe here, Kieran. I will bring you and your friend something to drink." The gentleman shook Kieran's hand before turning to Jillian. "Please, sit and make yourself at home, signora."

Jillian sunk into the soft couch, still trying to rationalize what she just experienced.

Giselle was real. Rouen was sent to another place after being momentarily human again, and Kieran belonged to an actual medieval order supposedly searching for Rouen.

Noting the distressed look on her face, Kieran settled a hand on Jillian's knee. "You okay?"

"No! I am definitely not okay. I just ran from a witch who showed up in a church of all places, to damn a human being. How many times has this happened?"

"Two other times that we know of. It's possible Giselle cursed Rouen more and the order just doesn't know about it." Kieran knew his answer wouldn't ease the confusion and panic Jillian felt.

Jillian wanted to scream at Kieran. *This is nuts, utterly insane!*

"That the order knows of? You have some serious explaining to do, Kieran Moreland. Let's start with what exactly is the Order of Saint John and how could you all lose Rouen in a town as small as Urbino, but I find him without even trying?"

"The Order of Saint John is the oldest group within the Knights of Malta. We are the keepers and guardians of England and Normandy's history. A few of us carry the special charge of looking after William the First's direct descendants, including Reynard Durrant's children." Kieran stopped to let what he said sink in. "And we are still trying to figure out why you found Rouen after we spent hours upon hours scouring every cobblestone and brick in Urbino for any sign of him. The only thing I can think of is Giselle worded the curse in a manner that prevented anyone who knew about him from seeing him. You being a complete stranger and not knowing who he was, for whatever reason, were able to see him."

The homeowner returned with two waters. "Sometimes things just defy logic. Magic, especially black magic like Giselle's, does not follow rationality. Kieran, you should call your father and share what has happened. He can offer some guidance on what to do next."

Kieran nodded, then pulled out his phone.

"I am Luca." The man offered Jillian a glass of water.

Jillian smiled, taking the glass. "Jillian. It's nice to meet you, Luca."

"Piacere mio." (The pleasure is mine.) Luca winked at Jillian, making her laugh. "And this is my grandson, Paolo."

Kieran stepped over to the side of the room to call his father, so he didn't disturb Jillian and Luca's conversation.

Jillian partially listened to Kieran relaying the events of the evening to his father while she sipped her water and chatted with Luca.

"Giselle cannot hurt you when you wear your necklace." Paolo randomly said, touching the medallion hanging around Jillian's neck.

"Che cosa?" (What?) Jillian recognized the young boy. She met him previously at the church.

"I see the knight sometimes too." Paolo advised, then looked over at Luca.

Kieran stopped talking to his father, overhearing what the boy said.

"The king gave you the necklace, so the witch could not curse you. The witch's magic is weakened by it." Paolo went back to playing with his car.

"How do you know that, Paolo?" The boy's grandfather sat down next to Jillian.

"He told me." Paolo kept playing with the car.

"Who told you?" Kieran asked after telling his dad to hang on a minute.

Paolo pointed across the room. "He did."

"Rouen?" Jillian wondered if he was still in Italy.

"That is not his name." Paolo rolled his little car across the coffee table. "He is Rouen's papa, the king. He likes you." Paolo laughed as if someone tickled him. "He says you must find the knight. The knight needs the necklace."

"William, if you are really here, I will do my best to find Rouen and return the amulet. That's what this is, isn't it?"

"Si. Follow the nobles and the crowns." Paolo answered for the king.

Jillian looked at Kieran. "The nobles and the crowns?"

Kieran shrugged; that could mean a hundred different things.

"He wants you to tell the knight he is sorry. The knight assumes his papa's sins." Paolo repeated what the king told him.

After Paolo went back to playing, Kieran brought his phone back to his ear. "Dad, did you hear all of that?"

Jillian thought about what William said. They needed more information than one riddle to find Rouen. "Paolo, is the king still here?"

"No, he left." The boy answered as if William the Conqueror visited him daily.

Kieran gently touched Jillian's arm, getting her attention. "We need to go."

"Go where?" Jillian doubted they could run from the events unfolding.

"England. My father believes we need to start looking for Rouen in England."

"I am not leaving Urbino."

Kieran took Jillian's hand in his. "I know this is scary and confusing, but Rouen needs you. Giselle has almost killed him on more than one occasion. The amulet assists in alerting him to her presence as well as provides some sort of healing protection. It just can't overpower her curses."

"Why hasn't anyone tried to kill her?" Jillian's thoughts reeled in a million different directions.

"We have. On more than one occasion. She has a mystical bodyguard that protects her. She usually sends a minion back to the places Rouen leaves behind. The order will take care of them whenever the henchman shows up. Going to England for a few days ensures you aren't around when the cleanup work takes place. We also must make sure the amulet gets safely to Rouen."

"And how do you intend to get it to him? Giselle sent him back to the sixteenth century. Or, at least I think she did. Don't tell me you and this order are time travelers."

"As far as I am aware, time travel is not possible. If we leave the amulet in the location Rouen inhabits, it will find him. I'll explain it better on the plane." Kieran pulled her towards the door now.

"On the plane?"

"Yes, on the plane. We need to get to Bologna. I'll take you back to your apartment, so you can pack a bag for a couple of days. We shouldn't need to be in England any longer than that."

**

Jillian shoved clothes into a carryon bag. She went into the bathroom to grab her toiletries. Seeing the outline of a woman in her bedroom, she dropped the toiletry bag and shampoo bottle.

"Eleonora." Jillian recognized the duchess from the paintings in the palace.

"Rouen was rather taken with you, Jillian. May you find him again."

Kieran ran into the bedroom. "I heard something hit the floor. Are you okay?"

"I am fine. Eleonora is here. She startled me." Jillian wondered why the specters chose to reveal themselves to her and not anyone else.

Ignoring Kieran, Eleonora smiled at Jillian. "There is something about Rouen that troubles your conscience. Speak whatever it is."

Half not wanting to know the answer, Jillian asked the Duchess the thing about Rouen that bothered her most, "Did Rouen kill the ambassador?"

"Rouen was the ambassador. The merchant story he told you and that you found in my records served to conceal his purpose in being here. There were individuals in England and Italy who did not want any alliance, commercial or military, between our two countries. The mysterious death of the ambassador allowed diplomatic flexibility in handling Rouen's cursed state. I would have been imprisoned or worse if I advised my husband or Henry Tudor that a witch cursed Rouen preventing any further correspondence between Urbino and England. Safe travels, Jillian."

"Thank you, Duchess." Jillian politely bowed her head.

Eleonora vanished from sight.

"She's gone now. What times is our flight?" Jillian picked up the items she dropped then placed them in her carry-on.

"Whenever we get there. My father chartered a private jet that will depart once we arrive."

CHAPTER FIFTEEN

"This is crazy!" Jillian broke the hour-long silence as Kieran drove them to the airport. "This can't be really happening! Tell me I ate something bad before I went to bed and the alarm clock hasn't gone off yet."

Kieran grinned. "I wish I could. How did you discover Rouen after five hundred years of him being invisible?"

"I think he found me. I saw him standing in the Piazza Republica my first night in Urbino. I thought he was a deranged lunatic when I met him the next morning in the palace courtyard. I wish I would have stuck with that opinion. I wouldn't be running away from a witch with some knight from a secret order, to look for an heir history forgot, just to give him a stupid necklace."

"Technically, I am a guardian, not a knight. Would it make you feel better if I shared that this isn't the first crazy thing I've experienced in my life? It could be worse."

Jillian found that hard to believe. "How could it be any worse or stranger than this?"

"Just trust me when I say it can be. There's a reason I am

an archaeology professor. Thought it would keep me out of the field if I did the behind the scenes stuff instead."

"That strategy doesn't seem to be working out too well for you." Jillian fell silent again.

Not liking the silence, Kieran reached to turn on the radio. He muttered under his breath when he couldn't get anything but static. "Are you in love with Rouen? I only ask because of how you got Giselle to alter the curse."

"No. Definitely not." Jillian ignored the cynical expression on Kieran's face. "I guess I'm just a romantic who hopes we all find our soul mates one day. Why not give Rouen something to hope for with being human again? He's bound to find someone."

"Maybe. From an outsider's perspective, it sure looks like you are falling for him after what I walked in on and the escape clause you gave him."

Jillian laughed.

Not wanting to take his eyes off the road for too long, Kieran glanced over at her. "That laugh and the kiss I witnessed says otherwise."

"We were caught up in a moment, nothing more. If I was in love with Rouen, I wouldn't have agreed to go to dinner with you. Besides, a sixteenth-century, moody, cursed merchant that only two people can see isn't exactly my type of guy."

"He isn't a sixteenth-century merchant. Technically, he's a bona fide knight in shining armor. One could even argue he's a prince of sorts. What girl doesn't want to be a princess?"

"I can honestly say I stopped wanting to be a princess around five or six. I am also not a fan of white knights in shining armor. Must be an English thing to hold on to that fantasy into adulthood." Jillian looked back out the window.

"So, what did you want to be, and what type of guy interests you?"

"A pirate." Jillian sighed, thinking back on her younger days. Rouen probably would have been her hero back then. "And I don't have a type of guy. The only consistent theme in the guys I find myself attracted to is dark hair."

"A pirate? Whatever made you want to be a pirate?" That was the last thing he expected to come out of her mouth.

"I don't know. I liked the idea of sailing the seas and seeing the world. The water has always been soothing to me. Maybe I was a sailor in a past life. What about you? Was it your dream to be an archaeologist?"

"Actually, it was. I've always loved the idea of exploring ruins and discovering the past." Kieran confessed, never having wanted to do anything different than his current profession.

"You are one of the lucky few who follow their passions and live the dream. I admire you for that."

Reaching the Bologna airport, Kieran drove to a security gate for the privately chartered aircraft. Once the guard checked their passports, they were flagged through.

He pulled up to one of the hangars and parked the car.

"I take it you regularly fly in and out of here via private charter since you know which gate and hangar to go to."

"It's the only way to travel when on official business." Kieran grabbed their bags from the back seat then ushered Jillian to the waiting jet.

Once on board, Jillian settled herself into a lush leather seat and fastened her seatbelt.

Kieran took the empty seat next to hers. "Is this your

first flight on a private aircraft?"

Jillian shook her head no. "I flew with the CEO of my old firm to two conferences on a company jet. Why?"

"Just curious."

The stewardess offered them a cocktail, glass of wine, or a bottled water. Jillian requested a water and a wine. She sipped the wine as the plane took off. Part of her thrilled at the adventure life presented, the other part of her was terrified of what awaited them in England. Neither she nor Kieran spoke for the first few minutes of the flight. The only sound that could be heard was the stewardess moving something in the front of the jet.

"What happens to Urbino, now?" Jillian broke the tense silence looming over the cabin.

Her question confused Kieran. "Nothing happens to Urbino. Why do you ask?"

"You said Giselle usually sends a minion or two to whatever location Rouen was in. What happens when they arrive?"

"Oh, that." Kieran took a drink of the scotch in his hand. "Urbino and its residents will be fine. The minion only looks for any of Rouen's associates to take hostage. Giselle likes to use them as leverage to try to force Rouen to do her bidding. You are safely out of the city, so whomever Giselle sends should only spend a brief time in Urbino."

"What about the Duchess? Will they harm her?"

"No." Kieran shook his head. "The Duchess is dead. Giselle's powers only work on the living. Eleonora is perfectly safe."

Jillian frowned, looking out the window. "What if Giselle finds us in England?"

"I am not sure. Prior to today, no one in the order has

encountered her since the Middle Ages, except for Rouen. Hopefully, we won't cross paths."

"So, Rouen is a Knight of the Order of Saint John?" With Rouen not liking the order, it surprised her to learn that he was.

"Not exactly. He never underwent initiate rights or took the oath. However, his father did."

"But he is a knight?"

"Yes. He's just not a Hospitaller. From what I understand, he was always suspicious of the order. Think of him as a knight of the realm if that helps."

"Is there any particular reason Rouen was suspicious of you guys?" Jillian found it odd Rouen trusted Kieran with her well-being, but kept the order at arm's length.

"No one has ever shared the reason. If we ever find him again, maybe you can ask him about that."

Jillian smiled at his answer. She doubted she'd ever see Rouen again. Time travel wasn't possible. It was insane to think they were going to try and leave the pendant some place he might find it.

Sensing Jillian didn't want to really converse any longer, Kieran picked up a newspaper. A half hour later, he noticed her yawning and turned slightly in her chair.

"I can ask the stewardess to fold down the seat and get you some bedding, so you can sleep if you like."

"That would be great. I assume we will have a long day ahead trying to figure out where Rouen went."

"More than likely." Kieran motioned for the stewardess to come over.

She happily provided Jillian with a pillow and blanket after reclining Jillian's seat.

Kieran woke Jillian once the plane landed in London.

She looked out the window on her right. Blinking runway lights and pitch-black sky filled the opening. "It's the middle of the night. Where are we headed?"

"A flat the order keeps available for times like these. We'll start looking for Rouen in the morning."

"Sounds like a plan."

Jillian folded her blanket then set it in an empty seat.

A car waited for them only a short distance from the jet. The driver politely greeted them then opened the door for Jillian. She climbed inside, nervous about what would happen next.

CHAPTER SIXTEEN

Jillian sipped her tea, waiting on Kieran to finish eating. "Where do we begin our search, Dr. Moreland?"

"I was thinking maybe the Tower since William built it."

"Sounds like a good place to start to me." Jillian trusted Kieran's expertise.

The two slowly walked the Tower grounds once it opened. After an hour of not seeing anything of significance, they went to the Crown Jewels exhibit.

Finding nothing there, they walked back to the White Tower. Kieran was adamant the clues they searched for would be there.

"All right. Let's think through this. William only spent limited time in England, correct?" Jillian tried to remember what she could about English history.

"About two years. He spent most of his time in Hastings, London, and York. He traveled northward in his conquest of southern England." Kieran pulled up a map on his phone to show Jillian the king's path.

"That is a lot of ground to cover. Rouen would have most

likely been in each location with him." Jillian looked down at the map, frustrated by the size of the potential search area.

"You mean Reynard."

"No," Jillian shook her head. "I mean Rouen. Rouen is Reynard, Kieran. Giselle even called him Rouen of Normandy. How could your family watch over the Durrant line and not figure out the person they looked out for is the same man going by a different name every few years?"

"Sons look like their fathers." Insult gave way to amusement as Kieran realized Jillian was right. "Clever bastard disguised himself by hiding in plain sight. By changing his name, he lessened the chance of anyone discovering his ties to the tale or William, and ensured he was never a threat to whomever sat on the throne."

Jillian laughed. "Or for whatever reason, the order duped you and your ancestors to keep track of him. No wonder Rouen doesn't trust them. Paolo said he spoke to Rouen's Papa-the king, not a knight or disinherited son. If Reynard or whoever Rouen's supposed father is in that cleverly crafted family tree spoke with Paolo, the boy wouldn't have called him a king."

"You do have a point. Either way, we are looking for your Rouen."

"Where was Rouen last in England? The witch was sending him back to the life he had before."

"If he was with William and it is the eleventh century she sent him to, York was the last place Reynard was seen in England. If it is another lifetime with this bouncing he appears to be doing, lord knows. He could be anywhere including some place new in Europe." Kieran wasn't sure what else to tell her.

Jillian put a hand on her hip, annoyed with everything. "He'll leave us some clue if he were here. Playing find Rouen is as irritating as his lying to me about being a merchant."

"That wasn't personal, Jillian. He is good at maintaining whatever ruse he needs. Rouen's hid who he is for so long to keep Giselle at bay, he probably was just trying to ensure the witch never returned to Urbino. He also needed to maintain Henry's confidence should he find himself back in England. I have a feeling Henry used Rouen to handle his more challenging and discreet affairs of state." Kieran advised as they walked back into the White Tower.

"Why Rouen, instead of Suffolk or Cromwell?"

"Cromwell was not well liked and was a politician, not a diplomat. Suffolk was too close to the king. Rouen was an outlier, on published paper, he was a low-ranking member of the aristocracy. He could move in circles Suffolk and Cromwell couldn't." Kieran noted how Jillian frowned. "Another thing to keep in mind is Rouen couldn't risk any strange time shifts that might forewarn the Pope of the alliance attempt. His revealing who he was to you may have altered history as we know it. Henry Tudor would not have reacted kindly to the real reason Rouen met with the Duke of Urbino becoming public. You must understand the tasking Rouen voluntarily undertook for England."

"That doesn't make me feel any better, Kieran. I hate to think what those duties might entail with as brutal a culture as existed in Henry's day."

"The downside of being one of the king's nobles. The king tasked you as he saw fit. The only way to sway the king was to be a master of subtly influencing him to change his position or risk your head."

"Speaking of heads, what else could have been meant by following the crowns and nobles? I am starting to think it wasn't the king and his men William referenced." Jillian asked as they walked the room where the Line of the Kings were on display.

"Besides the monarchy, they were coins." As Kieran said the words aloud, he knew what they were looking for.

"Coins?"

"Yes. Three large hoards of them were unearthed recently in Stafford outside Stafford Castle."

Jillian smiled. They finally figured out William's clue. "Looks like we are headed to Stafford."

***

Two hours later, they found their way to Stafford Castle. The castle was closed.

Kieran called a friend who opened the grounds up for them. The ruins that remained of the Norman stronghold brought visions of medieval grandeur to Jillian's imagination as she walked inside them.

Jillian looked through one of the arched windows and saw two riders speaking with one another on the south side of the hill.

A glimmer from between blades of green caught her eye. A round gold object rested in the tuft of grass now covering what was once the castle floor. She leaned down and picked it up.

"What did you find?" Kieran asked as Jillian handed him the coin.

She looked back out the window to see the horsemen still conversing.

Kieran held the coin up in the sunlight to get a better look at it. "My god, Jillian! Do you know what this is?"

"No idea, but it has the Tudor rose on it."

"It's a crown, Jillian! A crown of the rose to be exact, only two have ever been found. Henry commissioned the coins."

Jillian smiled as he hugged her and asked where she found it. As she pointed to the area, one of the riders turned their horse. She recognized Rouen.

"The nobles!"

Kieran wondered what caused Jillian to run towards the keep entrance.

She didn't slow down. Reaching the exterior walls of the structure, she shouted, "Rouen!"

"Rouen?" Kieran didn't see any sign of the knight.

Jillian kept following Rouen as he rode around the outer wall to the main gate. She ran out the large door trying to stop him from leaving.

"Rouen! Can you hear me?"

Kieran lost sight of her as she disappeared around a large chunk of remaining wall.

"Jillian! Wait! Don't go any further without me."

CHAPTER SEVENTEEN

Thinking she heard Kieran call her name, she turned and looked back at the keep. A fully intact structure now stood where the ruins once did.

"Kieran?" Jillian panicked, wondering where he had gone.

Rouen remained in her line of sight, but Kieran was nowhere to be seen.

Jillian realized she was no longer in modern day. "No. This can't be happening."

She sprinted after Rouen. His horse started to canter about a hundred yards ahead. There's no way she could catch up with him on foot.

"Rouen!" She screamed the man's name. He continued to ride off into the distance. *Had he even heard her?*

An icy rain began to fall from the sky after a loud clap of thunder on an already bone-chilling day. She tilted her face upward in disbelief before pulling her hood up over her head and zipping up her jacket in a feeble attempt to protect herself from the rain.

How in the hell am I going to survive alone in sixteenth-

century England, especially dressed like this?

Jillian kept walking in the direction Rouen rode.

Another horse and rider thundered past, splashing mud up on her, and sending her falling backwards into a newly forming puddle.

After a half hour of walking, her face and hands went numb. An hour into her journey to an unknown destination, she could no longer feel her feet or any other part of her body.

Only I would come to England chasing a fairytale. Any other normal person would have doubted their sanity or pretended the ghost didn't exist back in Italy.

Deciding to jog in an attempt to warm herself up, she tripped over a large tree root she hadn't noticed and face-planted in the wet grass.

"Damn it all to hell!" Thoroughly soaked now, she wanted to cry. "No ghost is worth all of this."

"The ghost may not be worth much, but you might be." A voice announced from above her with a chuckle.

Jillian found herself surrounded by a group of woods-men. The owner of the voice grasped her by the arm and pulled her up.

They certainly are a surly lot. She shivered, surveying the men surrounding her. They seemed as curious about her as she was of them.

"Her dress is strange. Is she a Viking?" One of them whispered.

"I do not know. She speaks English well enough." Another answered.

"My hearing is quite good, gentlemen, and no, I am not a Viking. They don't speak English and dress differently. I'm..." She paused as she realized they would have no clue what an American was. "I am looking for Rouen Durrant. Can you tell me where I may find him?"

"Never heard of him. Is he your lord or master? Wonder how much he'd pay to have you back?" The man who helped her to her feet tilted her face up and pushed the hood from her head to get a better look at the prize that stumbled into their ranks. The woman had all of her teeth and seemed to be in relatively good health.

"He is not my master. If you don't know a Rouen, perhaps you know someone who has this for their crest?" She pulled her chain out from under her jacket.

The Celtic symbol over the golden stone caused the men to jump back from her then suddenly cross themselves and spit on the ground.

A newcomer joined them and saw the amulet hanging around the woman's neck. "You kidnapped the cursed man's servant?!"

"I swear we did not. She came running down the road as if being chased by the devil himself. She must have stolen the man's coat of arms to wear it and be running as she does. Bet she got lost in the woods running away from the earl's house."

"He did ride through here a short time ago. Mayhap, he was hunting for the thief." The man who gave her the once-over before she pulled out the pendant remarked.

"I am not a thief, but I do need to find the man this belongs to."

"The only way you could have that is if you stole it. Droyn Hurrey would never let the pendant leave his house." The newcomer scoffed, "We return the stone to its owner and let him decide what to do with the girl."

"Droyn Hurrey? The man I am looking for is Rouen. I

swear I did not steal the pendant. He gave it to me." Jillian pleaded her innocence as the newcomer bound her hands. *Hell, that even sounded bad to her.*

"Then Droyn will send you on your way when we reach his home."

The man mounted the horse he left nearby.

***

Frozen and frustrated, Jillian walked on her makeshift leash behind the horse as the leader of the band took her to whoever this Hurrey was. While the cold made it feel like they walked for hours, Jillian guessed that they had only gone a few miles from the castle.

Reaching the top of a large hill, a stone manor home came into view.

Dread set in as the men who held her captive began to whisper and cross themselves again.

"Stop with the praying! The only one of us who should be worried about her soul is the woman if she stole the Hurrey crest." The band's leader scolded, crossing the threshold of the large gates before them. He looked back at Jillian and gave her a toothy grin. "Now you on the other hand, lady, you may want to ask God to protect your immortal soul. The earl is not a charitable man, even on a good day. I would hate to be in your place if you did steal from him. Hurrey will probably boil you in oil for doing so."

"Kind of a harsh punishment for petty larceny. Perhaps I can negotiate for having my hand chopped off or an hour on the rack instead?"

The rider laughed. "If you be knowing what is best for you, I would keep your mouth shut, lady. His lordship won't take too kindly to an insolent serf with a sharp tongue who stole his property."

Jillian rolled her eyes. If Hurrey wasn't Rouen, hopefully, the man would at least know Rouen.

***

Snowflakes fluttered down from the sky. The place seemed deserted. If it wasn't for a curled cloud of dark gray smoke coming from the chimney, Jillian would think no one lived at the country estate.

After knocking on the door, her captor jerked on the rope, bringing Jillian alongside him. She almost fell on the front door step from the force he used to yank her forward.

The master of the house appeared behind the steward who opened the door.

Jillian regained her balance. A gust of winter wind cut through her. She clutched her damp jacket tighter trying to find some sense of warmth.

"We caught the woman running through the woods with this." The man handed whom she assumed was Droyn the pendant she once carried.

Droyn's eyes sought the woman referenced. "Jillian!"

He descended the steps to retrieve the pale figure standing on his lawn.

Relief filled Jillian seeing that her ghost and Droyn were one in the same. "Rouen."

Rouen untied the rope from her wrists. He frowned, feeling how damp her clothes were and noting the crispness of wet hair turning to ice. *How did she end up in the state she was?*

"My god, your lips are purple. Come inside before you catch your death!"

He led her up the front stairs.

The steward appeared in the doorway with a blanket.

Jillian could feel the warmth radiating from inside the

house before she even crossed the threshold. The smell of baking bread filled her nostrils. Her stomach growled, reminding her that she had missed lunch.

Rouen settled the blanket around her shoulders. "Go with Brian."

Brian guided her through the door.

Once Jillian was safely in the house, Rouen turned to face the men who had brought her to him. He resisted the urge to wring their necks for dragging the woman through the countryside in the rain and snow. If he weren't so worried about her, he would have lived up to the false reputation brought upon him by the curse. He knew full well the lead rider may have tried to ransom or sell her if she hadn't been smart enough to show them the gem she wore.

"Thank you for returning her to me. She is not a thief. She is a family friend who went out in search of me earlier and became lost in the wood. We have been looking for her most of the day." Rouen handed the leader of the band several pieces of silver, well aware that the man would request a reward for returning the woman.

"She asked for a Rouen. Do you know him, your lordship?" The woodsman pocketed his newly acquired coin.

"I know him very well."

Not wanting any further dealings with the band of pilfers, Rouen walked back inside.

"She awaits you in the study." Brian, the steward, advised.

***

The study was the warmest place in the house at the moment. Rouen worked on the estate ledgers prior to the knock on the door. He walked down the hall worried about

He walked down the hall worried about his surprise guest. Reaching the study, he lightly rapped against the dark wood slab before opening it.

The woman from Urbino stood in modern clothing, shivering before his fireplace. She had removed the soaked down jacket she wore, but her wet shirt and damp jeans still clung to her.

Rouen crossed the room and gathered the bottom of her shirt in his hands.

"What are you doing?" Jillian didn't know what to think, feeling her shirt coming over her head.

"You need to shed those wet clothes immediately, Jillian. I am shocked you do not have hypothermia already with as cold as it is outside." Rouen held the blanket up between them. "Your undergarments as well."

Jillian smiled at how Rouen turned his head sideways and raised the blanket to give her some privacy.

Seeing her fingertips appear on the edge of the blanket, he draped it around her.

Brian entered the room with one of Rouen's nightshirts and a robe.

Rouen handed her the nightshirt. "Quickly now, woman! We need to get you warm again."

Jillian took the long sleeved, cream colored garment, slipped it up her arms then yanked it downward over her body.

Rouen knelt down to unlace her shoes.

Jillian wasn't sure how her stiff fingers moved to unbutton her jeans after Rouen tugged her hikers from her feet. She pulled the hem of Rouen's shirt lower to cover her hips.

"Put this on." Rouen held his robe open for her.

She slid her arms into the sleeves, happy to be in dry

clothing.

After picking up the discarded blanket Brian initially gave her, Rouen sat down in the oversized chair before his desk, watching Jillian tie the robe's belt around her waist. When she finished, he pulled her into his lap and settled the blanket over them both. He rubbed the woman's ice-cold hands hoping to restore their lost circulation.

Brian offered him a cup to give the lady.

Rouen took it. "Thank you, Brian."

Brian nodded. "I will bring another blanket after hanging up the woman's clothes to dry."

Rouen handed Jillian the mug. "Drink this."

Jillian took it from him and sipped the contents, making a face when the liquor met her taste buds.

Rouen chuckled, massaging her arms under the blanket. "A bit stronger than what you are used to?"

"Yes." She managed to get out now that the chattering of her teeth slowed. The strong flavor of the mulled wine didn't deter her from continuing to drink it. The hot liquid caused warmth to rapidly spread across her chest then down into her belly, gradually eliminating the quaking of her torso.

"While I am delighted to see you, Jillian, how is it that you are here?"

"I don't know. I am thankful those men found me and Droyn Hurrey is really Rouen Durrant." Jillian tried to muster a smile, looking up into the gray eyes of the dark-haired man who held her. She never imagined how bright those eyes would be if she ever saw him alive. "I knew you weren't a merchant or poor to be able to read Latin. Never would have guessed you were an earl or prince with the way you behave."

Rouen laughed. "Obviously, you have not met many nobles in your lifetime. I think I am more than making up for any of my ungentlemanly behavior at the moment."

"I suppose you are. Thank you for warming me up."

She still couldn't quite believe Rouen was as human as she was. As her body warmed, she could feel his chest against hers. His tall frame enveloped her, adding his body heat to that of the fire. The man definitely wasn't a ghost any longer. Giselle spared him that suffering this go around.

Having Jillian in his lap, baffled Rouen. She should have been in Urbino. "Now, explain to me how you are here in Stafford."

"Kieran and I came to England to send you the pendant. We thought if we found your whereabouts, it would find its own way to you. I never imagined it would bring me along for the trip. Your father left out that possibility in his instructions."

"My father?" The cold must have gotten to Jillian for her to claim his father guided her to Stafford.

"Yes, your father. William appeared to a little boy in Urbino. Paolo..." Jillian couldn't help smiling at the confusion growing on Rouen's face. "Paolo relayed a series of clues from William that led Kieran and me to modern-day Stafford. I saw you from the window in the castle ruins. Next thing I know, I am chasing you down a hill in the sixteenth century, then some woodsmen accosted me."

Rouen took in a deep breath, digesting the fact that his father had guided the woman to him. For whatever strange reason, that eased his fears of Jillian being an unsuspecting victim of Giselle's new curse.

Brian returned with a second blanket. He gave the two

of them an odd look as he set it on the desk, but didn't say anything.

Hearing the steward double check that the door firmly closed in place. Rouen chuckled.

The reason the steward seemed taken back dawned on Jillian. "It isn't normal for a woman to sit on a man's lap this day and age, is it?"

Rouen grinned again. "Normally, no. But with how cold you were, I took the actions I deemed necessary to remedy that. Do you object to what I have done?"

"I definitely have no objections, Rouen."

He stared down into hazel orbs. Compelled by raw desire, he tasted her soft lips as he had in Urbino. One breathtaking kiss melded into another. His fingers entwined themselves in her hair. Their tongues shared unspoken secrets; kindling the embers of passion that began in Italy to full flame. The flickering firelight only enhanced the allure Jillian presented with her lips slightly parted, her cheeks flushed and eyes closed, wearing his shirt and robe.

"Jillian…" For the first time, Rouen found himself searching for the words to ask permission to take a woman to his bed. In the past, if a woman he desired didn't protest his advances, he would have just taken what he wanted. But Jillian was not a woman from the fifteen-hundreds. She was not the type of woman to simply submit to a man. "Jillian, I want… I would like to… May I enjoy you as a lover? Do you understand what I am asking?"

"Je comprends." She whispered in the language of his birth.

Jillian unwrapped herself from the blanket then untied the belt of his robe. He shed his jacket and jerkin then pushed the nightshirt Jillian wore upward to discover the woman underneath it. Jillian gasped, feeling his hands traveling her torso. His knee parted her thighs when he pulled her back onto his lap. She moaned against his lips as his thumb brushed across the tip of her breast. The soft flesh became rigid as Rouen continued to tease it. She breathed his name after his fingers descended her belly, finding her core.

At first, he delicately strummed the tender flesh, slowly building the blissful tension between them. His own arousal heightened as her body began to tremor in response to his touch. Feeling her press closer to his hand, the tempo of his stroking quickened. She panted, writhing against him. Her fingers grasped his shoulders. Jillian freely lost herself in the passionate euphoria Rouen so perfectly created. Her barely whispered yeses and pleases intertwined with soft cries grew louder.

"Rouen!" Her fingers tangled in his hair, her body shuddering against his as they held one another.

A satisfied, deep chuckle caused her eyes to flutter open.

"I want you, Rouen of Normandy." Jillian brushed her lips against his before staring into gray eyes.

"You want me?" Rouen pretended not to understand her words. The way he brought her hips downward against his groin proved he more than understood the statement. "What is it you desire me to do, Jillian Mon Fitzalan of Urbino?"

Jillian smirked, sliding her hand down his chest.

An involuntary groan escaped his lips as Jillian reached between them and grasped him through his clothing.

"Make love to me."

"Happily, mon coeur." His mouth captured hers once more. He prolonged the kiss until Jillian urgently stroked his tongue with her own; wanting more from him, and his own body throbbed with undeniable need.

Rouen shifted her off his lap, spread the heavy blanket on the rug before the fireplace, then stripped away his remaining clothes.

Jillian took the hand he extended. She knelt beside him, taking a moment to admire the man she spent so many hours with in Urbino. The combination of cool winter air and his fingertips tracing their way across her skin made her quiver. She lay back, drawing him downward with her.

The cold became nothing more than a distant memory for them both. As the snow fell from the heavens outside, Rouen found himself a man lost in the bright sunlight of spring instead of the dark, never-ending winter that defined his existence.

CHAPTER EIGHTEEN

Waking in a warm bed, Jillian wondered if she had dreamed the night before. Every book she ever read referred to ancient beds as horribly uncomfortable and old stone manor rooms as cold and drafty.

No more wine and heavy meals before bedtime. She scolded herself, certain the familiar surroundings of her Italian apartment would greet her.

As she stretched, an arm encircled her, and two lips pressed against hers. The aroma of cinnamon and clove filled her nostrils. She did not need to open her eyes to know Rouen lay beside her.

"Bonjour, mon amour." Rouen admired her in the early morning light.

"Good morning." Jillian snuggled closer to him. The scent of winter spices grew stronger. "You smell like Christmas."

"Christmas?" Rouen grinned. No woman ever told him he smelled like a holiday.

"Or maybe pumpkin pie and wassail. Both of which I

love." Jillian gently pulled his face to hers for another good morning kiss.

Rouen gladly obliged, loving the sensation of her fingers dancing across his shoulder before settling on his back.

"I don't think I've ever seen you smile as much as you have the past twenty-four hours, Rouen. It is nice to see this side of you."

Rouen tickled her, enjoying how she shrieked with laughter. He experienced true happiness for the first time in half a millennium. The more Jillian smiled up at him, the higher he seemed to soar. His fingers could feel the smoothness of Jillian's skin and the plush velvet of the duvet that covered them. Her hands could caress him. He relished the sensation of a uniquely feminine touch as her fingertips skimmed down his arm.

"I don't know how it is possible, but I live again, Jillian. Twice now, you make a shade human once more."

"I doubt I am the cause, Rouen. You must have found the way back. I am curious how I ended up in the sixteenth century with you. Not that I am complaining; I am more than happy with ending up in your arms."

"Are you?"

Her lips meeting his again conveyed that she was.

Jillian's stomach growled, interrupting the round of lazy morning kisses.

"Since it sounds as if my lady is hungry, I suppose we should dress and find something for her to eat."

"Don't you have some form of room service this day and age?" Jillian wasn't ready to leave Rouen's arms or the warmth of the covers.

"Room service?" Rouen didn't know what that was.

"When you call down to the kitchen and have them

bring you breakfast in bed."

"Sadly, we do not." Rouen grinned at the way Jillian lightly nipped his earlobe then slowly trailed her mouth down the side of his neck.

"I think some earl in England invented it about now. My stomach can wait, my lord. Food isn't what I desire." The deep laugh that followed her remark made her want the man all the more.

Between the fresh snow on the ground and it being midwinter, Rouen contentedly indulged Jillian and himself by remaining in bed later than he normally would.

***

Jillian wrapped herself in Rouen's robe as he started dressing. She knew the layered clothing of the day had complex ties and buttons. "Do you need help?"

"No, I dress plainly when at home. We cannot make a routine practice of spending the morning abed, Jillian. I will be deemed a debauched lord who suffers from sloth if I do so."

Jillian watched him pull a pair of trousers from his wardrobe. "No hose this morning? I thought pants weren't a thing in England yet."

"I am impressed with your knowledge of men's garments, my lady. I brought a few pairs of trousers back from my travels in the East. They are much more comfortable than the hose and codpiece required when I carry out my official duties or attend court." Rouen frowned, looking back at his own clothing and pondering what he could give Jillian to wear. "We need to find you appropriate clothing."

"I took the liberty of securing a gown for the lady." Brian opened the chamber door. "Forgive me if I am intruding, but I heard you up and about. You slept in much later than

Tale of Rouen ❦ 177

normal, my lord. I shall tell the cook to start preparing your and the lady's breakfast."

Brian handed Rouen the garment he borrowed from a female member of Rouen's staff. The woman and Jillian looked to be close to the same size. He politely bowed to Rouen then disappeared into the hall.

"Does he always randomly come and go like that?" Jillian noted the puzzled look on Rouen's face as he closed the room door.

"Yes. His job as steward is to look after me and my estate. He does it exceptionally well at times."

Jillian put on the simple green dress.

"How do I look as a sixteenth-century woman, my lord?" She twirled, causing the wide skirt to fan out around her.

The whirling mix of green and smiling woman enthralled Rouen. If such a modest gown made her beam so, he looked forward to when she donned a finer gown befitting of her status.

He chuckled, offering her his arm. "What did you tell me the morning we met? The period suits you."

Whispers filled the house as the earl ate with the strange woman who appeared the evening prior. Rouen did his best to ignore the gossiping servants, well aware of the commotion Jillian caused in his household. The snow would offer them a few days of seclusion, giving Rouen time to craft an explanation for the woman and his interest in her before any unwanted guests stopped by. Inevitably, the lord of the county would start receiving visitors after word spread that he resided in Stafford again.

Jillian charmed Brian into finding her a pair of boots and a cloak while Rouen met with his estate manager. She was eager to explore the grounds of her new home.

"If you leave the main yard, you need an escort. We do not want you lost or in the hands of a brigand once again." Brian cautioned as Jillian started out the rear door.

"I won't go far." Jillian called over her shoulder before venturing outside.

The snow sparkled in the mid-day sun. White stretched across the countryside as far as she could see. Shimmering elongated and irregularly shaped patches of it disappeared into the woods on the far side of the property.

Jillian loved the sound of the freshly fallen powder crunching under her feet as she strolled through the dormant gardens then towards the cleared fields and barns.

***

Rouen stood outside of the stable chatting with one of his hired hands.

The stableman spotted Jillian sneaking towards them. The woman hurled a snowball in their direction. He paused mid-sentence, not believing what the woman had done.

Rouen noted the man's open jaw and wide eyes. Before he could turn to see what caused the expression, something hit him in the center of his back.

"Jillian! It is not ladylike to throw snowballs." Rouen held up his arm as she pelted him with a second one. He watched her bend down to rearm herself.

"Drop the snow in your hand this instant!"

He started towards her. Anyone else would have run from him in fear. She stood her ground, smirking.

"What if I choose not to?" Jillian threw the snowball without waiting for an answer.

Rouen ran towards her.

Both laughed as Rouen chased after her.

The groundskeeper stood stunned with the head groom. He had come out of the barn to see what was happening, when he heard a woman shouting.

Rouen playfully pushed Jillian backwards into one of the larger drifts.

"Rouen! This is the only gown I have to wear!" Jillian squealed as he dumped a handful of snow on her head.

"I will find you another."

She flung snow from the bank she sat in at him.

The two carried on like a couple of kids in mock battle. Neither noticed the small audience they attracted. Freedmen and servants working near the house looked in their direction. They had never seen Rouen behave as he did now. They were even more stunned when their lord pulled the woman to her feet and kissed her.

"Your subjects or whatever we call them are watching us." Jillian noticed how the two men outside the stables stared at them along with another three people from the adjacent field.

Rouen turned to see what she was talking about. "So they are. And they are freedmen and servants, madam. I would expect you of all people to know historical class structures better than those of us living in the period do."

Jillian wondered why they continued to gape at her and Rouen. "Are you that mean of an overlord that they find laughter and affection foreign things on your estate?"

"No! I am a generous master who treats his people very well. They just don't always see it, thanks to Giselle. They may also be shocked at a woman your age starting a snowball fight with a nobleman." Rouen had grown accustomed to his people's reaction to him since the witch revised the curse.

"I see. Well, we need to work on improving your standing in their eyes. I have an idea to start Operation We Love Our Lord and Master, regardless of what others say about him. Do you have vanilla? I know you have milk and sugar."

"I am certain the cook has some hidden somewhere. It is a luxury item. She may not be willing to give it to you. What are you planning?" Rouen thought her request was odd.

"Making something I haven't had since I was a kid as the first step in winning over a few friends for you. If the cook won't cooperate, I will tell her you will boil her in oil or something." Jillian headed towards the kitchen.

"Everyone knows I prefer drawing and quartering to boiling in oil." Rouen grinned, hearing her laugh.

"Is everything well this morning, your lordship?" The groundskeeper inquired, watching the woman disappear into the house.

By the expression on the groundskeeper's face, he worried about who Rouen contemplated boiling in oil or drawing and quartering that morning. Rouen smiled hoping to easing the man's angst. "Very well. I apologize for our antics. The woman brings out the boy in me."

"That can be a great blessing, my lord. It is nice to see you happy again. We prayed for this day after what happened." The groundskeeper suddenly smiled. The caring master they once loved emerged again from the cold, distant noble he had been the past few years.

The man's words puzzled Rouen. "After what happened?"

"I am not the dimwitted, superstitious fool some of the others are, your lordship. I know all that you do for us. I have seen you pay debts that were not yours. I see you work in the fields dressed as one of us when we fall behind with planting or harvesting. I do not know of a single noble, besides yourself, who would do such things in addition to all you must do for the king. I blame the rumors and nastiness on the devil that showed its face here five years ago. That harpy stole your soul. I think the good Lord sent you an angel to restore it. Begging your pardon if I spoke out of turn."

"No pardon is needed as no offense was given, John."

"That is another reason you are a good master. You know all of us commoners by name. Perhaps if the others meet the new countess, they will come to see that you are a good man, not the cursed monster they prattle on about."

The two watched Brian and the cook accompany Jillian outside with a large bowl. After testing a few mounds of snow, Jillian took the bowl from Brian and filled it. One of the maids joined them on the rear patio with the ingredients Jillian requested.

"Whatever is she doing?" Rouen wondered about the flurry of activity on the porch.

The groundskeeper chuckled, recognizing what was being made. "She is making snow cream."

Another maid appeared with bowls and spoons. Jillian gave each of the individuals around her a bowl, then walked towards Rouen with one in each hand.

"For you, my lord." Jillian offered a bowl to Rouen.

Rouen grinned, taking it from her.

She surprised the groundkeeper by handing him the second bowl instead of keeping it for herself.

"Thank you, my lady. This is a rare treat for an old man." The groundskeeper took a bite of the homemade dessert then smiled, enjoying it.

"You are most welcome. I will let you finish whatever business you were conducting. Eat it before it melts, Rouen. Sugar and vanilla aren't cheap these days."

Jillian departed to enjoy a bowl of the dessert herself.

"Hold on to her; she is a good woman. If you don't mind me saying, your lordship, she is much better than the last one you brought home with you."

Rouen snorted before taking another bite of Jillian's concoction. "The last one would not be caught dead in the snow, nor would she know how to make snow cream."

***

Jillian gave the last of the snow cream to some children peeking out of the rear barn doors.

Brian observed how she coaxed the three to come out of their hiding place. They declined the big bowl she offered to them.

"I know you! You are the earl's new friend." The oldest stepped forward first.

"I guess I am." Jillian wasn't sure if that was a good or bad thing yet with the way the boy spoke.

"My father says the earl is an ogre. You must be a witch if you are his friend." The middle child, also a boy, declared coming out of the shadows now.

Jillian tried not to laugh. "How can I be a witch? Aren't witches old, green, and covered in warts?"

"Aye, they are." The oldest agreed.

"Am I green or covered in warts?" Jillian tried to reason with them. She knew not to ask about being old with the three being so young.

"No." The younger of the two said, still eyeing her warily.

"Then I must not be a witch." Jillian used their logic,

sitting down on a small stool near them.

The two scampered backwards.

She pretended to ignore them, starting to eat the snow cream.

Brian smiled at how she handled the two little imps.

"No, lady, do not eat that!" The oldest grabbed her arm.

"Why ever not? I love snow cream, and you don't want it." Jillian brought the spoon back to her mouth, causing both boys to scream "no."

"It is poisoned, my lady!" A little girl ran out of the barn backing up her older brothers.

"Poisoned?" Jillian doubted her hearing.

"Yes, poisoned, you daft wench. Ogres give their guests food with poison then eat them for supper. See the brown color. That is poison!" The oldest pointed at the vanilla. "You take one bite, and the earl will eat you for supper."

Wow! What had these kids' parents been telling them? Unable to resist, Jillian ate a large spoonful

The three kids shrieked wildly.

Rouen heard all the ruckus and came to investigate what caused the horrified screaming.

Brian stopped him from interrupting the shenanigans. "There is nothing to be concerned about, Lord Hurrey. The lady is managing the three rascals rather well."

Brian chuckled as Jillian pretended to cough and gag, sending the children into another round of yelling about her eating poisoned snow and being supper that night. She fell forward on her knees then rolled over on her back, lying motionless in the snow.

"No! She was a nice lady! Why did you let her eat it, Thomas?" The little girl yelled at her oldest brother.

"Dare I ask why the children think she is poisoned?"

Rouen whispered, taking in the scene.

"It is better if you do not." Brian watched Thomas, the oldest boy, carefully approach the woman not moving in the snow.

"Is she dead?" The little girl whimpered.

Jillian waited until the snow crunched by her ear then grabbed Thomas's ankle, making him jump and the other two scream. She sat up laughing. "No, I am not dead. The brown stuff in the snow is called vanilla. It makes the snow cream taste good and is far from being poison. Come, try it."

She offered the spoon to the girl, knowing she would be the easiest to win over, being the youngest.

The girl cautiously approached Jillian then took the spoon. Her brothers watched to see what happened to their sister.

Jillian smiled as she heard the "mmm" from the little girl. "It's good, isn't it? We can eat it all since your brothers are too scared to try it."

Rouen and Brian grinned, watching Mary, the little girl, sit in Jillian's lap while eating the treat and telling her brothers 'it is very good.' Mary was normally terrified of strangers, but she took to Jillian.

Jillian held up two more spoons for the boys.

"I am not scared!" Thomas slowly came over, snatched the spoon from Jillian's hand, then defiantly shoved a spoonful of snow cream into his mouth.

A moment later, all three children sat talking with Jillian about life on Rouen's lands. They were the youngest working on the estate. The three proudly boasted of their contributions to Rouen's manor and their own homes. They eagerly shared their thoughts with Jillian on any subject she threw out to them.

Their hard work and how they agreed that the earl did a great deal to help them, even if he was an ogre, touched Rouen. *Could Giselle's curse be failing once more?*

The three siblings jumped as one of the adults started to shoo them away from Jillian, angry that their work wasn't getting done.

"It is my fault they aren't finished with their chores. I bribed them with snow cream to come speak with me. Please, do not be angry with them." Jillian took up for the children as Mary hid behind her.

"And who might you be to be distracting them? If you know what is best for you, I would get back to whatever tasking you should be doing before someone catches you loafing like these three brats."

"They are children, and from the sounds of it, they work just as hard as you do. There is nothing wrong with them taking a little break. As to who I am." Jillian squared off with the woman.

"She is the new lady of the house and deserves to be treated as such." Rouen stepped out of the shadows, halting the woman's challenge of Jillian as a newcomer to the area.

"Forgive me. I did not recognize her, considering the manner of her dress. My apologies, your lordship!" The woman retreated, seeing that the earl stood with arms crossed over his chest, staring her down.

"Jillian, what started this altercation?" Rouen noted Mary peering out at him from behind Jillian's skirt.

Jillian looked from Rouen to the woman, who fidgeted nervously. "A simple misunderstanding. As she states, she did not know who I was. I gave the children the last of the snow cream, so it did not go to waste. In doing so, I disrupted their chores. If anyone is to blame for it, I am."

"You there, hiding behind your lady's skirt. Come here." Rouen motioned for Mary to come forward.

The girl's parents anxiously watched from inside the barn.

"It is okay. Do as he asks." Jillian whispered, offering a hand to the scared little girl.

"He is so big! Thomas says he is a mean ogre." The little girl grasped the extended hand and slid herself around to stand before Jillian.

"He is a bit big, but he is far from mean. He is also not an ogre. Remember how Thomas said I was a witch, and we proved that I am not? We can do the same with your lord. Is he green or have horns and tusks?"

Mary glanced back at Rouen again and shook her head 'no.'

"Then he can't be an ogre. The earl is very kind. He just likes to scowl and act grumpy sometimes. Unfortunately, kings and counts have to do that, so people know when they act wrongly." Jillian reassured the girl he wouldn't harm her. She smiled at the momentary twitch of Rouen's lips as he suppressed a grin.

"I am waiting, little one." Rouen kept his tone stern, even though he felt like laughing.

"Yes, your lordship." The girl stammered, stepping forward, but not releasing Jillian's hand.

"Be brave and come closer. I will not hurt you. I only wish to ask you a question." Rouen knelt down, so his height didn't intimidate the child. "Your name is Mary if I remember correctly."

"Yes, my lord. Those are my brothers, Thomas and Michael." She inched closer to Rouen.

"Tell me, Mary, is what Lady Jillian said the truth?"

"Yes, my lord." Mary nodded, staring up at him.

"Did you enjoy the snow cream?" Rouen brought a smile to Mary's face.

"Very much. I like Lady Jillian. She is very kind to share her snow cream with us."

"I like Lady Jillian a great deal as well. Thank you for answering my questions, Mary." Rouen smiled at her. She returned the smile with a giggle, not afraid of him anymore.

"I do not think you are an ogre like Thomas said. You have pretty eyes. They look like the sky." Mary blurted out, never having been so close to Rouen.

Jillian choked back a laugh at the little girl's remark.

Rouen ruffled Mary's hair as he chuckled then stood up. "Thank you for the compliment, little one. Now, you need to finish your chores, so you and your brothers can play some more this afternoon."

"You are dismissed as well." He addressed the older woman who tested Jillian earlier.

"Good day, my lord, and to you, my lady." The woman did a quick curtsey, thankful Jillian did not lay the blame completely on her as others would have.

"I have a library full of books to keep you occupied, so you are not disrupting my household or estate. If you follow me, I am happy to show them to you." Rouen playfully chastised Jillian.

"Maybe you are an ogre after all, to lock me away in the library all day." Jillian protested as they walked together.

"All part of my plan to keep you where I can find you, so I can devour you later this evening."

Rouen greatly enjoyed the next few weeks he spent with

Jillian. She slowly won over his staff and those living under his care. More of the local people began greeting him whenever he walked or rode the grounds of the county he oversaw. The three children from the barn regularly approached him. No matter what he was doing, he stopped to play or speak with the three, knowing how much his attention meant to them. For a second time, the twenty-first-century woman changed the world he lived in for the better.

Jillian made him laugh more than he could ever remember. While he visited with her frequently in Italy, their new conversations face-to-face and the intimate moments he spent with her only deepened the affection he felt for her.

CHAPTER NINETEEN

Rouen went over the estate books in his study. He heard Brian attempting to deny someone entry to the house. By the man's protests and the sound of multiple footsteps in the hall, the visitor ignored the steward. The loud creak of the study door swinging open revealed the unwelcome caller. Shock kept Rouen from doing anything more than rising from his chair.

"Rouen, my love! I am so relieved to hear you returned safely from Italy. I prayed for it each night you were away." A woman cooed, pulling her gloves off then reaching out for him.

"I doubt your prayers were for my safe return. Why are you not at court, Vivian?" Rouen kept his distance, staring daggers into the woman.

"You wound me with that accusation, husband." She placed her hands on her hips and glared at Rouen.

Jillian prayed she misheard what the woman said. She stepped into the office to find a petite woman with blond hair and light blue eyes staring down Rouen.

"Husband? Did you lie about being divorced?"

"Yes," Vivian answered, as Rouen firmly said, "No."

"My, this is certainly out of character for you, my lord. Did you not tell your latest mistress about me? Wherever did you find this one, Droyn? She does not sound Italian. She dresses like a peasant." The elegantly clad woman surveyed Jillian's simple dress with a look of disgust on her face.

"She is not my mistress, nor am I your husband, *Viv*." Rouen intentionally used the nickname Vivian loathed. "The Church annulled our marriage three years ago after *you* demanded the separation. You have not answered my prior question, why are you here?"

Rouen placed himself between Jillian and Vivian, not liking the way Vivian circled her.

"It is amazing what can happen when there is a new queen on the throne. Kings are heavily influenced by their wives. Jane is championing my reinstatement as Countess of Stafford." Vivian smiled wickedly at Rouen and the growing panic on Jillian's face.

"I will kill you with my bare hands before that day ever comes to fruition." Rouen almost growled, glowering down at the woman who was once his wife. "Henry will never grant your request, no matter how close you are to the queen."

"Do not become too comfortable in Droyn's bed. You will not be in it much longer." Vivian addressed Jillian.

"Out!" Rouen pointed at the door.

"What?" Vivian feigned confusion at the barked command.

"Leave, Vivian! You no longer have any right to be here, and you certainly have no right to berate a guest in my home." Rouen grabbed the woman by the elbow and dragged her down the hall. She called him every derogatory name she knew in French and English.

He ignored the venom she spat at him. Reaching the front door, he almost ripped it from the hinges with how hard he jerked it open. He never broke his stride yanking Vivian through the open portal. He continued down the front steps then shoved her towards the waiting carriage. "Go back to your father's or London. You will not be offered any shelter here."

"You would not disgrace yourself by failing to offer me hospitality in this wretched weather, Droyn Hurrey!" Vivian shouted, watching Rouen walk back inside. She heard the snort he let out as he turned in the doorway to look at her one last time. "The king will have your head for this!"

Rouen slammed the front door.

May the wretched woman freeze to death!

A painting hung near the large wooden door rocked, threatening to fall from its perch.

Rouen turned to find Jillian, Brian, and his housekeeper -Sarah standing behind him. "She does not ever step foot in this house again. Vivian lost all rights to anything in Stafford when we divorced."

Brian and Sarah nodded.

Jillian fought back the sudden sting of tears in her eyes. Rouen tossed out his ex-wife. She shouldn't be upset, but knowing the woman wanted to once more be with Rouen and planned to leverage the king to get her way caused something to snap within Jillian. "I was stupid to come to England. To think I could ever change things for you."

"Jillian, you are far from stupid." Rouen crossed the room, concerned about her.

Jillian turned from him, attempting to hide her face.

He felt her shudder as his hand rested on her back. "Sweeting, do not cry over this. Vivian is not worth your tears."

"I just wanted to give you a chance at a normal life. You don't deserve the misery Giselle meted out to you." Jillian's lower lip trembled. Another tear ran down her cheek even though she tried to prevent it from escaping.

Rouen wiped it away. "You brighten my existence each day. Do not let something as trivial as Vivian's desire for status darken that."

"Vivian wants to remarry. What will you do if Henry orders you to do so?"

Rouen scoffed. "Vivian wants to be a countess and have access to wealth, not a husband. Furthermore, Henry would never marry that woman to any man that serves him in England. The king himself championed our divorce after Vivian claimed I could not get her with child. She condemned herself in the proceedings striking that raw nerve within Henry. Her temper worsened the situation when she drunkenly uttered the king and I must suffer from the same ailment as neither of us appeared capable of producing viable male heirs. Anne shared her remark with Henry. It's a wonder Henry didn't have Vivian and her father tossed from the Court then."

"If Jane Seymour is on the throne, Henry may change his mind about Vivian."

"He won't change his mind, and I would never consent to marry Vivian again, even if decreed by the king."

"Lady Jillian, you wished to see how the cook prepares the tarts." The cook's apprentice interrupted the tense moment.

"She did." Rouen smiled at Jillian and gestured for her

to follow the apprentice back to the kitchen.

"Rouen..." Jillian couldn't shake the feeling that Vivian's visit brought trouble to Rouen's doorstep.

Rouen kissed her cheek. "There is no cause for further concern, Jillian. Go enjoy your tart-making lesson."

***

Brian moved to stand beside Rouen after Jillian left with the chef's apprentice. "Mayhap it is time to call the seamstress, Lord Hurrey. When Vivian returns to court, she will tell everyone of Jillian in addition to confirming your return. While many around the estate believe the story of Jillian being an Italian woman, that tale will not suffice for the educated members of the aristocracy if they start questioning Jillian about her country of origin."

"Lady Jillian and I became acquainted in Urbino. No one should question my word when I explain her style of speech or any variations in her manners." Rouen frowned, eyeing his steward.

"If Lady Jillian is from Urbino than I am the king of France, Droyn." The steward laughed, noting the warning look Rouen gave him not to challenge the narrative further. "I do not care where the lady is from, but others will, once they realize Jillian doesn't speak Italian fluently or hear tales of her dress when she appeared on the doorstep. Not to mention her English is very different from ours. You know Vivian as well as I do. Once scorned, that woman will stop at nothing to decimate whoever made her angry. Protect Jillian and yourself, Droyn. Sooner or later, more visitors will be on your doorstep, or worse, a summons to court may arrive. Prepare the lady while there is a chance to, so Vivian or any of the other vipers in the king's court cannot shred her or your reputation to tatters at the first opportunity presented."

"You address your lord with too much familiarity." Rouen reprimanded Brian for speaking so bluntly.

Brian guffawed. "Forgive me, my lord. Having served your family since you were a young child, I forget my place. When should I tell the seamstress to visit Lady Jillian?"

Rouen knew his time alone with Jillian would eventually come to an end. None of the nobility ever successfully avoided at least one trip to court a year, unless Henry was displeased with them. "I will resolve the matter of Jillian's wardrobe."

CHAPTER TWENTY

Jillian sat with Sarah learning how to do needlepoint. Rouen read a book in a chair across from hers. On occasion, the two stole flirtatious glances at one another. Brian and Sarah noted the smiles and looks the earl and lady shared.

"You have the stitchwork down, my lady. Why don't you finish this section of border? My old hands are tired after a long day's work." Sarah held the loop out to Jillian.

Jillian took it and slowly embroidered another rose on the wall hanging.

Brian winked at Sarah, knowing the woman could sew all night long if needed. She just subtly encouraged Jillian to be more confident in her newly acquired skill. After Sarah smiled back at him, he took in the idyllic scene of Jillian quietly embroidering across from Rouen, who seemed engrossed in whatever text he read. The dark-haired, hazel-eyed woman was a nice match for the earl. She was intelligent and charming. The two were close in age. Jillian's sense of humor and adventure complemented Rouen's restless nature.

Rouen lowered his book, and started to address Jillian when someone knocked on the door.

Jillian set her needlework in her lap. "Who could that be at this hour?"

If Vivian is on my doorstep once more... Rouen scowled, worried that the spoiled daughter of the Earl of Sussex returned to cause more discontent.

"My lord, a messenger for you." Brian announced as a gentleman joined them.

"Giovanni, it is good to see you again." Rouen stood and shook the man's hand.

"You as well, Droyn. I am afraid I cannot stay long as we are riding through to London. The supplies from Italy arrived safely this morning." Giovanni's statement caused Rouen's brows to raise.

"That is excellent news. May the king enjoy his long awaited wine."

Jillian knew more than wine found its way from Urbino to England's shores.

Their guest's eyes settled on the brunette woman watching the two of them. "The rumors appear to be true. You did bring a woman back from Urbino with you."

Rouen already knew Vivian set in motion whatever retaliatory scheme she came up with. "Where did you hear such a tale?"

Giovanni chuckled. "You and Lady Jillian are one of the more popular stories circulating at court. Vivian is most vindictive, considering she is the one who spurned you. Other than curiosity about the mysterious Italian woman, nothing has changed your fellow nobles' perspective of yourself. Henry wished for me to extend his thanks for your expeditious work in Urbino. He welcomes you to visit him whenever you wish, but understands if you would prefer not to, with Vivian present."

"Perhaps I will find my way to Windsor or London when Vivian undertakes her spring sojourn to her father's home."

"My Lord Stafford, forgive me for interrupting, but I am wondering who our guest is." Jillian suspected Giovanni Battista was the gentleman calling on them.

"Lady Jillian, Giovanni Battista Castiglione; Signore Castiglione, Lady Jillian of Urbino." Rouen politely introduced them.

"It is a pleasure to meet you, Lady Jillian. I must apologize for the abrupt departure, but I am expected at Hampton Court." Giovanni politely nodded to Jillian and Rouen.

Brian escorted their visitor to the front door.

"England just got you back." Jillian set her hand on Rouen's arm. "I also don't want to lose you again so quickly. Be careful with the dangerous things you do for god and king."

Rouen grinned down at the woman learning to navigate his world. "I am not in any peril, Jillian. I acted under the king's order, not anyone else's."

CHAPTER TWENTY-ONE

Brian sent a messenger to inform Rouen that the seamstress arrived. Rouen grinned, thinking about how pleasantly the day progressed. It started off with a fruitful morning hunt, Jillian's dresses finally arrived, and for a change, he had minimal things to attend to. He would easily be home in a few hours. After taking care of his official duties in town, Rouen returned home.

John took the reins of Rouen's horse as Rouen rode up to the manor house. "You would think it was Christmas morning with the way the women are carrying on."

"That is exactly how I hoped it would be." Rouen entered the house hearing laughter and compliments from inside.

Brian pointed upstairs. "Follow the giggling. Adelaide, the seamstress, and Lady Jillian are enjoying themselves. Adelaide would make a perfect lady's maid to assist Jillian going forward."

"I will keep that in mind." Rouen ascended the stairs eager to see Jillian's reaction to the gowns.

Adelaide and Jillian laughed as the seamstress finished pinning the gown Jillian wore. The dark rose-colored velvet dress with purple accents was the first one the seamstress suggested to Rouen after Rouen described Jillian's coloring. Adelaide finished decorating Jillian's hair with matching ribbons and white glass pearls.

The maid nodded to him and whispered to Jillian that he watched them. He caught the subtle glance Jillian cast him as the seamstress told her not to move just yet.

"I am blessed to have such an angel at my side, my Lady Jillian." Rouen flirted with her from the doorway.

Jillian turned from the mirror, irritating the seamstress. Though the woman bit her tongue with the earl present.

Rouen offered Jillian a polite bow. She laughed and extended her hand to him. The moment he took it, she dropped into a low curtsey and bowed her head.

"You are too kind to me, Lord Hurrey. It is I who am blessed with such a generous and handsome lord. You humble me with your actions, dearest knight."

"Nay, fair maid." Rouen placed a finger under her chin and raised her face to look at him. "'Tis you who brings the earl to his knees each morning and evening, to pray for just half your heart and wisdom. Verily, he selfishly prays that his love is enough to keep the spring you bring him everlasting. That nothing on heaven or earth shall cause such a rare flower to wilt or take the sun he so adores from him."

"How romantic." Adelaide whispered to the seamstress as Rouen brought Jillian's hand to his lips and helped her to her feet.

"Never thought I would see the day Droyn Hurrey would go to such lengths to woo a woman." The seamstress continued her alterations.

Rouen shot the seamstress a disdainful glance.

Jillian laughed. "Pay her no mind, Rouen. As always, you amaze me with your words and deeds. Thank you."

"Lady Jillian, you have a guest who is anxious to see you." Brian announced from the doorway.

"A guest?" Jillian didn't know anyone outside of Rouen's estate.

"Yes, madam. Lady Mary wishes to visit you. She is curious to know what was in all the trunks delivered earlier today. Additionally, the earl requested her presence."

Mary peeked in the room from behind Brian.

"I did?" Rouen raised a brow then smiled. Brian chuckled, knowing he jested. "Oh, yes, I did. Now, I remember the invitation."

Seeing that Mary was clean and dressed in what must be her Sunday best, Jillian knew Rouen invited the girl to the house.

"Come in, Lady Mary. You look very lovely today." Rouen bowed to the little girl and gestured for her to join them.

Mary shyly walked into the room, not sure how to respond to Rouen's greeting.

"Tell him 'thank you, my lord.'" Jillian whispered to the little girl.

"Thank you, my lord." Mary repeated. "You look like a princess, Jillian. Are you going to marry Lord Hurrey today?"

"I am afraid not. Rouen was nice enough to buy me some dresses. Would you like to see them?" Jillian took her by the hand and showed her the dresses on the bed.

"Jillian, sweetheart, are you almost done with the fitting? I invited Mary to join us for an afternoon repast as she has been working extra hard just as she promised she would." Rouen inquired, after Mary got to see the trunks that perked her attention earlier.

"Let me change. This is the last one I needed to try on."

Rouen picked up Mary. "I think Lady Jillian should wear her new dress to eat with us. What do you think, Mary?"

Mary nodded her head yes, wrapping her arms around Rouen's neck.

"Leave the dress on and come downstairs as that is what your lord desires. You can change later." He walked out the door speaking with Mary.

"Yes, my lord." Jillian rolled her eyes, dropping a quick curtsey to his back, and then followed him to the dining room.

The plate of pastries and cups set out for them fascinated Mary.

Jillian couldn't stop smiling, watching Rouen play the role of honored host with the little girl.

Rouen winked at Jillian as he noticed her admiring him while she sipped the hot cider from her glass.

The three spent the next hour laughing and talking.

Anne, Mary's mother, entered the room to bring her back home.

Seeing Anne in the doorway, Rouen set his glass down and reached under the table then handed Mary a doll. "For you, Mary. Thank you for all of your help taking care of my animals."

Mary shyly took it from him. "She is for me?"

"She is. She reminded me of you. She has brown eyes and hair, just as you do." Rouen pointed out what the two had in common.

"Mary!" Anne gasped from the hall as Mary forgot her manners and suddenly hugged Rouen.

"She is merely excited about her gift." Rouen reassured Anne he did not take any offense to the little girl's actions as he hugged Mary back. "Let us go show your mother your doll."

Mary patiently waited for Rouen as he picked up two small, wooden swords from the shelf behind him then extended his hand to Mary. The little girl bounced alongside him, holding onto his fingers as they crossed the room.

Rouen gave Anne the toy swords he purchased for Thomas and Michael. "Here is something for your two sons as well. I noticed the children are starting to outgrow their clothes. Brian delivered a bolt of cloth along with some venison I killed this morning to your husband. Are you in need of more than meat and cloth?"

"No, my lord. You are too kind, my lord. God bless you and Lady Jillian." Anne teared up, thinking about all the times she and her husband spoke ill of him. She hurried Mary out the door before anyone could notice.

"My dear Lord Stafford, I do believe your people are now seeing the man you truly are. Charity and love can conquer the witch's ill intentions." Jillian whispered beside him.

"So, it seems, Jillian."

CHAPTER TWENTY-TWO

Jillian excitedly walked the streets of Stafford with Rouen. Today was their first venture together off the estate. He grinned as she marveled at the buildings along the main road and explored the various stalls of the weekly market.

Nearing the butcher's stall, Jillian gagged. "Oh, the smell is awful!"

"You are spoiled with how your merchants refrigerate your meats. We do not have that luxury."

"I am shocked more haven't died from food poising with the meat being kept in the open like this." Jillian halted their walk after noticing the eyes of an animal staring at them from its recently severed head. "We can end our tour of the market now."

Rouen laughed. "Squeamish stomach, my love?"

"All of this doesn't bother you?"

"Not particularly, but as it does you, we will turn back. There other less pungent sections of the village you will probably enjoy."

The stench of freshly butchered meat faded as they

strolled up the medieval rows of the commercial center. Jillian's hand settling against Rouen's chest halted their walk. Rouen followed Jillian's gaze to see what caught her attention. An old gray stone church was the reason for the unexpected stop.

"That is Saint Chad's Church."

"May we go in?" Jillian always loved visiting old churches due to their unique architecture and the artwork concealed within their walls and windows.

"We can." Rouen escorted Jillian inside.

***

The arched nave immediately drew Jillian's eyes upward to the colorful stained-glass windows behind the altar. She silently admired the elaborately carved stone columns.

The priest noticed Rouen and started towards them. "My lord, how may I be of service to you?"

"The lady wished to visit your church after hearing of its carvings and wheeled window."

"Lord Hurrey!" A loud voice echoed through the silent chapel as someone thrust the door open. One of the young men working for the sheriff approached Rouen. "You are needed at Croxden. Armed men are at the abbey trying to take it. They claim the abbey must be surrendered by order of Cromwell and the king."

"What?" Rouen wondered if he misheard. Why would the abbey come under attack from Henry?

"It's true, Droyn." An out of breath Bryan joined them. "I rode out there myself after a messenger visited the estate to confirm their report. We have managed to keep Cromwell's men at bay, but they grow ever impatient, saying they act under the order of the king."

"Cromwell must be starting to enforce the Dissolution

of Monasteries Act." Jillian came toward Rouen.

"The Dissolution of Monasteries Act?" Rouen wasn't familiar with the law.

"You most likely know it as the Suppression Act. It disbands monasteries, convents, and priories. Cromwell's men will raid the property of anything worth any value and seize its assets to line royal coffers along with their own."

"The Act of Supremacy and the Suppression of Religious Houses Act is what these men claim as their authority to takeover Croxden." Brian confirmed Jillian was right.

"Like hell they will. Croxden is under my oversight. Take Jillian back to the house and meet me at the abbey." Rouen turned to leave with the young man who initially sought him out.

Jillian grabbed his arm. "Rouen, I know the laws better than you. Let me go with you. There is a chance we could negotiate a royal license allowing the abbey to remain as it is."

"It is a two-hour ride to Croxden. With the men arriving armed, peaceful negotiations could quickly deteriorate into violence." Rouen hoped to deter her desire to ride with him.

"Please allow me to assist you with this." Jillian feared Rouen's lack of knowledge about the Acts might worsen the situation.

"You may come on the condition you do exactly as I tell you; failing to heed my direction can place all of our lives at risk."

"One other thing, is it 1536 or 1537?" Jillian should have asked him the year long before today.

"February 1537." Rouen led her out the door, towards their waiting horses. "My life picked up as if my travels to Urbino went as originally planned. I've been back in Stafford since August of 1536, just as the uprisings you once mentioned began. I helped Suffolk quell them in September and October, then was discharged from service to tend to my estate after being gone so long."

***

More men joined them as they rode through the countryside to Croxden. Jillian assumed they were a mix of constables, keepers of the peace, and Rouen's men-at-arms. Rouen only acknowledged them with a nod of his head. By the time they reached the abbey, the group had grown to about forty men including Rouen.

The red and beige stone walls of the abbey made a colorful display against the dormant grass and barren trees surrounding it. Rouen halted the group several yards from the abbey grounds. The abbot stood with the sheriff. A small group of men that worked for Cromwell, judging by the way they were dressed, waited across from them. Jillian counted fourteen men in total, only one of Cromwell's hired Visitors rode with a group of that number.

"I've read Thomas Leigh was Cromwell's man in this area. He was rumored to ride with fourteen men when he appeared at a location." Jillian whispered to Rouen. "I thought he came through the Midlands during the summer last year. What is he doing here now?"

"Perhaps Croxden only now caught his attention. Leigh is the man in the black and brown coat across from the sheriff. You mentioned the law allows for a royal license." Rouen kept his voice low.

"Yes. From what I understand, a place could pay a fine and gain licensure to remain operating as long as they were not deemed a threat to the new church. It's a long shot, but if Leigh is here to dissolve the abbey, it's the only peaceful option you have."

"I want you to stay here. I will leave one of my men-at-arms with you. If I cannot negotiate with Leigh and our discussion degrades into conflict, you are to ride to Stafford. Stop for nothing until you reach the house and await my return."

Jillian nodded, confirming she understood his direction. She worried about Rouen, watching him ride toward the sheriff and Leigh. Leigh had a reputation for being cruel in his treatment monks and nuns. He was also greedy and arrogant.

The soldier who joined her noted the fear in her expression. "Hopefully this matter will be resolved quickly, Lady Jillian. The earl is an excellent negotiator."

"Lord Hurrey!" The sheriff greeted Rouen as the earl rode towards the waiting group.

"Your men are interfering in legal and royal matters. Tell them to disband at once." Leigh snapped at Rouen.

"Sir Leigh, had you extended the courtesy of notifying me that you would be conducting whatever business it is that you have in Staffordshire, this unfortunate standoff could have been avoided." Rouen didn't dismount. "That is standard protocol, is it not?"

"I ride under the King's order."

"Let us be perfectly clear as to who your employer is, Thomas. You conduct visitations for Cromwell. If the king himself sent you, I would have been notified as Henry's lieutenant for Staffordshire."

Leigh loathed Droyn Hurrey and the interference his men caused at the abbey. "Careful with your tone and corrections, Lord Hurrey. You do not wish to upset an agent of the Lord Privy Seal as he has your king's favor."

Rouen laughed. "The Lord Privy Seal? Is that his highest honor now? Tell me, Sir Thomas, have your coffers or Cromwell's run dry to be once more terrorizing poor monks and nuns in Henry's name?"

The man reached for his rapier and took a threatening step towards Rouen.

Brian and Rouen's men-at-arms raised their crossbows or pulled their swords.

Unfazed by the commotion around him, Rouen grinned down at the hot-tempered lawyer who overstepped his bounds. "Remove your hand from your blade should you wish to leave Croxden today."

"I would do as Lord Hurrey recommends, Sir Thomas. He has almost fifty men present to your fourteen." The sheriff kept an eye on both men, worried he may have to choose a side in the argument if things escalated.

Thomas looked around him then dropped his hand away from his weapon. "Cromwell will hear of your obstruction here."

"You may tell Cromwell he is welcome to discuss his concerns with my actions anytime he wishes. In the meantime, there will be no further visits of any agent to Croxden. My family has protected and patronized this abbey since the day it was consecrated. The monks here are loyal to Henry and to me. I understand the law allows a license to be purchased for any institution that maintains their religious practices and their loyalty to the Church of England. This should be more than enough to cover whatever assessment you or Cromwell require for said license."

Rouen tossed a bag of coin at Leigh.

"Please also advise the Lord Privy Seal, the king will receive a petition of exception drafted by myself on behalf of the abbey within a fortnight."

"Your lord spares your home, abbot." Sir Thomas motioned for one of his underlings to retrieve the bag of coin. "Droyn, pray your actions do not condemn your petition."

"The proper way to address me, Leigh, is Lord Hurrey or Lord Stafford. It amazes me how new men forget that they can fall as quickly as they rise, if they anger those above them. May I also remind you Cromwell no longer shares the favor of the queen nor is his reputation beyond reproach with the king as it once was. That bodes ill for he and you long before my actions condemn my petition. Leave. Do not stop riding until you reach the next county. You and your men are not welcome in Stafford."

Leigh and his livery rode past Jillian and her escort. Leigh slowed his horse, staring at the woman dressed in blue velvet with a matching fur trimmed cloak. She shot him a scathing look.

Not trusting the passing envoy, the man-at-arms directed her to go to Rouen.

Leigh looked back over his shoulder to see the earl ride forward to meet the woman. Seeing how Hurrey stopped his horse beside hers, Leigh surmised she was the earl's rumored new mistress. Odd that she would accompany Hurrey to the abbey. He would be certain to report her presence as well.

CHAPTER TWENTY-THREE

"I want you to share with the Duke of Suffolk what you reported to me." Thomas Cromwell brought Sir Leigh into the elaborately decorated chamber in which the Privy Council frequently convened.

Charles Brandon, Duke of Suffolk, sat with Edward Seymour, Earl of Hertford, discussing the revolt in Lincolnshire the previous fall. Neither aristocrat cared for Cromwell. Both noblemen fell silent with the loud interruption.

Charles scowled at Cromwell. "Whatever the issue is that Sir Thomas is facing, I have full faith and confidence that it is a matter you can resolve, and is not a situation requiring my or Seymour's attention."

"Has the king not charged the two of you with quelling the rebellions against him?" Cromwell shot back.

After exchanging glances with Seymour, Charles let out a breath then looked at Leigh. "Share whatever news you have about further insurgencies against the new Church and our king, Sir Thomas."

Leigh stepped forward. "Lord Hurrey and an armed

faction prevented my visitation to Croxden Abbey."

"Droyn Hurrey?" Edward wanted to confirm the man Leigh referenced. Droyn maintained a reputation of fierce loyalty to the Crown. It made no sense that he would stage a rebellion in Staffordshire.

"Yes, my lord." Leigh nodded. "He paid for a temporary licensure and intends to petition the king requesting an exemption for the abbey, instead of allowing our rightful possession of the property."

Charles grinned. "Did you notify Hurrey of your intent to dissolve the abbey prior to attempting to do so?"

"I did not see a need to. We have not done so with previous properties."

"The passage of the law serves well enough as notification to any religious house that they may no longer exist. There is no need to alert Hurrey to one of my agent's visitations." Cromwell supported Leigh's decision not to reach out to the earl.

"And therein lies the root of such a poorly conceived decision. It is no wonder Droyn and his men greeted you with hostility. Lord Hurrey has longstanding personal ties to the abbey. You should have enlisted his help. Leigh, you are a fool if you believe he would allow you to harm the Cistercians living there." Charles chuckled at the embarrassed expression on Leigh's face.

The duke's lackadaisical response perturbed Cromwell. "As you do not take this matter seriously, I shall present it to the king for resolution and visit Lord Hurrey myself."

Henry Tudor joined the three members of his Privy Council. Charles and Edward started to rise, but Henry motioned for them to sit down and disregard formalities.

"What has Droyn allegedly done that requires my

attention?"

"Droyn hostilely removed Sir Leigh from Croxden after the Visitation Officer failed to inform Hurrey of his intent to dissolve the abbey." Charles smirked as he spoke. "Lord Cromwell and Sir Leigh are seeking my assistance with convincing the earl to apologize for his actions and to talk him out of drafting a petition of exemption for the abbey."

"Lord Hurrey appears to harbor Papist sympathies." Cromwell pushed the king to either send Suffolk to Stafford or to stymie any sort of exemption request.

Charles scoffed at the accusation. "Droyn is not a recusant. He supports the new church and our king. This is simply a misunderstanding and his honoring a vow made by an ancestor to protect the abbey."

"I had forgotten Droyn's forebearers granted the Cistercians the land the abbey was built upon." Henry stared thoughtfully at Charles then Cromwell. "Does the same abbot who refused to lease the land as we requested still head the order that lives there?"

"Yes, your majesty." Cromwell hoped the abbot's earlier disobedience would prove the need to reprimand Droyn. "Lord Hurrey supported the abbot's refusal then just as he supports the abbey by paying the fine for a temporary licensure."

Edward didn't see anything troubling about the events. "If Droyn paid the fine, there is no issue with the abbey remaining open."

Cromwell shook his head. "This is not solely about the abbey. The Earl of Stafford freely took up arms against a king's representative. Furthermore, he defended Catholic interests on our shores after shortly returning from visiting an Italian court loyal to the Pope. I fear future revolts against England and the new church will occur in Stafford as they did in Lincoln. One can never be too careful when protecting England's interests. Lord Hurrey has a great many men loyal to him. If for some reason he changed allegiances after being in Italy for so long, he is an adversary to be wary of going forward."

"Enough of this conjecture, Lord Cromwell!" Charles knew he attempted to sow seeds of distrust between Henry and Droyn. "Your man disregarded common courtesy and, humiliated, had to return to London with his hat in hand for failing to seize assets after tangling with one of the most devoted Englishmen to serve the Crown. The earl you accuse of having Papist sympathies assisted me in ending the revolts in the North. A man loyal to the Pope would not have done so. You waste the King and Council's time. I, for one, will not listen to another word of this drivel."

"The new Lady Stafford was with him at the abbey. I saw her myself. Her coloring is consistent with that of an Italian. Being from Urbino, she is more than likely a Catholic. Love makes even the greatest men behave poorly." Sir Leigh threw further fuel on the fire Cromwell stoked.

"Lady Stafford? I was not aware he married the woman." Henry's temper flared at the possibility one of his nobles married without permission.

"Droyn has not wed the woman. She merely resides with him." Charles interceded on Rouen's behalf. He committed the same infraction with Mary years ago. No one should have to unnecessarily endure the king's wrath stemming from a false accusation.

Henry looked over at Charles again. "Are you certain of that?"

"Vivian spent an hour complaining to Katherine about

Droyn's new mistress. If Droyn wishes to marry the woman, he would seek your approval before doing so."

"Perhaps, Charles, you should pay Droyn a visit to ensure he has not done something as foolish as you once did, and to assure Cromwell of Hurrey's support for the Church of England."

Charles politely inclined his head to the king. "Yes, your majesty. I will depart immediately."

"I shall accompany you." Cromwell stood as Charles made his way towards the exit after Henry gestured for him to go.

"Hurrey is very particular about those he allows in his home." Charles hoped to deter Cromwell from following him.

"One of my cousins resides just outside of Stafford. I will stay with him, so I do not impose on Lord Hurrey."

CHAPTER TWENTY-FOUR

Charles woke early on the third day of the ride to Stafford. They hoped to reach Hurrey's house around midday. Not wanting to surprise Droyn with the impromptu visit, Charles dispatched a messenger to warn of his and Cromwell's pending arrival. Regrettably, he could give Droyn no more than an hour or two's notice.

Brian read the note the messenger delivered. He shook his head, knowing the chaos that was about to erupt. "I will take the note to the Lord Hurrey. You go to the kitchen for a glass of cider and some breakfast."

Happy out be out of the cold, the young man thanked Brian for the hospitality.

Upon hearing Brian enter the study, Rouen looked up from reviewing an estate contract with two of the local guilds. The perturbed expression on the normally jovial man's face warned he did not come to share glad tidings. "Yes?"

Brian handed Rouen the note. "The Duke of Suffolk sends you this. He and Lord Cromwell will be arriving by midday."

Rouen quickly skimmed the note. "It appears my coin was not enough to satisfy Leigh. Ready the household and guest rooms. Suffolk will most likely have two other men with him. I have no idea how large an entourage the Lord Privy Seal travels with as this is the first visit he's paid me." Rouen put away the paperwork to prepare for his unexpected guests.

"Shall I inform, Lady Jillian?"

Rouen tapped the note against his hand, debating what to do about Jillian. "Where is Jillian?"

"She attends her riding lesson with Jonathan."

"Send Oswyn to find them and request that she return to the house once her lesson ends."

***

Jillian ended her riding lesson early. Something wasn't right for Oswyn to deliver the message that he did. She hurried back to the house.

The household staff flitted about both floors of the home. Jillian wondered what caused the flurry of activity. She found Brian and Rouen in the dining room.

Rouen wore a doublet, breeches, and hose in gold and black hues as he would at court. His ambassadorial collar once more rested against his chest.

"Go change into one of your new gowns. Brian will send Adelaide to style your hair. We are about to have important visitors."

"Who?"

Rouen offered her a reassuring smile. "You shall see soon enough. We don't have much time. Go dress as I asked."

Jillian nodded, then started for the stairs. *If Rouen was*

smiling, whoever headed their way wasn't anyone to worry about.

***

Changing into the many-layered gowns of the day was time-consuming, requiring running laces through holes to secure what wasn't sewn or pinned in place. Jillian chose to wear her hair uncovered, contrasting with customs of the day. She quelled Adelaide's objections to not donning a gable or rounded hood. Accepting that Jillian wouldn't wear either item, Adelaide set to work on braiding, arranging, and decorating Jillian's hair in a presentable manner.

Looking out a second story window, Brian could see Suffolk and Cromwell approaching the house. Protocol required Jillian to be at Droyn's side when their guests arrived. The steward knocked on the master bedroom door. "Lady Jillian."

"Come in." Jillian smoothed the front of her gown as she looked in the mirror.

"Lord Hurrey wishes you to wear these." Brian opened a lined case holding a pair of earrings and a matching garnet and pearl necklace.

"These are incredible." Jillian admired the gems.

Brian held out the earrings to her, so she could put them on. Once they dangled from her ears, she turned back to him. He held an end of the gold chain in either hand.

"If you could kindly move your hair from your neck, Lady Jillian, I will assist you with the necklace. The clasp can be difficult to close."

Jillian could hear muffled voices from downstairs as Brian settled the necklace in place.

"As Lord Hurrey already entertains our guests, may I have the honor of escorting you to him?" Brian offered Jillian his arm.

Jillian settled her hand on his then walked with him to the great room where Rouen stood speaking with two well-dressed gentlemen.

His back to the entryway, Rouen didn't notice Jillian and Brian coming down the hall.

The taller of the two gentlemen spotted the woman clad in a wine-colored gown trimmed with gold, black, and brown embroidered ribbon complementing the golden embroidered patterns decorating Rouen's clothing. "This must be the Lady Jillian we hear so many stories about."

Rouen grinned as the sounds of skirts swishing came from behind him. He turned and offered Jillian his hand. "Indeed, it is."

Jillian's hand lightly touched Rouen's as he started to step forward to make introductions.

"Your grace." Jillian dropped into a low curtsey before the gentleman who spotted her first. "It is a pleasure to make the Duke of Suffolk's acquaintance. I have been an admirer of yours for some time now."

"Rise, Jillian. There is no need for courtly manners in your own home." Charles smiled, impressed the lady knew who he was.

Jillian couldn't believe that Charles Brandon stood before her. He was her favorite Tudor courtier.

Rouen cleared his throat after Jillian continued to stare at Charles. "Jillian, our other guest, Lord Thomas Cromwell."

In contrast to how she greeted Suffolk, Jillian only gave Cromwell a quick curtsey and a nod of the head.

Cromwell ignored the snub and politely bowed to her, and in Italian, stated it was a pleasure meeting her.

Charles noted Jillian's immediate dislike of the Lord Privy Seal. "The feeling does not appear to be mutual. Perhaps your Italian needs some refreshing."

"My apologies, my lords. I meant no disrespect. I am still learning all the English customs and ranks." Jillian hoped her reaction to Cromwell did not reflect poorly on Rouen.

"No harm done, mia bella." Rouen took her hand with a smirk, well aware she liked Cromwell even less than he did.

Jillian followed the three men to Rouen's office. She sat quietly listening to the polite exchange of news and political discourse, waiting for the formalities to end. Etiquette amongst aristocrats always entertained her. The conversation continued, now delving into proposed legislation and other happenings.

Rouen chuckled and looked over at both men. "The two of you did not ride to Stafford to provide me a personal update on court gossip and parliamentary proceedings."

Charles's eyes shifted in Cromwell's direction before they met Rouen's once more. "Regretfully not, Droyn. We are here on official business after the Privy Council received a concerning report about a conflict between Sir Leigh and yourself at Croxden Abbey. We would like to hear your version of the events that morning."

Jillian set aside her sewing and sat straighter in her chair. She stared directly at Cromwell, wanting to gauge his reaction to Rouen's side of the story.

"I had a feeling that is why you were here." Rouen smiled as if unworried. "Leigh and his men behaved in a manner unbefitting for their office and charge. Before my arrival, they brutalized two of the monks, tore the cloth vestments from the chapel altar, and attempted to steal a jeweled chalice, a crucifix, and the tithe collected that week. My men-at-arms halted their malicious mischief. As the situation escalated to a violence, I was summoned to resolve the matter. Charles, you know Croxden has enjoyed my family's protection since the Hurreys arrived in England. While I support the king and his new church, I cannot simply turn a blind eye to abuses and greed as abysmal as the ones we seek to end with the reformation of religion in this country."

"I assumed Leigh's conduct contributed to the conflict he reported." Charles paused as if weighing what Rouen shared with him.

Angered that Charles was disregarding the seriousness of Rouen's offenses, Cromwell spoke up. "Lord Hurrey, under the law and the king's reform efforts, difficult changes must occur. That includes the dissolution of certain institutions with their wealth entering the king's coffers for redistribution as he and Parliament see fit."

Rouen loudly laughed at Cromwell's claim. "From what I observed that day, the accounts of what Leigh and his men obtained from the alms box and the church would be drastically reduced on royal ledgers. We both know Leigh intended to keep some of the king's wealth for himself. And do you yourself not receive a commission from many of the properties Leigh visits?"

"Now, now, Lord Hurrey. Do not lower yourself to the level of common drivel by making unfounded remarks without proof of such actions. As you paid the required licensure fine and acted in good faith to protect those under your care, you shall receive a warning to more diplomatically resolve such incidences in the future." Charles balanced his role of Lord President of the Privy Council and his long-standing friendship with Rouen in the reprimand.

"If Sir Thomas Leigh notifies me of his arrival and behaves as one with the title of Sir should, I will more than happily assist him with any visitations he may have in Staffordshire." Rouen yielded to Suffolk's direction.

"Those terms are reasonable, Lord Hurrey. Thomas, please remind Sir Leigh that representatives of the Crown are expected to conduct themselves as gentlemen, even if they are not of that status."

"I will speak with all the men who serve as my visitors, your grace. My apologies for Sir Leigh's behavior, Lord Hurrey. We look forward to more amicable interactions and your support of our reform efforts in the future. While it may not appear so, I am empathetic to the people being afraid of this new change." Cromwell chose his words carefully, well aware that the earl would be quick to take arms against whomever threatened Croxden.

"Empathetic?" Jillian muttered, a bit too loudly as the men all looked over at her. Realizing they heard her, Jillian stood and stared directly at Cromwell. "Empathy is not the word I would use to describe your treatment of the clergy or the common man, Lord Cromwell. I think your actions are better described as despotic. If you truly worried about the people accepting the reformed church, you and your employees would not behave in a manner that caused rebellion in the North. Instead, you would behave more as Christ did with kindness, patience, and charity."

"Jillian." The way Rouen growled her name cautioned her to be careful.

"Forgive my remarks, my lords. I shall check on the midday meal. I assume the duke and Lord Cromwell have not eaten."

Cromwell's expression remained a mix of shock and anger watching the woman exit the room.

Charles and Rouen hid smirks at the woman's upbraiding of their peer.

"Italian women are such passionate creatures." Charles broke the tension in the room with a chuckle.

Rouen appreciated Charles's downplaying of Jillian's actions. "Jillian is very passionate about many things. Lord Cromwell, I hope her remarks did not offend you. Charity and compassion are two virtues Jillian holds in high regard. She chides me if I deviate even slightly from them. Similar to the people, she is still seeking to navigate our new faith."

"With her being raised in a Papist region of Italy, I understand how reformation may be difficult for Lady Jillian to embrace. Rest assured, I will give Jillian more time before rendering any sort of opinion about her character." Cromwell diplomatically brushed off the offense.

***

Brian appeared in the doorway and advised the midday meal was prepared.

Jillian sat next to Rouen and only minimally engaged in the mealtime conversation. She answered any inquiries directed to her and avoided the topic of religion. By the way Cromwell keenly stared at her whenever she spoke, he scrutinized every word she said.

Needing a break from her role playing, Jillian left the dining room. She stared out the window at the hills and woods. Rouen did a good job of only clearing as much land as he needed to. In a few years, sheep farming would obliterate England's wooded landscape as the wool industry boomed.

"Lady Jillian." Cromwell pulled Jillian out of her

thoughts.

Jillian thought it odd he approached her alone. "Lord Cromwell."

"I can understand how a woman raised in a location that strongly supports the Pope finds our splitting from the Church incomprehensible. You must trust me when I say it is for the best if we wish to end corruption within the clergy. Surely, you have seen those abuses yourself in Urbino."

Jillian forced a smile. "One man's sin does not provide justification for another to commit an equally grievous action. I can honestly say, the conduct and behavior of Sir Leigh far exceeds anything I have personally witnessed from a Catholic priest or nun."

"And as I promised Lord Hurrey, I shall take Thomas to task for his behavior. May I suggest an accord between us, Lady Jillian? For Lord Hurrey's sake. I think you will find we have much more in common than you realize. I once resided in the Italian Peninsula myself and greatly admire your homeland."

"Your admiration of my homeland does nothing for England nor does it garner any further goodwill. But as you stated, for Lord Hurrey's sake, we may engage one another cordially from this point forward." Jillian reined back the original response forming on her tongue. The men of the age considered women beneath them; speaking her mind might harm Rouen more than herself.

"As we are now friends, may I request your assistance in influencing Lord Hurrey to consider a broader perspective on how to properly patron Croxden?"

Conniving bastard. Jillian took a deep breath. "A woman's place is in managing domestic matters, Lord Cromwell. Commercial and military matters remain Droyn's jurisdiction."

"If Lord Hurrey does not learn to see matters as the king and I do, his Papist sympathies could lead to future harm. Neither of us wishes for that to happen."

"One who deceives will always find those who allow themselves to be deceived, Lord Cromwell?" Jillian recited Machiavelli, knowing Cromwell would have read him.

"Nicolo Machiavelli. You are a well-read woman, Lady Jillian."

"Allow me to speak freely, Lord Cromwell. I am not a disciple of Machiavelli as others claim you to be. While I do not believe in the principles Machiavelli preached, I heed his lessons wisely and recognize when a person deploys them. Do not underestimate Lord Hurrey or myself. May I also recommend you cease whatever scheme you are deploying against Lord Hurrey before you become a victim of your own conspiring."

"What incites such a remark from my lady?" Rouen stood in the doorway.

How long had he been there? Jillian hadn't heard him come down the hall.

"Lord Cromwell was requesting my assistance in managing your Papist sympathies."

Rouen shot Cromwell a glare. "My Papist sympathies?"

"In other words, he wants you to force the abbot to lease the land to whatever local man he has in his pocket, so he and Leigh may benefit."

"Lady Jillian, the revenues from such a lease go to the king's treasury." Cromwell corrected.

"The majority of them, but not all of them. Why else seek to lease these lands? Your wealth has grown substantially with the implementation of the Acts, and that isn't due to solely the king's generosity."

"Jillian." Rouen's tone once again cautioned her to be careful.

"It's the truth. Honorable men like Cromwell here freely exploit leases and wardships to climb the social ladder, and as long as Henry gets his cut, he doesn't care."

Cromwell found the way Jillian spoke strange, but he comprehended the message in her words. "I hope you do not imply that I exploit the masses for my gain, Lady Jillian. I execute the king's commands and am a moral man."

"A moral man!" Jillian snorted, no longer holding her temper back. "What kind of man allows many to be slaughtered for standing up against tyranny? Do you really think that the rioting in the North results from your upstanding morality? If you were a moral and fair man, Suffolk wouldn't be serving as Lord Marshall in Lincolnshire. Churches wouldn't be looted and many people wouldn't have needlessly lost their lives due to your righteous policies. History will remember you for the tyrant you truly are."

"Enough, Jillian!" Rouen crossed the room and grabbed her by the arm to ensure he held her attention. "I think it best you depart, Thomas. You wear out your welcome."

Rouen's raised voice brought Brian to the room.

"Lord Cromwell, if you follow me, we will wait in the other room for your horse to be readied." Brian helped to defuse the escalating argument.

"Thank you for your hospitality, Lord Hurrey." Cromwell only uttered the words as formality dictated he do so, then followed Brian down the hall.

Once Cromwell and Brian were out of earshot, Rouen released Jillian's arm. "You know better than to speak so carelessly, Jillian! To say such things to Cromwell, of all people! You are well aware that man is vindictive and never forgets a slight paid to him."

"His manipulative, holier-than-thou nonsense got to me. Does he think women are complete idiots? That we don't realize when games are being played? I am not about to stand there and kiss his ass or flatter the man."

Rouen shook his head. He had never seen her this angry before. "The next time a man slights you or angers you, come find me. I will address those situations on your behalf. You have done so well with remembering your surroundings until today."

"I am sorry, Rouen. There is just something about him that makes me so angry."

"I can see that." Rouen grinned, feeling that way himself. "Perhaps we can repair any damage done by sending Thomas a written apology this evening."

"Like hell I will apologize to that royal ass-licker!"

Charles laughed, entertained by the term he overheard from the hall. "Royal ass-licker? Crass, but an appropriate description of the man."

Not realizing the Duke of Suffolk had rejoined them, Jillian let out an exasperated sigh. "Me and my big mouth. My apologies, your grace."

Charles gently took Jillian by the shoulders. "You have nothing to fear, Jillian. Many of us feel the same about Cromwell."

"Thank you, your grace."

"My friends call me Charles, Jillian, not your grace."

Jillian stared up at the duke, unsure of how to respond.

He reassuringly patted her upper arms then shifted his attention to Rouen. "Droyn is correct. A short, simple note of apology will remedy any wrong, and those of us who know Droyn well will stymie any other actions that may result from such a minor altercation."

"If it is all right with the both of you, I would like to take a walk to clear my head." Jillian knew fresh air would help calm her down.

"It is fine, mon coeur. Use the rear entrance and stay to the back of the house in case Cromwell hasn't departed yet."

The two men watched the woman disappear down the hall.

Charles lifted a brow at Rouen. "She is not Italian, is she?"

Rouen knew he couldn't lie to Charles. They had been friends too long.

"No. We did meet in Urbino, but that is not where she was born."

"From where did she come?" Charles patiently waited for an answer.

Rouen doubted Charles would understand the complicated relationship between Jillian and himself.

"The New World. I can say no more, Charles."

Charles knew the only reason Hurrey would rather remain silent than confide in him. "Her presence here ties in with the undertakings of the order."

"Yes." Rouen sat down, contemplating the events of the afternoon.

"As I told Jillian, you have nothing to fear, Droyn. Cromwell is not a stupid man. He will not cross one that has friends on the Privy Council and the king's favor. If he is foolish enough to tell anyone of the minor altercation, Henry will more than likely demand Cromwell apologize for offending Jillian and yourself. The Lord Privy Seal no longer walks on water as he once did. Tell me of your time in Italy. I assume you did more than woo Jillian."

CHAPTER TWENTY-FIVE

After paying a visit to Croxden with Charles and Rouen, Cromwell returned to London. Charles spent a week in Stafford catching up with Rouen and enjoying a few days of relative calm.

Jillian carefully guarded what information she shared with Charles. She appreciated that Rouen had Suffolk as an ally on the Privy Council. It eased her worries about retaliation from Cromwell. The morning Charles departed to return to Lincolnshire, Jillian found herself feeling an odd mix of disappointment and relief. Charles's ability to maintain Henry's favor for a lifetime, even with some of the things the duke did, always impressed her as a historian. To actually meet the man only furthered that admiration. Rouen teased her about being star-struck by the duke.

The month following Charles and Cromwell's visit passed peacefully. Jillian focused on perfecting the speech patterns and mannerisms of the day, and took on routine duties around the estate. Rouen's day-to-day obligations as Lord Marshall followed a predictable routine.

"I think we can declare victory over Giselle and

Cromwell." Jillian brought a grin to Rouen's face.

Rouen chuckled, pulling the woman who lay beside him closer. "I pray for that every night, Jillian."

"With how calm things have been, I would say your prayers were answered."

"Perhaps with Cromwell. It is too early to believe we've beaten Giselle and her latest curse. The witch always reappears when least expected."

"I disagree with you, my lord. The people you look after appreciate you, the king and Privy Council are happy with you, and even though it's a bit of an adjustment living in sixteenth-century England, I am more than happy to find myself in the arms of a formerly grumpy ghost every day."

"Your formerly grumpy ghost thinks you need to go to sleep. We both have early appointments in the morning." Rouen didn't want to think about Giselle or curses any further tonight. He wouldn't waste the potentially limited time fate granted him and Jillian worrying about things beyond his control.

***

Screaming and a frantic knocking on the front door woke Rouen and Jillian. Rouen pulled the curtain covering the window aside. An orange glow in the distance paired with the late-night visitors and shouting told him all he needed to know. He yanked on the pants he wore the day prior and pulled a clean shirt from his wardrobe.

The sound of muffled voices and Brian and John making their way towards the stairs further alarmed Rouen. He met the two men at the bedroom door then dashed back to the bed to pull on his boots.

Jillian tried to rouse herself to a more conscious state. "Rouen? What is it?"

"Get dressed, Jillian." Rouen tossed her a gown.

He opened the door to the large cabinet where he stored his sword and armor then put on his hauberk and secured his sword to his side.

"What's happening?" Jillian resisted the panic she felt watching him arm himself.

Rouen tossed a lightweight saber and a small crossbow on the bed. "Bar both the doors and do not open them for anyone other than me. You should be safe here. If someone enters, you know how to use these."

Jillian followed Rouen, John, and Brian down the stairs. Adelaide and Sarah helped Jillian bar the doors. The three women went upstairs to watch what occurred from the window.

The lands around the house glowed orange as fire swept across them. Raiders burned what had become Jillian's home. She could see the outlines of men fighting. *This kind of crap should have ended with Henry VII. What in the hell was happening tonight?*

The dull screaming grew louder as the fighting moved closer to the house.

Forget the crossbow and sword! Jillian ran back to the bedroom for the wheellock pistol and arquebus Henry had sent to Rouen. He was not comfortable with either weapon yet.

None of the invaders carried guns from what she could hear and see. She would have a limited tactical advantage if the gunsmith properly forged each weapon.

"What are you doing, my lady?" Adelaide starred wide-eyed at Jillian as she prepped and loaded the two weapons.

"I am not exactly sure of that myself."

After cracking open the upstairs window, Jillian trained the weapon's sight on a man fighting Brian.

Let the barrel be straight and my aim accurate.

She opened the pan and brought the lit fuse down into it. The loud bang of the weapon firing reverberated around the room. Jillian choked on the lingering haze of smoke the ignited powder left behind.

Brian looked towards the house as the man fell dead.

Jillian pressed herself back against the wall. "Sarah, hand me the small leather pouch hanging off the belt there."

"Where did a lady learn to use such weapons?" Adelaide had never seen the earl fire either one. It dumbfounded her that Jillian knew how to use them.

"My father is a gun enthusiast and I once dated a guy that only used black powder for hunting. It also helps having interned at several historical sites that demonstrated these and muskets in college." Jillian knew neither woman would grasp what she told them as she cleaned the barrel and prepared another round of powder and shot.

Would it be wrong of me to put the idea in some early gunsmith's head that they could make the whole loading process a lot easier with a few tweaks?

She heard more screaming from outside and the room brightened, letting her know the fire moved closer to the house.

Who to shoot next? Her eyes scanned the men fighting in the yard. *Armies fall apart without cavalry and leaders,* she told herself, recalling her military history lessons.

The armor of the knight she targeted reflected the glow of flames. The end of the black barrel followed his movement. He wasn't one of Rouen's men with the uniform he wore. Jillian brought the lit fuse into the open pan once more, creating another cloud of sulfur-filled smoke in the bedroom. The smell briefly conjured memories of fireworks on the 4th of July. She'd much rather be watching her friends and family lighting off fireworks than fighting some weird band of rogue knights.

She smiled when the knight slipped from his horse as the ball penetrated his breastplate. *Two down.*

Grabbing her gloves to try and protect her hands from being burned by the hot barrel, Jillian guessed she could probably take another shot before the arquebus was too hot to fire or the raiders located the marksman firing on them. She ran to the opposite window and looked for another rider not wearing anything that identified him as Rouen's men. After a third knight fell, one of the enemy footmen spotted her. He ran towards the house.

Jillian dropped the gun. It needed to cool before it could be used again.

The repeated thudding against the front door warned others mercenaries joined the lone footman trying to break into the house.

The distinctive high-pitched crash then the tinkling deluge of shards falling against wood floor alerted Jillian to something shattering a window the next room over. Jillian wrapped herself in one of Rouen's thick leather jackets then picked up the pistol and sword from the bed. She cautiously made her way towards the room where glass had shattered

Flames from whatever they threw moved from the floor and up the walls. A second window breaking in the master bedroom caught her attention. Adelaide's screaming confirmed whoever attacked Stafford firebombed the house. The two women met Jillian in the hall.

"Is anyone besides us in the house?" Jillian demanded as

the heat grew more intense.

"No, my lady. The others returned to their homes or are fighting." Sarah answered, starting to cough from the smoke.

"I want you to go downstairs and hide in the pantry. I will join you in a minute." Jillian had one last idea of how to take out a few more men. "Then we will find a safe way out of the house."

Sarah nodded, then led a terrified Adelaide down to the kitchen.

Jillian covered her face and crouched down to make her way to Rouen's weapons cabinet. She retrieved the extra powder keg and lead rounds. The crash of a table along the far wall succumbing to the flames climbing its legs caused Jillian to jump. Forcing herself to focus, she crawled to the window directly above the men trying to break down the door. She tossed the keg and shot onto the flat roof covering the entryway.

Sprinting down the stairs and into the small stone pantry, she yanked the door closed behind her.

The fire sparked the gunpowder as she, Sarah, and Adelaide huddled in what Jillian deemed the strongest corner of the storage space.

A thunderous boom rattled the house; shattering the stone and wood front. Lead launched into the air. Splinters and stone shard shrapnel mixed with the lead balls bombarded the men at the front door and a few others nearby.

Hearing the explosion, Brian and Rouen turned. What had caused it?

"Jillian!" Rouen ran towards the blaze, fearing that she might be trapped inside.

Brian grabbed his arm to keep him from entering the

burning structure. They couldn't afford to lose the earl to the flames.

Once the house stopped tremoring, the three women opened the pantry door. Ignoring the heat and the haze, they crawled to the back door and managed to lift the heavy bar securing the back entrance. Jillian shoved the door open and waved for the other two women to run. After they safely made it across to the tree line, she sprinted in the same direction.

A large knight stepped in her path, grasped her by the throat, and snarled something in French.

Jillian frantically worked at the hands around her neck.

Thomas came out of nowhere and smashed the man in the back of the head with a shovel.

The knight released Jillian and swung his sword, killing the boy.

Jillian shouted Thomas's name as she fired the one remaining shot in the pistol, killing his assailant.

The echo of a gunshot over the crackling of the fire brought Rouen and Brian to the rear of the house. Rouen recognized Jillian holding the pistol.

Mary and Michael came out of their hiding place in the barn when they saw Jillian.

"Turn back! It isn't safe!" Jillian screamed at the children running into the fray.

As she feared, one of the mounted men rode after the siblings. Seeing Brian and Rouen coming towards her with Jonathan behind them, she pointed towards the two kids trying to make their way across the yard.

Brian and Jonathan charged forward, attempting to reach the two children directly in the rider's path.

Rouen took aim at the rider with his crossbow.

The arrow struck the man, but it only wounded him.

Rouen grabbed Jillian from behind already foreseeing what would happen next.

She wailed and stretched her hands towards the children.

"Look at me, Jillian." He prayed she'd turn her face in his direction.

Before she could fully turn towards him, the rider clubbed Mary then trampled Michael.

The haunting sight of the children being killed and the anguish in the cry that left Jillian's lips tormented Rouen. He restrained the woman frantically trying to go to the little ones lying on the ground.

"There is nothing you can do for them. They are gone." Rouen hated uttering those words.

"They can't be." Jillian whispered, still struggling to cope with what she just witnessed.

"Jillian, we need to leave." Rouen knew this was the first time she saw the horrors of ancient warfare. He needed her to understand the longer they stayed in one place, the more they endangered themselves.

"Why would grown men kill children?" Jillian now faced him. She was taken back by what she saw. Blood and mud splattered his face and the white shirt partially covered by mail. Dried blood on his fingers shared that Rouen directly engaged the men in swordplay or hand-to-hand combat.

"Unfortunately, some believe in annihilating everything in their way. This is not a raid for plunder. These men were sent to destroy Stafford. Come with me."

She nodded, taking the hand he held out to her and followed him to the darkened tree line where Adelaide and

Sarah disappeared earlier. She hoped they remained safe.

Rouen led her deeper into the woods where a mounted rider waited with a Rouen's favorite horse.

"Up you go." Rouen whispered before helping her into the saddle. Once she settled herself, he handed her the reins. "Ride to Croxden. I will meet you there when this is over."

"Rouen, you can't," Jillian started to beg him to come with her.

"I am needed here, Jillian. I have more field experience than almost all of those fighting. I will come to you as soon as I am able." He turned to her armed escort. "Ride quickly. Stop for nothing. Make sure she reaches the abbey safely."

Rouen slapped her horse on the rump. The horse bolted forward, sending Jillian and her escort into the night.

***

Jillian's escort banged on the large door of the abbey. The wood slab opened, revealing a brown robed monk. Rouen's man identified himself as a soldier of the earl escorting a member of the earl's household.

The abbot led Jillian to a small room. "I apologize for the accommodations, my lady. This is the best I can offer you."

"I am thankful to have shelter for the night. There are many who will go without."

"May I get you something to eat or drink, Lady Hurrey?"

"No, thank you. I would like some water to wash my hands and face." Jillian could still smell the gun powder on her skin.

Finding no solace in her small room, Jillian slipped away to the chapel and prayed for the battle to be over quickly.

The abbot smiled as he saw the woman kneeling before the altar in silent vigil. He noted how she crossed herself and paid her respects before leaving it. The priest nodded to her as she passed him.

Jillian eventually succumbed to weariness after staying awake as long as she could. She woke alone on her cot. Sunlight shone in the small window of her room. *Had Rouen survived the night?*

"Any word from Lord Hurrey?" Jillian asked finding the abbot and her escort in the hall.

"None, my lady." The man-at-arms stood up. "As soon as news arrives, we shall share it with you."

"What is your name, sir?"

"Adam, my lady."

"Please be certain to keep your word, Adam."

At midday, Jillian grew restless. She stepped outside into the abbey yard and stopped one of the men walking past. "Where are the horses kept?"

"The stable is a bit of a walk. Shall I have someone bring your mount, my lady?"

"Yes, please. I would like to go for a ride."

The man returned the smile Jillian gave him. "We will ready your horse. As it will take a few minutes, you may be more comfortable waiting in the church than out here."

"Thank you." Jillian went back inside the church.

The abbot overheard Jillian and the stable hand's discussion. He went to alert Adam of what Jillian planned.

Adam ran into the church. The earl would have his head if Jillian left Croxden. "You cannot ride to Stafford, Lady Jillian. It is not safe."

"I cannot stay here knowing there are wounded that need tending and dead buried at the manor. If you fear for my safety, ride with me."

"Please, my lady. Lord Hurrey would not approve. He

was very specific in his orders that you not leave the abbey."

"I don't give a damn what orders he gave you! We don't have any clue whether or not the earl lives." Jillian snapped, sliding her arms into Rouen's jacket.

"The earl lives and breathes, madam." Rouen announced from the main entryway. The wooden door of the church banged shut behind him. "You should listen to Adam. I absolutely would not approve of you riding back to Stafford."

Seeing Rouen survived the battle, Jillian sprinted down the aisle towards him. He only managed to take two steps forward before she embraced him. Fatigued from a night of fighting and putting out fires, she almost knocked him over as her body collided with his. Jillian's lips found Rouen's; the urgency of the kiss intimately conveying her relief at his safe arrival. Her hands pulling him ever closer, shared her fears of him not returning. Strong and reassuring arms enfolded her, silently promising he would always do his best to return to her. The intimate way he returned the kiss inscribed that unspoken oath on her heart.

Brian cleared his throat, ending the amorous display. "We are in a church, my lord. I do not think Christ would appreciate you taking the woman in his house."

Rouen chuckled, still holding Jillian. "I believe our Lord and Savior would understand after what we survived."

"I am willing to face the inferno if it means I have you." Jillian whispered, making Rouen laugh once more.

"We will just enjoy our reunion in a location more appropriate for carnal activities. I secured lodging for us nearby. As I see you have everything you came with, are you ready to leave?"

"More than ready." Jillian brought a smile to his face.

Rouen obliged her request to ride with him versus waiting on her own mount.

Brian helped her into the saddle behind Rouen then advised he would retrieve her horse.

Jillian wrapped her arms around his waist. She held him tighter when the horse moved forward. Her chin briefly rested on his steel covered shoulder. In contrast to the cold mail, the man who wore it was warm when she turned her face into his neck and hair.

Rouen closed his eyes, enjoying how it felt to have her in the saddle with him.

Jillian felt his chest shake through the mail as he chuckled at how tightly she held onto him.

"Does the idea of my death truly frighten you that gravely, Jillian?"

"Yes, it does. The worst thing I could imagine is being stuck in the sixteenth century without you."

"We will have to strive to ensure that nightmare never becomes reality." Rouen urged his horse into a lope. "I have no intentions of making the woman I love spend the rest of her days alone in the sixteenth century."

"The woman you love?" Jillian smiled, catching his words.

"Aye, Jillian. And you should well know that by now."

"Can you not just say the words, Rouen? We both could have been killed last night and would go to our graves having never told each other how we feel."

Rouen laughed. "If it will soothe thy angst. I love you, Jillian Fitzalan."

"And I love you, Rouen Durrant." Jillian whispered in his ear.

"We are quite the hapless pair, aren't we, Jillian?"

"I think the word you meant to use was lucky. So tell me, Lord Stafford, did we win if there is such a thing, or are we retreating to fight another day?" Jillian brought a grin to his face.

"You ride with the victor, my naive woman. I won the field just before dawn. Do you honestly think I would let anyone take Stafford or my home?"

Rouen requested a bath be drawn for him when they reached the inn where he had rented rooms.

The innkeeper looked startled by the request, but did as the earl wished.

Rouen escorted Jillian upstairs to a private room then left to speak with Brian about what still needed to be done for those that survived. He dispatched a rider to the king with a warning that the French waged war on English soil.

Jillian watched as several men dragged a tub into the room and began filling it with buckets of boiling water. She realized how spoiled she was with the bathing room in Rouen's house. She had no idea how long it took to fill the tub they used. Unlike many of the time, Rouen was adamant about taking an actual bath every few days and washing daily. His travels introduced him to the benefits of bathing to prevent disease and heal a sore body.

With the messenger dispatched, Rouen returned to his room.

Jillian helped him remove his mail and shirt. Discovering two gashes on his upper arm and chest, she realized some of the blood on the shirt was his.

"How did you get these?" Jillian placed her fingers underneath the one on his chest.

"While the mail helps, it is not foolproof. One or two of the bastards got a lucky shot in on me. You still smell like gun powder, Lady Marksman. I am impressed you could use the weapons as you did." He undid the jacket she wore then threw it on the wooden chest next to his shirt. "I believe a woman should smell of perfume and flowers, not sulfur. Undress, so you may help your master bathe and wash yourself."

"Are we not returning to Stafford to assess the damages?" Jillian thought Rouen's direction odd. By the way he diverted his eyes to the floor, Jillian knew he had bad news to share.

"Tomorrow, mon coeur. After the fires burn themselves out and the ash has time to cool. I left men behind to guard the estate and tend to the wounded."

"The house?" Jillian wondered if anything of the home remained.

"Gone, Jillian. It is just stone and wood. I have all that I need with me." Rouen kissed her; grateful she escaped the house before the flames overwhelmed it.

CHAPTER TWENTY-SIX

Jillian and Rouen's raised voices rang throughout the inn as she followed him down the stairs and out the front door.

"No, Jillian! That is my final word on the matter." Rouen snapped, having enough of the disagreement and swinging up into the saddle of the horse waiting for him outside.

"You are a pigheaded ass, Rouen Hurrey!" Jillian hated his leaving her behind for the afternoon.

He leaned downward and gently grasped Jillian by the chin. "This is not twenty-first century Urbino, madam! You will do as instructed. Now, enough of this childish outburst! Go back inside and await my return."

"My earlier question was not a request, it was a rhetorical statement. And I am not going back inside."

Brian chuckled as Jillian stepped closer to Rouen's horse and held her head higher, glaring back at him.

"I will follow you on foot if need be, Lord Stafford."

"You will do no such thing. Do as your lord has ordered and return to our room."

"No."

"Jillian, if I have to get off this horse and carry you up to the room myself, I will do so. Save yourself that humiliation and retire to our chambers." Rouen resisted the urge to take her over his knee, reminding himself the woman was new to old customs and ways.

"I dare you to do that." Jillian defiantly glared up at him.

Rouen ignored the taunt in her words.

She grabbed a hold of the horse's bridle to keep Rouen from leaving. "Stafford has become my home. I wish to help rebuild it in whatever way I can."

"You can help by doing as you are asked. Step back and allow me to depart."

"You there!" Jillian called to the stable boy watching the disagreement.

"Yes, my lady?" He stammered, wondering what she wanted.

"Bring my horse."

"Do not bring the lady's horse!" Rouen halted the stable boy.

"As I stated, please, fetch my horse." Jillian smiled at the boy who was not sure what to do.

"Do not take a single step towards the stable. I own the woman's horse and withdraw my permission for her use of it. As the Earl of Stafford, I decree that the horse is not to be used or leave the barn without my explicit instructions that it may do so." Rouen usurped any authority she had.

"Yes, your lordship." The stable boy sat back down on the front porch.

"I hate this patriarchal, backwards place!" It irritated Jillian that everyone just followed whatever direction a noble issued. *Stupid hierarchy of classes!*

"Fine, your high and mighty *lordship*, I will stay here." Jillian sneered the word 'lordship' with a mocking half bow.

"Woman, you try what little patience I have left!" Rouen growled, locking eyes with Jillian once more.

Since arguing didn't work, Jillian decided to try another approach. "My Lord Hurrey, my gallant protector, you leave me fearing for my life. I, a poor, defenseless woman, will stay at a strange inn with a pitiful excuse of a lock on the room door. A lock easily broken by lustful men who view women as nothing more than chattel, mere objects to sate their lust on. You will come to hate yourself for forcing me to stay behind if I am raped or worse."

Rouen laughed at her dramatic change in tactics. "With the racket you are making, you scare any would-be attacker into the next county, madam. You also forget no man would dare touch the property of the ruling magnate."

"Your rank and this supposed code of chivalry you live by did not prevent an attack on your estate. What makes you think another man wouldn't ravage your woman to avenge the loss a night ago?" Jillian shot back, striking a nerve.

Rouen fell silent and the angry tick in his jaw returned.

"She makes a valid point, Droyn." Brian interjected, earning an irritated glance from Rouen. "The prisoners are secure, and there are no signs of any stragglers roaming the countryside. She can help tend the wounded and boost morale by appearing with you. People will ask about her welfare if they do not see her at your side."

Rouen let out an exasperated breath, aggravated that his steward now aided Jillian's cause. "Who scouted the area for remaining troops?"

"I did. The area is clear and safe. We will be with her at

all times if something were to happen." Brian wanted peace between the earl and the woman.

"Boy! Bring the lady's horse, and be quick with tacking the animal. I am losing daylight." Rouen caved, not entirely sure it was wise to do so.

"Thank you, Brian." Jillian smirked, pleased Rouen changed his mind.

"You are most welcome, my lady. What you won today is a rare victory. I advise you not to challenge Droyn in such a fashion again. I cannot afford to make it a routine practice to contradict my lord's orders." Brian curtly replied.

"You are a troublesome woman, Jillian Fitzalan. A lesser man would have beaten you for your ranting this morning." Rouen scolded, noting how she now smiled up at him.

"Then I am fortunate that I love a great man with such control over his hand. I ask my lord's forgiveness for angering him. My intent is just."

***

Jillian felt ill as they came onto Rouen's lands. Only an exterior shell of his great house remained. All but one barn was burned to the ground. The barn left standing was used to help the injured.

The homes of those that lived nearby were in various states of disarray. Some missing walls; others, portions of their thatched roofs. Charred walls, holes in roofs, and broken framing members could be repaired. They only passed two properties with black ash eerily forming the outline of what was once a home.

"Did Cromwell do this in retaliation for the abbey?" Jillian speculated about the reasons Stafford was attacked.

Rouen shook his head. "If Cromwell were behind the attack, Leigh or Seymour would have led the men. I also would have received a warning from Charles."

"You and the Charles really are good friends."

Rouen half-smiled. "We share a mutual hatred of Cromwell and respect one another."

"If Cromwell and Leigh didn't do this, who did? I don't believe French troops would cross the Channel to randomly attack you."

"I am not sure, Jillian. After we see to the citizens of Stafford, we will figure that out."

***

Rouen glanced over at Brian after seeing Anne, the children's mother, standing with her husband staring out at the decimated fields.

Brian smiled sadly, aware that Rouen worried about Jillian discovering the three little bodies. The steward lowered his voice, so Jillian would not hear what he said. "I and their father took them to the church for burial this morning. I know how seeing them would devastate Lady Jillian."

"Anne." Jillian dismounted and walked over to the silent woman.

Neither woman said a word, but embraced one another.

Rouen watched the two grieve together. Helpless to do anything more for either one of them, he left the two women alone to check on the others present to ensure they all had food and shelter. After he and Brian met with those living directly on his property, he returned to Anne and Tobias's cottage. The two women still stood outside, quietly speaking to one another with tear-streaked faces.

"Jillian."

Hearing Rouen call for the lady of the manor, Anne looked up at the earl as he rode toward them.

Rouen worried about what she would say with the pain in her eyes; having overheard several people repeating that the devil punished them all for showing leniency to a cursed lord who disobeyed the order to dissolve the abbey.

"I, I am so sorry that you lost your children; that I could not save them."

"You did not kill my children, my lord." Anne took Rouen's hand in hers. "We are grateful that you protected those that you could, and for generously ensuring we have food and shelter after your own home and stores were destroyed. May you bring those that did this to justice."

***

Jillian and Rouen visited the yeoman farms on the borders of Rouen's lands to learn what assistance they needed. Rouen admired the woman's courage and charitable side. She took everything head on.

When they returned to his property, she walked beside him into the barn serving as a hospital. She blanched several times while helping tend to the wounded, but still managed to complete whatever tasking the physicians gave her.

Needing fresh air and to escape the horrendous injuries she saw, Jillian left the barn. She spotted Rouen standing outside what was once his home, staring at the remaining portions of stone and brick walls. Even from a distance, Jillian could see the frustration on his face. She wished there was something more she could do for him, for his people, for all of them. He looked over at her as she drew near.

"For what it is worth, I am sorry, Rouen."

His brows came together. "This is not your fault. The houses and barns can be rebuilt."

"Can we salvage anything from the ashes?" She stepped through one of the openings in the wall.

"Careful, love. The remains are not very stable." Rouen cautioned, following her.

Both of them walked the footprint of the house, finding a few items still usable in the rubble.

Flecks of gold glinted up at Jillian from a pile of black ash. Her fingers brushed aside the ash. She smiled, retrieving the Durrant crest.

"You are a tough old thing, aren't you?" She muttered, walking over to a small pail of water Rouen had drawn to assist with cleaning anything that they salvaged.
Surprisingly, neither the pendant nor chain had melted in the heat of the fire. The emblem almost gleamed after she polished it against her skirt.

"What treasure did you find, Lady Hurrey?" A soldier asked, coming out of nowhere.

By the heavy French accent, Jillian assumed he wasn't one of Rouen's men. She took a few steps back towards the burnt structure behind her.

Giselle appeared. "I should have known it was you interfering with my plans."

"Rouen!" Jillian yelled, glancing around for him.

He stepped out from behind one of the remaining walls; his eyes quickly skimming the landscape for Jillian. Rage replaced worry in his expression seeing Giselle standing next to Jillian. The witch's presence confirmed his suspicions about the culprit behind the attack on his home. Wrath seized his soul with her destruction of a third community under his care. The only thing keeping him from attacking Giselle at the moment was Jillian's proximity to her.

Brian came from the other side of the house concerned about Jillian's shouting. He halted beside Rouen unsure what to think about the oddly dressed woman and knight near Jillian.

A group of men wearing multiple liveries surrounded them. The two calmly surveyed the well-armed men.

Rouen noticed Jillian starting to turn towards him. "Stay where you are, Jillian."

Giselle walked over to Rouen. "You have lost everything, yet again, Rouen. Come back with me. Seize the throne from your brothers. You can rule England and France as God intended."

"Are you certain I have lost everything, witch?"

"Look around you. Your lands are burned. Your people hate you for failing to defend them. Your fortune is gone. Soon, you will receive word that you have fallen out of favor with Henry due to your defeat here. Cromwell will pounce on the opportunity to send you to the Tower for denying him and Leigh Croxden. What do you possibly have left, Rouen?"

"Even with all that was lost here, I am still richer than most men, Giselle."

Giselle scoffed, looking back at Jillian. "The woman is hardly worth the dirt she stands on. I can give you all the women, land, and gold you desire. You will no longer be the bastard son time forgot. Instead, you will be one of the most powerful kings in England's history. All you have to do is return to Saxony with me and challenge your father. Unlike you, William is far from being a man of honor. He'd sell his own mother if it benefited him to do so. Did the king you so adamantly defend not abandon you for his other sons?"

Rouen stared down at the sorceress who enjoyed finding new ways to torture him. He was tired of the centuries old game they played. "Not all of us are driven by greed or lust for power. When are you going to learn, no matter what you offer, I will never accept it?"

"Perhaps, I am making the wrong offer to the wrong person." Giselle smiled up at Rouen then sidestepped the knight.

"Tell me, lady, would you not desire to be married to a powerful king? Imagine being immortalized in tapestries, poetry, and songs." The witch pulled Jillian from the sidelines into the game.

"I would rather have love and live poorly than have all of the money and power in the world." Jillian replied, bringing a smile to Rouen's face.

Giselle turned, glaring at the Norman as he laughed at Jillian's answer.

"Your power wanes even further, witch. The lady is not even the slightest bit tempted by your offer."

Giselle ignored Rouen's taunt, placing an arm around Jillian's shoulders. "There is something else I can offer you, Jillian."

She turned Jillian, so she stared directly at Rouen.

Rouen frowned, not liking how friendly the witch acted with Jillian.

"I can give you the knight. I will cast a spell commending him into your care. He will have eyes for no one but you. You will spend each night sleeping beside him and each day doing whatever you desire."

Jillian realized Giselle shifted tactics out of desperation. "I prefer he wants me of his own freewill, not because of some spell."

"Freewill is fickle, my dear." Giselle brushed off her decline. "What if I gave Rouen his freedom from the curse?"

"His freedom?" Jillian wondered why the witch thought her to be so naive that she would fall for whatever slick line she crafted.

"Yes, his freedom. I will revoke the curse if you can persuade him to return Saxony to its former glory."

"What interest do you have in the kingdom to desire its restoration to a former age?" Jillian wondered what drove the witch to demand William's death.

"Does one need more incentive than to see the Norman king destroyed? William was brutal to live under. He humiliated and tormented us. The man killed his queen. He poisoned your hero's mother. They say he added hemlock to the water she was given as she birthed his son. Can you imagine a being so cruel as to murder one wife and poison the other who gave Rouen to the world?"

"No, I cannot." Jillian stared at the man she had fallen in love with. *How could he live with these rumors, or worse yet, the horror of the tales if they were true?*

Rouen's face remained stoic as Giselle escorted Jillian to him.

The empathy and concern written across her features juxtaposed against the cruelty in Giselle's and the burnt landscape around them strengthened Rouen's resolve to outwit the witch.

Jillian stared up at Rouen amazed by his fortitude. Nothing ever seemed to faze him. He remained confident and strong in the face of a vindictive enemy that greatly outnumbered his small rank of three.

"Rouen, my love." Jillian whispered, gently placing her hand against the side of his face. She felt the dark stubble covering his cheek under her palm. Those coarse whiskers always felt like velvet to her whenever she stroked them or he brushed them against her skin. She looked over at Giselle. "He more than deserves his freedom."

"Jillian, no." Rouen caught her wrist as she started to pull away. "The witch never does anything without the recipient of the request paying a steep price for her favor."

Jillian smiled and reached for him again.

Rouen was not sure how to react to the sudden embrace.

"I do not need the witch to break the curse, Rouen. I asked you once before, don't you remember how fairy tales work and curses are broken?"

Giselle slinked forward, feeling an odd sensation of impending defeat.

"I am afraid to admit I do not recall." Rouen confessed in a hushed tone.

Giselle paled. Fear surface on the witch's face for the first time in five hundred years.

"You have an escape clause this time. You've found a love that supersedes time. Five centuries technically separate us. We are from vastly different periods, but somehow manage to make things work. We're literally the past melding with the present." Jillian brought a grin to the knight's face.

Rouen's grin broadened to a smile. Jillian's impulsive addition to Giselle's spell back in Urbino provided him a chance to gain his freedom. He knew what he needed to do. His arm settled around Jillian's waist, drawing her to him.

"Mon coeur, we aren't the past and present, we are today and the future."

"No." Giselle realized the modern-day woman tricked

her.

Jillian tilted her face to his. "Kiss me, Rouen. With Giselle present, you'll break the spell."

Rouen claimed those soft, pink lips anxiously and freely awaiting his. Time stopped as the kiss deepened. The chains of obligation that bound him to his prior fate fell free.

Giselle shrieked in anger.

Rouen opened his eyes as the howling came closer.

Giselle charged them.

He pushed Jillian from him.

The knight standing behind him pulled Jillian away from Rouen and Giselle.

Jillian grasped the Frenchman's arms, watching Giselle hurling herself at Rouen.

Giselle's eyes widened in surprise as Rouen's dagger found her belly.

"You should choose more reliable minions for the war you attempted to wage, sorceress. Once defeated, the mercenaries were quick to turn to the service of the victor. Your false messenger to Henry lies in a fresh, shallow grave. Your captain happily agreed to draw you out of whatever cave you hid away in. You will never cast another spell or curse another soul, Giselle. The forgotten Duke of Normandy stands victorious before you, just as he was in the conquest of England as William's right hand." Rouen declared his triumph over her as the witch drew her final breaths. "My father's legacy remains as is, and I fulfill my last promise to him."

The sorceress's eyes rolled back. Her vibrant champagne-colored locks disintegrated. She turned into a hunchbacked old woman. Lean muscle vanished and her skin withered around her bones. Giselle embodied the true monster that she was when the last grains of sand in the hourglass of her terrible life ran out. The beastly body of the witch crumpled to the ground, lifeless.

Rouen looked at the knight standing with Jillian. "Burn her remains, Jordan. I do not want any chance of her returning."

"It will be done, my prince. Are you certain you do not wish to return to Normandy with us? The king will be disappointed you chose to remain in England." The Frenchman surprised Jillian with his respectful response as he released his hold on her arm.

"My life is here now." Rouen's gaze rested on Jillian as he spoke.

"You will be missed, Rouen. Shall I give Frances your regards?"

"Please do. Thank you for your assistance in defending my home and today." Rouen shook the man's hand.

"I regret we did not arrive fast enough to prevent the damage done." The knight gestured at the charred house.

Rouen shrugged. "Buildings can be replaced. While I can't recover the lives lost, I can make the lives of those still remaining better."

"Others before self always, mon prince. Bonne chance until our paths cross again, Durrant." The knight placed his fist against his heart then headed towards a group of similarly dressed men on horseback.

It dawned on Jillian that the knight knew Rouen's real identity to address him as his prince. "He knows who you really are?"

Rouen smiled, placing an arm around Jillian. "He does."

"I wondered why you were not concerned when the

French knights appeared."

"Did you not recognize their coat of arms, Lady Historian? They wore the colors and crest of Normandy. The herald they march under now flies over the ruling palaces of France and England. The man who protected you when Giselle charged is the Captain of William the First's personal guard."

"What?" Jillian thought Rouen misspoke.

"I will explain everything when we return to the inn."

Fortunately, things turned out as he, Brian, and Jordan planned. Even though it was a well-played gambit, it distressed Rouen a great deal when Giselle brought Jillian into the fray. If Jillian had not stood her ground about returning to the estate, he might still be a servant to the curse.

CHAPTER TWENTY-SEVEN

Jillian sat with Katherine, the Duchess of Suffolk. Charles and Katherine extended an invitation for she and Rouen to stay with them until Rouen secured temporary lodgings elsewhere as plans to rebuild Stafford were drawn up. The two women became friends over the two weeks she and Rouen spent in Lincolnshire. They continued to correspond with one another when Rouen and Jillian took up a residence in London.

Rouen and Charles stood on the other side of the room. Both smiled and laughed about whatever topic they discussed.

Jillian cast a nervous glance Rouen's way, worried about why the king had sent the invitation to join him at Hampton Court. She had seen Vivian in the hall as they made their way to the king's private study.

Katherine smiled and placed a hand on Jillian's forearm. "Stop worrying, Jillian. Droyn assured you earlier that everything is fine. If there was ill intent behind Henry sending for Droyn, Charles would warn the two of you. We also would not be waiting in the royal chambers for the king."

"The king is on his way." Sir Wriothesley, the king's secretary, alerted Charles and Rouen.

Charles and Rouen set down the wine glasses they held and moved closer to the door, preparing to great their monarch.

Rouen reassuringly grinned and winked at Jillian as she and Katherine stood, but remained off to the side.

The door opened once more, but Cromwell entered instead of Henry. Several guards accompanied him.

"Arrest Droyn Hurrey for treason."

"On what grounds?" Jillian asked before Rouen could voice the same question. She watched the guard seize the man who loyally served Henry.

"Be quiet, Jillian." Rouen worried she would endanger herself.

Cromwell handed Henry the bundle of letters discovered in Rouen's temporary residence as the king entered the hall. "Someone alerted the Bishop of Stafford to your Papist sympathizing. We found the written correspondence between the Duke of Urbino, the Pope, and yourself, Lord Hurrey. These should be all the evidence you need, your majesty, to see that the man conspires against the Crown."

Rouen kept his composure. "The existence of those letters is explainable."

"I am well aware of the correspondence, Thomas." Henry sorted through the letters unconcerned. "I sent Droyn as my delegate to meet with Duke della Rovere as a gesture of friendship. I hoped to ensure continued trade and good will between Urbino and England."

"Then I assume you are also aware that Hurrey funded the insurrection in the North, and under Papal decree, was assisting in bringing in a Roman assassin to make an attempt on your life." Cromwell produced another letter neither Rouen nor Jillian recognized. "The Roman hired to execute your assassination is in the Tower. He provided us with this letter along with Hurrey's name a short time ago."

"I have done nothing of the sort, your majesty." Rouen knew Cromwell considered him a threat, but never suspected the Lord Privy Seal to stoop so low as to create this farce of funding insurrection and supporting a plot to kill the king.

Henry skimmed the letter. "While I do not believe you capable of such a deed, Lord Hurrey, a king may never be too cautious. Take him to the Tower until this matter may be investigated further."

"No!" Jillian whispered, not believing what the king just ordered.

Rouen looked over at the Duke of Suffolk. "Please, Charles, watch over Jillian."

Charles nodded then caught Jillian by the arm as she tried to get between Rouen and the guards. "Do not make matters worse, Lady Jillian. I am certain this misunderstanding will be resolved in due course."

"Rouen!" Jillian looked back at the man being shackled.

He mouthed the words, "Go, Jillian."

Katherine stood, stunned by the scene unfolding.

Charles smiled at his wife. "We should tend to Jillian, my dear. This is undoubtedly an upsetting turn of events for her."

"Yes. Come with me, Lady Jillian." Katherine took Jillian's other arm and escorted her out of the palace.

Jillian hated how the duke and duchess did nothing to assist Rouen. "You know he did not do this!"

Charles flagged over a groom and requested Rouen's horses be tacked and brought around. "What I believe does not matter. Cromwell is power hungry and dangerous. Droyn isn't the first to fall victim to the Lord Privy Seal's political maneuvering." He turned to his wife and whispered he would return shortly.

"Even more of a reason you should be demanding Cromwell drop the charges and arguing for Droyn's freedom." Jillian fumed that Charles let his friend be sent to the Tower.

"Jillian, I will do what I can. In the meantime, we need to get you to Sir Moreland."

"Sir Moreland? I do not know a Sir Moreland."

"Lady Jillian, you are very well acquainted with Moreland." Charles thanked the groom for bringing the horses. "Quickly now, Jillian."

Not really having any other options at the moment, Jillian climbed into the saddle. "Where are we going?"

"You will learn where we are going soon enough."

"Why should I trust you?" Jillian glared over at the duke.

Suffolk took an exasperated breath. "What other choice do you have? With Rouen in the Tower and the argument you had with Cromwell, how do you believe you will fare navigating life in England? Do you honestly think Thomas has not devised something to ensure you are never a threat to his standing?"

"Did you just call Droyn, Rouen?"

Charles grinned, pleased she caught his use of the earl's real name. "Evidence enough of my trustworthiness?"

"For the moment." Jillian followed Charles out of the gates of Hampton Court.

They rode a short distance to Syon Abbey.

"What are we doing here, Charles? With the charges leveled at Rouen, the last thing he needs is for someone to report you and I were at an abbey."

She and Charles walked to the large wooden door on the front of the building. Charles knocked on it twice.

"Jillian, I know who you really are. Rouen told me everything about Urbino, Giselle, and you. You must trust me."

"If he told you everything, then you know he would not ever kill Henry or support any usurpation attempt."

The nun answering the door seemed surprised to find Charles Brandon with a strange woman standing before her. Charles pulled a medallion out from under his shirt. The nun nodded and motioned for them to follow her.

Jillian recognized the citrine emblem Charles concealed under his clothes. "You're a member of the order?"

Charles did not respond as they hurried down a darkened hallway.

The sister knocked on a wall and a panel slid open, leading to a stone staircase. They descended the staircase to a secret chapel beneath the abbey.

A man with hands folded behind his back stood before the altar looking up at the crucifix and images above it.

"Sir Moreland." Charles's voice caused the man to look in their direction.

"Yes?" The man stepped into a better-lit part of the aisle to see who addressed him. "Charles Brandon?"

Jillian recognized the other person in the chapel. "Kieran?"

The shocked expression on Kieran's face shared his surprise at who joined him. "Jillian?"

Kieran took her hand in his to make sure he wasn't hallucinating. She seemed real enough.

"It's really me, Kieran." Jillian smiled as he hugged her.

"I've been worried sick about you. Are you all right?"

"I'm fine. But Rouen isn't." Jillian hoped Kieran could help him. There had to be a way to clear Rouen's name if the order sent Kieran back in time.

"What do you mean he isn't? What's happened to Rouen?"

Charles spoke up before Jillian could. "Cromwell arrested Rouen under charges of treason and heresy. Rouen requested that I bring Jillian to you for safekeeping."

"Rouen was arrested and told you to bring Jillian here? To me?" Kieran seemed confused by everything.

Suffolk now eyed Kieran as if he didn't trust him. "Are you not Sir Kieran Moreland, son of Sir Richard Moreland?"

"That would be me."

"Then you are the man entrusted with Lady Jillian's safety."

"Rouen is to be executed." Brian announced, coming down the steps.

"You can't allow that to happen, Brian! He has done no wrong!" Jillian hoped one of the three men in the room could save Rouen.

Charles took her by both shoulders, wishing he could offer her stronger reassurances that Rouen would be okay. "Stay with Moreland. I will try to convince Henry or whoever sentenced Rouen to reverse the execution order."

Loud voices from above interrupted their conversation.

They could hear Cromwell and Edward Seymour demanding to know if Suffolk and a woman sought shelter there.

Kieran, Charles, and Jillian looked at the ceiling.

Brian crept back up the underground chapel steps with his hand on his sword should Edward and his men force their way into the hidden chapel.

Cromwell's voice sounded once more. "The woman is to be tried as an accessory to the plot her lover, the Earl of Stafford, concocted to kill the king."

"Neither the duke nor woman are here." Mother Superior stared the two noblemen squarely in the eye.

"Witnesses advise they rode up to your door."

"Again, Lord Cromwell, I do not know where the Duke of Suffolk rode. We have seen neither Suffolk nor a foreign-born woman this evening."

"Then you will not mind allowing us to search the premises, Mother Superior." Edward pushed the door all of the way open and motioned to the men-at-arms with them to enter. "Harboring a fugitive is an act of treason against the Crown. If you are lying, you and your sisters will find yourselves imprisoned and your home will be no more."

"They are not here." Mother Superior watched the group of soldiers split up and begin searching the grounds.

Footsteps traveled to just above Charles and Jillian.

Cromwell loudly muttered, "Jillian's head will be placed beside that of Rouen's once she is found."

"No!" Jillian softly cried, hearing what befell Rouen.

Charles clasped his hand over her mouth and shushed her to prevent any future utterances then whispered, "He would not dare execute Rouen that quickly. Henry would hang Thomas from the Tower if he did so. Cromwell is hoping you will betray your presence. He knows we are here."

CHAPTER TWENTY-EIGHT

Someone shook Jillian, saying her name.

What was going on? Jillian opened her eyes. Finding herself in Urbino, she looked around at the familiar surroundings of her apartment dumbfounded. Kieran sat next to her with a smile on his face.

"Kieran?" Jillian hugged him.

The professor chuckled. "That must have been some dream. The way you screamed, I thought someone was murdering you in here. I have never been so thankful to find a door unlocked in all my life."

"What? I...I am in Urbino?" Jillian could swear she really had been in England.

"Where else would you be?" Kieran grinned as if surprised by her question.

"England, with Rouen."

Kieran picked up the notes and copies of manuscripts scattered around the bed, then neatly stacked them on the nightstand. "I've heard of people becoming too attached with their living research subjects before, but this obsession of yours with an ambassador is challenging whether or not that can occur when research subjects are long deceased."

"He's not..." Jillian stopped herself from finishing her sentence.

"He's not what?" Kieran raised a brow, waiting to see what she'd say.

Jillian wondered if she was crazy. *Had she fallen asleep working and dreamed everything?*

Sunlight reflected off the ring Kieran wore; drawing her eyes to it. The miniature emblem over the stone reminded her that the secret order Rouen belonged to was real, only adding to her confusion about everything.

"Maybe I need to focus on something else and give this a rest." Jillian mustered a smile still working through her thoughts.

"I think that is an excellent idea. You've been working on this pet project way too much. You should be enjoying Italy as much as you are scouring the archives for this supposed ghost of yours." Kieran returned her smile. "Can I make you some breakfast?"

"Breakfast sounds wonderful."

CHAPTER TWENTY-NINE

On her last day in Urbino, Jillian received a call from one of the curators at the Palazzo Ducale. They invited her to come see an artifact they found hidden in the archives.

Kieran joined her outside the courtyard entrance, curious to see what had the archivist and curator so excited.

They took Jillian into the back office and unveiled a painting they stumbled across the day prior. It wasn't in any of the archival records.

Jillian smiled, reading the title in sixteenth-century Italian, "A Guest of the Duchess."

The painter captured Rouen's likeness perfectly. Her ghost almost lived and breathed in the intimate strokes of the master's brush. The intensity of the Englishman's eyes immediately drew her gaze. The gold collar and the Hurrey crest popped against the black velvet they laid upon.

"We believe this may be the man you are researching. We found an odd entry in one of the older inventories of the palace about one portrait of an unknown courtier. Simonetta went looking for the piece, and sure enough, it was hidden under several others. We are the first to see it in almost four hundred years." Silvia excitedly explained how the painting appeared after telling Jillian no images of a so-called English ambassador existed.

"It's him. Look at the ambassadorial collar and the crest. They are exactly as the texts described. It has to be Rouen based on everything I've read." Jillian would recognize him anywhere. "May I take a picture for my records in case he gets lost again?"

"Of course." Silvia shifted the painting into better light.

"I'll be damned." Kieran muttered beside Jillian as her iPhone captured the image.

Jillian wondered if Rouen left her the painting to substantiate her research. "When I publish his story, I would like this painting to be on the cover. What do I need to secure the image permissions? Any idea who the artist is?"

Francesco smiled. "We have no idea who painted it. We will work to get the appropriate permissions for you. I will also send you a professional reproduction and proofs for your book once the conservation team has a chance to clean the painting up."

***

That evening she and Kieran took one last, sunset-colored walk together. The crisp air tinged her cheeks as she looked out at the rolling countryside.

Nothing made sense. It should be late spring or early summer in Urbino, not still winter if she had been in England with Rouen for several months. Had she imagined it all?

"He was real, wasn't he? I didn't just dream those days in England."

Kieran frowned, wishing the green hills and history around them distracted her from any more thoughts of

Rouen.

"He was real. It was all real. I am supposed to convince you it was only a dream, but I just can't bring myself to do that."

Jillian took Kieran's hand in hers. "Why does the order want him to be such a secret?"

"Honestly, I don't know. Giselle no longer exists, so it should be no big deal if some obscure noble is discovered." Kieran drew her against him.

"Thank you, Kieran." Jillian smiled up at him.

He wasn't exactly sure why she was thanking him. He had spent the past week or so withholding the truth from her. "For what?"

"Having the courage to not let me think I was crazy or obsessed with a dead man. I know the risk you take in telling me the truth. You have powerful, spiteful bosses it seems."

"I just can't lie to you any longer, Jillian. Even if it means my head." Kieran looked down at the wine-colored brick they stood on, knowing there'd more than likely be hell to pay. Jillian squeezing his hand brought his eyes back up to hers. "I truly do like you, and hope one day, you might be interested in seriously dating a lowly archaeologist. If his bosses let him live after breaking his oath to them tonight."

"I am a pretty good shot with a crossbow and gun. The order would be stupid to attempt to harm one of my favorite archaeologists."

"My fearless historian." Kieran kissed her.

Jillian enjoyed the kiss, but something felt off about it. "I am not sure I am ready for this, Dr. Moreland."

"We will take things at whatever pace you prefer, love. What do you say to coming back to Cambridge with me?"

"As tempting as that offer is, I need some more time. I will let you know when I am ready to pursue this further."

"You really did fall for him, didn't you?"

Unlike the previous time he posed the question, Jillian laughed. "Yeah. I guess I did. But I am going to have to learn to let him go. A relationship with a man who died in the 1500s isn't something for me to hold onto going forward."

Kieran could appreciate that she needed to sort through things on her own. "In that case, when you find yourself ready to move on, you have my number."

He kissed her cheek then left her standing alone on the outer wall.

Jillian turned to admire the Palazzo Ducale behind her. The moon lit the night much like it had the first time she saw Rouen standing on the third-floor balcony. Tonight, the white stone structure stood empty, driving home that her ghost rested soundly in the afterlife; free of Giselle and all the secrets time charged him with keeping. The thought of Rouen finding peace after all he endured helped soothe the painful sense of loss she now felt.

CHAPTER THIRTY

Jillian changed her flight home, so she could spend a few days in London. She needed to know what happened to Rouen. Did he really face the gallows on trumped up charges of treason?

Jillian sighed, frustrated after finding no mention of him in the British Museum archives or the National Archives about him. *What was it with Rouen and disappearing?*

She walked through Beauchamp Tower, looking at the carved graffiti centuries of prisoners left behind.

Come on, Rouen. Give me some sort of clue about how life turned out for you.

Her heart sank spotting a worn-down area with the faint outline of a shield, two swords crossed behind it, and the Eagle from the Montefeltro coat of arms along with Rouen's initials set in its center. The words "pour mon coeur" were etched just under the shield, as if he knew she would one day discover the carving.

"You did not deserve this, Rouen. After all you endured for England, this was the last thing you deserved."

A Yeoman Warder passing through the crowd caught

Jillian's eye.

"Sir!" She stepped between the two tourists behind her and waved at him, hoping to catch his attention. "Excuse me, sir. Mr. Beefeater."

He smiled and stopped to see what she needed. "What can I help you with?"

"Do you know which prisoner may have carved this?" Jillian directed him to Rouen's engraving.

"That is one of the carvings where the creator is a mystery. The coat of arms isn't English, nor do the initials match anyone imprisoned here. We do know it was carved in the sixteenth century, most likely under Henry VIII's reign based on the others carved around it. I wish I could tell you more."

"Thank you for what you could tell me."

Jillian studied the other images decorating the stone-wall before deciding to move on.

She strolled along the Thames before turning to make her way past Parliament and on to Westminster Abbey. A sign hung on the church gates stated that a private service closed the church for the day. Disappointed, she turned to head back to the Tube station.

"Jillian?" A familiar voice halted her.

"Kieran?" She recognized the man standing across from her. "What are you doing here?"

"I have a meeting with the Dean of Westminster. Yourself?"

"Sightseeing before going back to Texas. I was hoping to see the abbey one more time, but I guess I will have to come back on another trip."

Kieran smiled. "There isn't a service any longer. It ended an hour ago. They are just taking advantage of the closure to do some maintenance in a few areas. You can accompany me inside if you'd like."

The dean met Kieran and Jillian at the door. Jillian expected an academic professional, and was surprised to learn the title dean actually referred to the senior clergy member overseeing the abbey.

Kieran politely introduced the two of them. Jillian grinned, hearing Kieran refer to her as his research assistant then ask the dean if Jillian could explore the grounds while they discussed the upcoming excavation on the property. The dean politely said of course.

Kieran captured her hand as she turned away from him, not liking the strange feeling of something being wrong. "Maybe you should come with the dean and me."

"And miss out on the opportunity to admire this place with no crowds and to translate some of these lesser known headstones? Not a chance, Dr. Moreland. I will meet you at the front door in an hour."

Jillian stopped before an old, black marble crypt tucked away in one of the side chapels. The gold paint highlighting the Latin engraving faded over the centuries. She read the placard beside it stating 'Individual unknown. Potential relation to the Bishop of Canterbury.'

"Unknown?" She muttered, startled that the placard described such an elaborately carved grave with the words 'individual unknown.' They had to be someone of status to be buried here. She knelt down to get a better look at the inscription. The quote was familiar to her, but held no clue as to who occupied the ancient crypt. After pondering where she read the phrase before, she noticed the odd faded emblem at the top of the tomb. She unlocked her phone and thumbed through to the painting of Rouen. She laid the phone beside the engraving. The engraving and citrine pendant were an identical match!

Jillian grabbed her phone and texted Kieran.

Rouen is buried here. Henry honored him with an unmarked tomb as grand as any king's.

Her phone immediately buzzed as the word 'read' popped underneath the text.

Kieran stopped his meeting and called her. She explained where she was. The dean's voice raised in the background after learning one of their mysterious eternal guests had been identified after all this time.

"Do not go anywhere, Jillie. We're en route to you."

"I promise. I will stay right here." Jillian laughed, hanging up the phone and sliding it into her purse. She turned around and found herself face to face with a man listening in on her conversation.

The man smiled. "Rouen escaped the Tower along with any charges of treason. He would be pleased that Kieran is looking after you."

She was about to ask if she knew him when he shifted his style of speech.

"A member of the order paired with the beloved of the last Durrant is an outstanding match, Lady Jillian."

Rouen's friend and steward stood before her.

"Brian? How?"

"It's possible, Jillian, and I can't tell you how. It is good to see you well. Stafford is a very different place without you and Rouen. Both of you are deeply missed." Brian looked down at the marble holding the man they both knew. "I figured you would come here sooner or later."

Jillian recognized the citrine ring on Brian's hand. "You're a knight?"

"Tell no one of the box." Brian breathed in her ear, capturing her hand between both of his as he kissed her cheek like they were old friends.

She felt something press against her palm. Her fingers closed around whatever he wanted her to have.

Once he knew Jillian had a good hold of the small box, he slowly pulled away, buying her time to slip it into her coat pocket. Seeing her hand hidden between the folds of the woolen pocket, Brian cleared his throat. "Someone wants to have a word with you."

"Kieran is on his way with Dean Smith."

"Then I better be quick." A second gentleman extended his hand to her. He had dark hair and strong build though a bit of a belly.

After grasping his hand, she turned it slightly to look at the amethyst ring he wore. It bore the same symbol Brian's had.

"I wanted to extend condolences on behalf of the order. Brian explained how devastated you were. It is good Kieran is helping you through this difficult time."

There was something about the man that bothered Jillian. She wasn't sure what it was, but it made her not trust him.

"Thank you. I think you and Brian have the wrong perception of Kieran and me. We bumped into one another this afternoon. I haven't seen him since leaving Urbino a week ago. It is going to take some time to move on from..."

The order representative noted how the woman worked to compose herself. "If you had another chance with Rouen, would you take it?"

"Rouen is free of the curses he lived through. I do not think he would want to endure all of that again. I would rather be without him and know he is finally happy wher-ever he is."

The man stepped closer to her, giving her an intense stare. "I don't believe you. If I could conjure Rouen right now, right this very instant for you, you would simply pass on the opportunity if it meant he'd suffer any ill? You would honestly put his welfare before your wants and leave him in the grave?"

Jillian surprised him as she moved forward into his per-sonal space. If witches, fires, and warring knights no longer frightened her, one man sure as hell wouldn't.

"I don't care what you believe. Let the poor man find peace in the afterlife since he didn't have it on earth. Does the order have no mercy for a man that served them well?"

The man laughed. "Loyalty and courage were the things Rouen prized most in those he called friend. He will remain at peace, Jillian."

He casually strolled off, leaving her alone beside Rou-en's grave.

Jillian checked the vault to see if the order had disturbed it.

A third man now stood beside her.

"Rouen still sleeps where Henry laid him. Do not fret. We watch to ensure he is not disturbed along with all the other prominent people in this room. Jordan enjoys ma-nipulating and intimidating people. Do not let him get under your skin."

Jillian recognized the name of the man who just depart-ed. "Jordan D'Aberon?"

"So, you and Sir D'Aberon are better acquainted than I realized."

"We've never met before tonight."

The newcomer grinned. "The two of you met, in a dream, after a witch and her minions burned an estate long ago."

"And you are?"

"William. I oversee the Order of Saint John. Jordan and another man, Michael, are my seconds. Droyn was one of a kind."

"Yes, he was." Jillian guarded her words.

"I can see that you do not trust me. I cannot blame you for that after Jordan's behavior. I wanted to say thank you for freeing him from the curse. Without you bringing some light into his dark existence, I am not sure he would have ever found a strong enough incentive to slay the witch. You may not realize it, but the people of old England are indebted to you. If there is ever anything we can do for you, just ask. Kieran knows how to reach me."

"The only thing you can do for me is promise that Rouen will never be placed in the position he was previously. Do not do anything that would disgrace his memory or torment his soul."

"You have my word. The order will do nothing that would cause him strife, Jillian. I value his peace and happiness as much as you do."

Jillian snorted. "For some reason, I doubt that."

"You shouldn't. Seeing how much Rouen's welfare means to you, you mustn't ever publish your research on him."

"Why? What harm can come from it if no one knows where his body lies?"

"Jillian, the only way to protect Rouen is to keep him a myth. You publish the information you have, and we both know the body in this tomb will be exhumed for DNA testing. The property at Stafford will be excavated. His whole life will be exposed. Is that what you want for him?"

"No, not at all. I can publish without disclosing the grave or other identifiers." Jillian wondered what the order had to hide.

"Why do you feel the need to tell the world of him?"

"His story is one that deserves to be told, William."

"He once asked you to keep his secrets." William raised a brow as if challenging her to deny Rouen had. "Do you love him enough that you really would do as you told Jordan?"

"I love him with my entire being, and yes, I would rather he be dead and happy than have the order conjure him out of thin air; forcing him to endure whatever curses he does for your little deranged organization."

William grinned. "Giselle's dead, Jillian. He'd be curse-free."

"You sound a lot like Giselle, William. Rouen taught me never to accept offers like this. Maybe you should ask him what he wants since it sounds like you can speak with the dead. If he chooses to come back, he'll know where to find me. This conversation is over. Both you and the order can sod off, Sir William."

"Watch your language, Miss Fitzalan. You are in a church." William chuckled, amused by her words. "I see I don't have any options left when it comes to you and Rouen. You both are so very stubborn. Taking that into consideration, be forewarned. If you publish one word about Rouen, we will discredit you and the text in ways you can't imagine, Miss Fitzalan. Do not test us."

Kieran came around the corner. The surprised expression on his face gave away that he knew the man standing with her.

"Good night, Jillian." William noted her new hero jogging towards them. "One other thing... Rouen's eyes are from his mother, not any other noble or one who wore the crown preceding him. Pity we will never know if the ones that followed him would have his eyes or their mother's."

She didn't respond to the odd statement now that Kieran joined her.

"Is everything okay?" He noted the fury on her face.

"Associates of yours just paid me a visit." Jillian looked back in the direction the three men had come from to find them gone.

Kieran hated that they harassed her after everything that happened. "That explains why the dean wanted to chat so much about the discovery of Richard the Third. They obviously wanted to speak with you alone. What did William say?"

"They extended their condolences. They don't do that in a friendly way."

"I am honestly surprised they extended any at all. They normally keep to the shadows."

"My research into Rouen frightened them. They only came to warn me not to publish any of my findings."

"If you want to publish your work, Jillian, I will negotiate something for you. We can easily withhold whatever information they don't want disclosed. Give me a few days to speak with William and straighten all of this out." Kieran hoped he could do exactly as he promised. "There is an excellent restaurant not too far from here. Why don't you let me treat you to dinner tonight?"

He called his father on the way to find out why the order threatened Jillian.

The waiter brought Kieran an envelope as the two ate. He opened it, knowing exactly whom it was from after the events of the day. He smiled, handing Jillian its contents.

She may write her book since it means that much to you and her. His grave remains lost along with the exact location of his home destroyed by a fire from a lightning strike in the early sixteen hundreds.

"Shall I tell William you accept the terms?"

"If I ever write a book about Rouen, I can live with concealing his gravesite and the house. You do know, sooner or later, someone is going to research the estate or start looking into that unknown grave. If not a scholar or writer, someone who is just curious about the history of either item."

"You would be surprised by what can be erased or how many dead ends information seekers can encounter. If William doesn't want information found, it rarely ever is."

Jillian and Kieran split a bottle of wine in the quiet dining room after the waiter cleared their dinner plates. The two of them laughed about memories from Urbino.

Kieran really is charming. Jillian stared over at Kieran in the candlelight. She slowly swallowed the red wine in her mouth that suddenly became a heady mix of smoky and bitter.

"You came to Urbino to stop me from finding the ducal records on Rouen."

Kieran's shoulders rising gave away the deep breath he took as he sat back in his chair. He remained silent, neither confirming nor denying her accusation.

"I bet you thought I forgot about the green folder Rouen gave me."

Kieran chuckled. "I should have guessed that's how you

got it. No one else could have gotten into my room's safe."

"Why didn't you destroy the painting or hide the letters? Why did you let me find them?"

Kieran ran his fingers across the white tablecloth before meeting her gaze again. "Rouen was a man I admired. His legend is the real reason I became an archaeologist. When I heard a woman was in Italy making strange requests of librarians and the university archive about our lost knight, I knew you had to be the one who could end the cycle of curses. The one who could set him free. No one should endure an eternity of torture. Never imagined you'd fall for him or he for you, being from such different backgrounds and centuries."

"Thank you, Kieran."

Kieran shook his head. "You thank me for the strangest things, Jillian. You know, I was rather surprised by your disappearing from modern day Stafford. When I called William and Jordan about you vanishing, neither seemed concerned. I think they knew it would happen."

"Did I imagine you at Syon Abbey or did you really go there?"

"I was there. I was walking out of a meeting with Jordan D'Aberon when he set his hand on my arm telling me you were in trouble, that I needed to get you home; the next minute, I was in the chapel. I almost had a heart attack finding myself in the sixteenth century, especially seeing you and Charles Brandon walk down the stairs."

"Never time travelled in your role before? I figured you guys did that all the time." Jillian smirked, taking another sip of her wine.

"I had no idea time travel was even possible for anyone other than Rouen."

"How did we get back to 2018?"

Kieran pulled the sleeve of his jacket back to look at his watch. "You've got an early flight out, Lady Jillian. May I drop you at your hotel?"

"Avoiding my inquiry, Sir Moreland?"

"Who told you I was a Sir?" Kieran offered her his arm to escort her to the car.

"Suffolk. I thought he was crazy when he said I was well acquainted with a Sir Moreland. With everything going on, I didn't realize Sir Moreland was actually Dr. Moreland. So, why did you hide that you are a knight from me?"

Kieran gave her a sheepish grin. "I prefer to be called Doctor Moreland. People act strangely when I use Sir with my name, especially you Americans."

"You never answered my question." Jillian nudged him as they walked back into the cool night.

"What question?" Kieran grinned down at her, then opened the car door for her.

"How did we get home?"

Kieran shut her door and settled himself in the driver's seat before answering. "I am not exactly sure. I think Brian or Charles sent us back. I remember Cromwell and Seymore arguing with someone then hearing shouting and footsteps above us, but nothing else; besides waking up next to you in Urbino. When I came to, I didn't know what to think. After looking around the room, I realized we were in your apartment and found a note on the bed with my name on it relaying the order to convince you everything was just a dream."

"Wow." Jillian didn't know what to say. "Pretty scary if the order keeps secrets from their own members."

"In some ways, I am glad they do. Can you imagine the

trouble there would be if the ability to time travel ever became general knowledge?"

"I don't even want to start contemplating that."

It was a quick ride to her hotel.

Kieran put the car in park. "I guess this is good night."

"I guess so. Thank you for bringing your research assistant to the abbey today. It ended my trip on a high note, even if your bosses are assholes."

Kieran laughed. "You are most welcome, Jillian. Safe travels home tomorrow."

He waited to leave until she was safely inside. Seeing her wave to him from the lobby window, he waved back then pulled out into the street.

Before going to bed, Jillian took one last look around the hotel room to make sure she hadn't forgotten to pack anything. She sat down on the bed, holding the box Brian gave her. She had wondered about it most of dinner, but dared not pull it out in a public place or in front of Kieran. She carefully lifted the lid after undoing the delicate gold clasp. She gasped at what lay inside.

"Oh, Rouen! The world so misunderstood you in your day. I wished things had turned out differently."

CHAPTER THIRTY-ONE

Texas seemed more of a foreign country now than Italy or England ever did. Jillian threw her keys on the dining room table and sat down after another job interview. Reheating leftovers for a quick dinner, she stared at the picture of Rouen on the balcony. She missed him.

When her marriage dissolved, she could talk to family and friends. Not having that option with losing Rouen made his absence even more painful. People already thought she had experienced a mid-life meltdown when quit her job and went to Italy "to find herself." Someone would want her committed if she ever said a word about being in love with a medieval knight that she met in a Renaissance town. That kind of thing only happened in movies, not real life.

The microwave beeped, snapping her out of her musings. She opened her laptop, letting it boot up while she retrieved her dinner.

Her eyes skimmed the rough draft of the last chapter of her manuscript. She ate another forkful of spaghetti before scrolling down to the blank area on the page.

How do I end it? With the standard 'nothing more is really known of Droyn Hurrey as no further records can be found to date?'

A loud ding and her messenger app popping up unexpectedly broke her train of thought.

Did you finish your book, yet?

Jillian looked around her apartment, wondering if someone was watching her, before settling her hands on the keyboard once more.

No. Still working on the last chapter. Not sure how I should close the book out.

The white message box popped up, flashing blue again. Jillian read the response.

How do you think it should end?

"How do I think it should end? Really?" Jillian muttered, thinking either Kieran or one of her friends who knew she was working on a book messed with her now.

Considering this is a nonfiction historical work, not a movie, it has to end with where the sources leave off. That Droyn Hurrey was sent to the Tower for some time as evidenced by the carving he made on the wall.

Jillian waited for whoever was on the other end to respond. After a few minutes passed without a new message, she started to add a sentence to her manuscript about the inscription. A third, annoying, ear piercing ting interrupted her writing. Shaking her head, she moved her mouse arrow, so it hovered over the flashing blue and white text box then clicked on it.

Droyn Hurrey's story didn't end in the Tower, but you already know that.

Jillian's hands shook as she typed back.

Unless you have sources that confirm otherwise, Droyn escaping the Tower is pure conjecture.

Blue and white flashed once more almost immediately after she hit enter.

Maybe, you aren't looking in the right place or asking the right person the right questions to find the evidence you need, my Lady Historian.

"My Lady Historian" made her heart skip a beat.

Who is this?

A minute passed with just Jillian's cursor flashing on the screen. Almost afraid to hope, she simply typed, Rouen?

No, not Rouen, but someone who knows you both. Dig deeper. Figure out the right question to ask, Jillian.

Someone who knows us both? From modern day?

Still not the right question. Try again.

"Try again?" Jillian stared down at the laptop mad at

whoever messaged her.

What source did I overlook?

No answer came.

Are you still there?

Jillian frowned as the chat box didn't move. She started to exit the conversation figuring whoever messaged had logged off.

You never struck me as the type to give up so easily.

The words made Jillian laugh.

Thought you had left. Where do I start looking?

Where did you last see him?

Under a marble slab, in Westminster Abbey.

I asked where did you last see him, not where his grave is.

I am not flying back to Stafford or Hampton Court on some wild-goose chase. Learned my lesson the first time doing that.

Was Stafford or Hampton Court the most recent place you saw him?

Jillian sat back, thinking about any other place she and Rouen traveled her last few days with him.

Well? Where did you _**SEE**_ him last?

"See him?" Jillian noted the way 'see' was typed. *What did they mean by see him?*

The top of her research portfolio poking out of her bag caught her eye as she looked around the room. At the end of the interview earlier that afternoon, she had pushed it down and zipped the leather bag shut.

She got up and pulled the portfolio holding her notes and a print of Rouen's portrait found in Urbino out of the bag. A cream-colored parchment envelope now lay between the notes pocket and the one holding the photograph.

Elegant calligraphy spelled out her name in black ink across the front. She flipped it over. Someone closed it with a wax seal. The Tudor rose distinctively stood out on the red disk.

She broke the seal to find an airline ticket and a note directing her to fly to Vienna. There she would find more information on Rouen's last days. The flight left the next afternoon. Jillian walked back over to her laptop.

Where do I go once I get to Vienna?

A package with further instructions will be waiting for you at the Left Luggage Services area. Give the clerk at the counter your name. Pack light, dress warm, and may what you find help you craft the ending to Droyn Hurrey's tale.

Why not just send me a copy of whatever documentation is in Vienna?

It is best you see the original work in context. Do you know what a pain it would be to have the archive ship sixteenth-century works to the US, not to mention arranging for a proper storage location where you could view it? Just get on the flight, Jillian.

CHAPTER THIRTY-TWO

Why do I do this to myself? Jillian hiked the mountain trail, searching for the landmark referenced in the note. She was crazy to be on another overseas adventure set in motion by the order.

What was the Order of Saint John's deal? First, the warning not to publish anything. Now this crazy insistence that her book be accurate. Only a medieval order would hide evidence in the mountaintops of some Viennese National Park. I should have called Kieran before getting on the plane. Maybe he could have come with me or knew who sent the message.

"I don't see any monuments up here." Jillian searched the snow drifts for any sign of a medieval marker. "Damn illuminati rejects and their random crap."

Stepping off the trail to get a better look at a stone tip sticking out of the snow, her feet slipped on a hidden patch of ice. Feeling her legs go out from under her ended her grumbling.

Tumbling towards the edge of the trail, Jillian frantically tried to grab anything she could. The winter weather covered the landscape with snow, ice, and frost, making it hard for her gloves to grip anything.

Whatever she was looking for had to be in the mountains. It couldn't be some place where early spring spread warmer temps.

Her lungs seemed frozen as her feet lost any sensation of ground. She managed to grasp two large tree roots sticking out of the edge of the mountainside.

You are going to die! Fear screamed inside her after she looked down to see the closest ground almost a story below her.

It's survivable. If I don't hit anything on the way down. She silenced the panic growing within. *I made it through living in the sixteenth century. I will survive this.*

She mustered the courage to pull herself upward toward the ledge just above her head. The thick root slid an inch forward.

"Don't break! Please don't break!" She glanced down again. "Help! If anyone can hear me, help!"

Her shouting caught the attention of a hiker and two skiers not far from where she was.

"Hang on!" One skier shouted, making his way towards her.

The other skier pulled off his skis to assist him.

Jillian reached for the hand that extended towards her. The snapping of the root echoed throughout the silent landscape. Snow, rock, and dirt accompanied Jillian towards the ground below.

The second skier jerked their friend backward, preventing him from following the mix of human and mountain plummeting at an ever-accelerating rate. The two watched the hiker on the path below run towards the collapsing hillside.

"Are they nuts?" The younger skier asked the local ski coach he hired for the morning.

The ski instructor recognized the hiker. "He's doing his job. He's a park employee. She's lucky he was nearby."

***

The sensation of free falling disappeared after a blinding pain rippled from the back of Jillian's head throughout her body.

Bright sunlight vanished into pitch black.

The hiker called out to the woman lying on the ground in each language he knew, hoping to hear a response of some sort. When none came, he feared the worst. He forced his legs to move faster through the deep snow. Finally reaching her, he ripped off a glove and laid his fingers against the side of her neck. A steady heart beat pulsated against his exposed skin, bringing a slight smile to his face. She survived the fall.

The stinging sensation of a hand tapping against her frozen cheek caused her eyes to flutter open then shut.

A muttered mix of French, German, Italian, and English reached Jillian's subconscious.

The damp cold and agony traveling through her body made her long for the peace she felt only seconds ago. Rouen looking down at her while they lay in his bed only strengthened her desire to return to the unconscious place someone dragged her from.

You must wake up, Jillian! Rouen stroked her cheek.

I don't want to leave you again. Jillian stared up into gray eyes that stirred an incredible longing for the man she missed since finding herself back in modern day.

Wake up, Jillian! Rouen shouted at her as the strange, distant voice grew louder. He suddenly began speaking to her in French, then Italian, followed by French again.

Rouen faded and the voice in the background became louder.

"What? I don't understand..." She mumbled, not sure if the voice speaking to her in French was real.

She heard a loud sigh from whoever spoke to her, along with what almost sounded like a brief laugh.

"I will use English since you seem to know it."

Maybe I am dead. Jillian allowed her eyes to shut once more.

"Come on. Open those eyes again." The man cradled her face between two gloved hands. "Miss, can you hear me? Please answer me if you can."

"I can hear you." Jillian shivered as a winter breeze passed over them, "Things are blurry."

"Give your eyes another minute or two. With the fall you took, it's not unusual for your vision to be impaired. What is your name?"

"Jillian. Jillian Fitzalan."

The man's hands traveled her arms and legs.

"Let me know if any place I touch hurts." He gently applied pressure anytime his hands stopped, checking to see if she had broken anything.

"I hurt everywhere, if that helps. How much pain should I complain about when you squeeze?"

He chuckled, moving to her other leg. "We will both know if there is something to be concerned about. You will let me have it when I find a problematic spot."

"Are you ski patrol or a paramedic?"

"Park ranger."

"Park ranger. Great. Here I was thinking I got lucky, and a doctor was nearby. I assume you know first aid to be doing what you are."

"I have a lot of field experience with injuries of all kinds. You're not the first person to take a tumble in the park." He felt her collar bone. No signs of it being fractured. "Well, the good news is nothing seems broken. Can you wiggle your fingers for me?"

Jillian did as requested, then slowly moved each arm and leg as he asked her to do so.

"You are a lucky woman. A few bruises and a concussion are all that you appear to have. I expected much worse."

Since it was his day off, he didn't have his radio. He pulled out his cell phone and called the main park station. The dispatcher on the other end of the line advised that help was already en route to them as the skiers called in the woman's fall. He confirmed their location then hung up.

Jillian drifted off while he was on the phone.

"No sleeping just yet, Jillian. We need you conscious. Ski patrol will need to ask you about your medical history and a few other things. You can nap after the doc checks you over."

"My passport's in my bag." Jillian started to roll to her side. A sharp pain and burst of light blurred everything, making her wince.

A firm hand on her shoulder prevented her from sitting up. "You need to stay down until the paramedics get here."

Her aching body, not being able to see normally, and knowing no one in Austria broke what was left of Jillian's courage. The more she thought about everything, the angrier she became.

"Goddamnit! This is typical order-caused chaos. I should have expected some random awful crap to happen. It always does. I couldn't have just ignored the stupid text and minded my own business. No, I had to be all, 'let's see where this leads.'" Jillian took a jagged breath, not caring if the ranger thought she was crazy. "You know what else, Mr. Park Ranger, I hate not being able to see clearly! This is bullshit! This whole damn trip is just another cluster fuck caused by an organization I shouldn't have trusted. I should have known better. Now, I am stuck all alone in the middle of nowhere, in some stupid foreign country. No offense by the way."

The ranger chuckled and took one of her hands in his. "None taken, and you aren't alone. I promise I will stay with you until ski patrol reaches us, then you will have four very capable people taking care of you."

"I am sorry. I am scared. I came here thinking I was going to the archives or a museum, not some friggin' mountain top park."

"No need to apologize, Jillian. How does one plan to go to the archives and end up hiking in the mountains?"

"You wouldn't believe me if I told you."

"Oh, I don't know about that. With all the strange occurrences in my life, your story is probably pretty believable."

"You're just trying to keep me awake."

The ranger laughed. "Yes, but you also have my curiosity piqued now. So, tell me, what brought you out here?"

What was it about his voice that was so soothing? She slid her hand from his and pulled off her gloves. The cold immediately made her fingers feel stiffer than her sore body.

"You will get frostbite if you leave your gloves off too long."

"With what all I've endured the past several weeks, I couldn't care less about potential frostbite." Her fingers climbed up his jacket sleeve towards his shoulder. "What did you say your name was?"

His face briefly came into focus, then became a blurred mix of colors blending into the countryside again.

"I am Henry, Jillian. It's nice to meet you." He once again held the hand that didn't explore his face.

Jillian felt the soft stubble of a few days' old beard. Her fingers traveled over a small mole between his ear and lower jaw. For a brief second, the familiar scent of winter spices filled her nose. She ran her hand down the side of his neck. *It had to be there.*

"You know, Jillian, I really must insist we get those gloves back on."

She felt him pull her glove over the hand he held. His leaning forward allowed her to grasp his shoulder.

Like hell you are putting that last glove on! Not before I have the chance to check.

Feeling his jacket and shirt collar, Jillian reached inside them. She heard him inhale sharply when her icy fingers slipped down the warm skin of his neck. The uneven texture of rope chain against her fingertips made her smile.

"Henry, is it? You always were a horrible liar."

"You must have me confused with someone else."

His fingers closing around hers then giving them a gentle squeeze contradicted the denial.

"No, I don't. I don't need to see you clearly to know who you are." Jillian smiled as he slipped her other glove back on.

"I am starting to think you hit your head harder than we both realize."

"So, you're a park ranger this time around? I figured if you ended up in the twenty-first century, you'd choose a more lucrative career." Jillian let out a short laugh. "Field experience with injuries in the park my ass."

"The cavalry's arrived, Miss Fitzalan. Hopefully, once the swelling on the back of your head goes down, those delusions you are having will go away as well."

"Thank goodness she's conscious. We've got her from here, Henry." One of the paramedics interrupted their conversation as the medical team arrived.

The ranger moved back, allowing the EMTs to take care of Jillian.

She let out a loud cry when they attempted to slide a blanket under her head to make her more comfortable while they triaged her.

"Bring the toboggan and a neck brace. She's not going to be able to walk out of here on her own." The lead medic sent one of the junior team members back to the equipment they brought with them.

"The pain is from my head, not my spine." Jillian felt the paramedic starting to brace her neck.

"You never want to take any chances with a neck or back injury, Miss Fitzalan."

Henry helped the team carefully ease Jillian onto the waiting sled.

Everything rattled her. She squinted against the bright sunlight, trying to pick the ranger out of the blurred group of faces looking down at her. "Henry, are you still there?"

"I am here." The ranger reassuringly set his hand on her shoulder. "They are going to take you to the ambulance waiting at the lodge. It'll be a bit of a ride, but you will be warm and in good hands soon."

"We need to strap her in, Henry."

He nodded then stepped back. "May your recovery be quick, Miss Fitzalan."

Distracted by the paramedics asking her questions, Jillian wasn't able to say goodbye to the park ranger who initially took care of her.

One of the paramedic's radios went off. Jillian couldn't make out what the dispatcher said.

"You probably want to get home or to the nearest station yourself. Another storm is making its way in." Jillian heard someone behind her say. She guessed they were talking to Henry as he was the only one not part of the medical team nearby.

"Wait! Henry, we need to talk."

"With how fast that storm is coming in, we really need to get going, Miss Fitzalan. You can talk to the ranger later."

"I need to talk to him now."

"We'll arrange a meeting between the two of you tomorrow."

A tap sounded above her head, then the sensation of movement and wind against her face followed.

"Henry, tell William, I know the answer to the eye color question." Jillian yelled as the team started to take off.

"Who's William?" The last of the ski patrol asked Henry, wondering what the woman shouted about.

The park ranger shook his head. "I have no idea. The woman's been saying strange things since she came to."

"Totally normal after a head injury. See you tomorrow, if the roads aren't blocked and we can all make it into work." The paramedic skied down the slope.

CHAPTER THIRTY-THREE

With the excitement over and the storm warning, Henry picked up the pack he set aside to tend to Jillian then made his way back down the mountain. The wind picked up and dark clouds rolled in. He decided to shelter in a nearby ski lodge until the storm blew through. The last thing he needed was to be stranded out in bad weather.

A welcomed blast of heat hit him as he opened the lodge door. The owners had taken him under their wing shortly after he started working at the park. Henry enjoyed visiting with the husband and wife team who ran the place. Locally owned and operated hotels always added a caring and inviting touch for vacationers. Seeing no one at the front desk, he headed for the hotel lounge. If Yannick wasn't at check in, he was usually serving drinks and food along with telling stories to the guests over the lodge's trademark wooden bar.

Henry grinned, finding Yannick doing exactly that in the cozy lounge with a massive stone fireplace centered on the far wall. He set his pack down on the floor then walked over to the bar. The lead paramedic for the park EMT team sat without his jacket and gear, drinking something out of a mug, and engaged in conversation with Yannick.

Henry knew the paramedic should be at the main ski resort. He looked at his watch, checking the time. There was no way the team could have dropped the American off and gotten back up here.

"Lars, what are you doing here?"

The paramedic smiled at the ranger. "The storm moved in faster than we could get back. We hunkered down here."

"Did the ambulance get the American to the hospital?"

The paramedic shook his head no. "She's in one of the guestrooms. A doc flew in with the crew that came to get her. We hoped to fly her out of here, but that didn't happen. Thank goodness she is stable or the odds wouldn't be in her favor."

"Sit down, Henry. We'll have you a room key in just a minute. Lars told us you were with our guest of honor. We figured you might wander in and spend the night with us too." Yannick handed the park ranger a warm drink and gestured to a nearby table.

"Thank you." Henry appreciatively took the drink then chose a seat in front of the fireplace.

He stared at the flames, contemplating the events of the day. It had started off calmly enough. He enjoyed the peacefulness of the woods and sunshine until the American fell from the trail. That path was closed to hikers for the winter due to past incidents from black ice patches developing under the snow and a landslide earlier in the year. *What was she doing hiking it?*

Her last words to tell William she knew the answer to his eye color question repeated in his head. *What did she mean by that?*

***

"How is the patient, Dr. Leitner?" Yannick asked the physician walking towards the bar.

"She is doing well, all things considered. I would like to order dinner for her and myself."

"Of course." Yannick nodded. "Will you be eating here or with your patient?"

"I'll take Miss Fitzalan hers and then join you guys here for mine."

Yannick turned to ask his wife Annika to prep dinner for Jillian. Having overheard the conversation, she already headed toward the kitchen.

"Is Miss Fitzalan's vision any better, or is it going to be a few days before the concussion heals enough for it to clear up?" Henry inquired.

Dr. Leitner smiled, aware the ranger came to her rescue earlier that day. "I cannot answer that. Miss Fitzalan would need to give me permission to discuss her condition with you. All I can say is she appears to be stable, and will more than likely be fine in a few days."

Annika set Jillian's tray on the counter. "She and the baby are both lucky you hiked nearby today."

Henry choked on his drink. "The baby?"

Lars thought it odd Henry didn't know Jillian was expecting. Most injured pregnant women tended to worry more about their unborn child than themselves. "She didn't tell you?"

"No. She didn't." Henry set the drink in his hand on the table and sat back in his chair. The dazed expression on his face gradually faded into a thoughtful one.

He watched Dr. Leitner pick up the tray from the

counter. "Doctor, if it is all right, may I take her dinner to her? I would like to check in on her."

"Be my guest. She will probably appreciate the change in company. She did ask if any of us knew if you made it home before the storm hit. She seemed worried about you." Dr. Leitner handed Henry the tray.

"I'll show him to Miss Fitzalan's room. Have a drink on the house and I'll get your dinner when I get back." Annika stepped from behind the bar, knowing the doctor had a long day. "This way, Henry."

Henry followed Annika to Jillian's room. He politely opened the door for Annika.

"Dinnertime, Miss Fitzalan!" Annika announced, settling the tray on Jillian's bed.

Jillian smiled, enjoying the aroma of roasted chicken and vegetables wafting in her direction. She was starving. Dr. Leitner allowed her only water earlier until he finished her exam. "It smells wonderful!"

"I cut up everything into small pieces for you, dear. There is chocolate cake for dessert behind the dinner plate."

Jillian felt for the fork beside the plate and hesitantly picked it up.

Annika guided her hand toward the plate. "Your eyes will be back to normal in no time. It's amazing what we can adapt to."

"Well, at least I am not totally blind. I can see bright blurs and outlines." Jillian tried to have a sense of humor about everything.

"I'll be back to check on you shortly." Annika smiled at Henry, who still stood in the doorway. She patted him on the arm as she passed.

He watched Jillian take a couple bites of her meal, not saying anything.

Jillian didn't notice him standing there. She cursed as she managed to dip her fingers in cake frosting, reaching for her water glass.

"Allow me." A baritone voice broke the silence.

She felt someone take her hand as a blurred shape appeared at her bedside, cleaning off her fingers before placing them alongside the water cup.

Cool glass seemed to be such a stark contradiction to the warm hand that she felt seconds ago.

"You do not sound like Dr. Leitner or Lars. Your accent is different." Jillian smiled. "I am glad you are safely out of the storm, Henry."

"I guess fate intended for us to spend a little more time together, for both of us to end up in the same place."

"So it seems." Jillian picked up the dinner tray.

Henry grasped the portable tray, worried she'd spill it on the floor. "Aren't you hungry?"

"I am, but it is rude to eat in front of a guest. I also want to talk with you a bit more. I can't turn towards you with the tray in the way."

"Manners aren't required of anyone who fell from a cliff, Miss Fitzalan. You can eat and talk to me at the same time."

"Then I am not hungry, Ranger..." Jillian realized he never shared his last name.

"Strauss." Henry set the tray on the desk behind him.

"Strauss? You don't sound like a Strauss." Jillian resisted the urge to laugh at his last name.

"You are a strange woman. You have definitely said the most outlandish things I've ever heard today." He watched her hand sliding up his arm as it had earlier on the mountainside. "I did not realize names had certain qualities to them."

"Oh, they most certainly do." Her fingers traveled across the tops of his shoulders to his neck then stopped to feel the outline of the chain under the soft sweater he wore. "They share more than our families' nationalities. One could argue they tell the story of who we truly are."

"If they tell the story of who we are, care to explain what a Strauss sounds like to an American?"

She laughed. "Not like you. There is no hint of a German or Austrian accent in the way you pronounce things."

"Maybe you don't know your accents as well as you think you do." He pulled his necklace from under his sweater, knowing something about it intrigued the woman. "I'm not sure what the deal is with you and men's jewelry, but I am curious to learn why you are so fascinated by a simple rope chain."

He closed the woman's fingers around the twisted gold strand.

Her hand moved downward until she felt a bail. She smiled again, holding the pendant. "This is special for you to wear it under your shirt."

"Family heirloom."

By how a mix of musk and spice floated on the air, Jillian knew he leaned forward in his chair. She closed her eyes, enjoying the scent of man and cologne.

"You smell good."

The ranger chuckled. "Do I?"

"Yes, you smell like home."

"Home? Where is home for you, Jillian?"

Her thumb brushed over the medallion hanging from his chain. She did not need to see the metal and gemstone to recognize what she held.

"Stafford."

"Stafford, Virginia? You don't sound like the Virginians I've previously met."

"I am not a Virginian, just as you aren't a Strauss."

"There you go again, saying crazy things. What makes you think I am not a Strauss?"

"Your accent is a blend of English and very old French, even using modern diction." Tears formed in Jillian's eyes as she spoke. She settled her hand over his heart. "Hurrey is Norman for Henry, if I recall correctly. And only one man could ever smell like winter evenings at home to me."

His fingers enfolded hers. "That mind of yours is going to get you into a lot of trouble one of these days. You are too damn smart for your own good, Jillian." He brought her hand to his lips.

"I thought you were dead."

"I was. I still am without you."

"Rouen, I will call you any name you like as long as you don't leave me again."

Rouen drew her against him, now that he knew he could do so without harming her. "I am just a common man now. I do not have lands, title, or wealth. Another can offer you a much more comfortable life."

"You promised you would not leave me. That you would stay with me until help arrived. The only person who can truly help me is you. Will you break your oath, my lord? Are you no longer a man of your word?"

"I am still a man of my word. I will more than happily keep it if that is what you truly desire. Our new life may be difficult, Jillian. I still have a duty to confront Giselle if she ever returns as part of my agreement with the order. Can you live with that?"

"I am not afraid of witches, Rouen. I can live with any thing as long as I am with you. Why didn't you at least contact me, so I knew you were okay?" Jillian wished she could see him clearly.

"I understood you were now with Kieran."

"Kieran? Who told you that?"

"Are you not seeing Kieran?"

"How many times must I tell you a few dates doesn't equal a betrothal? I was only seeing Kieran as I was told you were gone forever; no chances of you ever coming back. If I had known otherwise, I'd come looking for you long before today. I love you, Rouen. There is something I need to tell you."

"I already know of our child, Jillian. Annika remarked about how lucky you and the baby were that I hiked nearby. I fully intend to make you my wife since I don't need to wait on the king's permission in this day and age."

"Is that why we went to Hampton Court?" Jillian realized why Henry sent for them. Rouen petitioned the king, requesting permission to marry.

"How else could I fulfill my promise of not abandoning you in the sixteenth century?"

He finally claimed the lips only a breath away from his.

"Henry Strauss!" Annika shouted, walking in to find the ranger and Jillian lip-locked. "Yannick! Lars!"

The men she called for along with Dr. Leitner came running down the hall.

Lars laughed, seeing the embarrassed expression on Jillian's face and the surprise on the ranger's. "Really, Henry! The poor woman has been through enough today without you accosting her."

"He can accost me anytime he likes." Jillian shocked the group gathered at the door.

Jillian's remark further appalled Annika. "What would your baby's father say about such a fling while you were abroad?"

"As long as it is me she is kissing, I wouldn't have an issue with it at all." Rouen added to the mayhem.

"She's the woman from Italy? Small world for you two to find one another again." Lars remembered Henry mentioning an ex he met in Italy that he wasn't over when they went out drinking a couple of weeks back.

Yannick gave Rouen a hard stare. "I thought better of you, Henry. How could you leave her if she was pregnant?"

"He didn't know. I came here hoping to find him and tell him." Jillian hated the accusation in the man's tone. "Ro, Henry is a good guy. It is a long story, and if you don't mind, I'd rather enjoy a peaceful reunion with him versus explaining it right now. We both have been through enough today."

Dr. Leitner cleared his throat. "As her doctor, I agree that it is better none of us stress Miss Fitzalan any further. Ranger Strauss, I must advise against any activities of too romantic a nature. Once she is fully examined, we can decide when those may resume."

Jillian smiled, hearing the door close, giving her and Rouen some privacy. "I am sorry you learned about the baby as you did, Rouen."

"You needn't apologize, Jillian. It is welcome news." Rouen set his hand on her belly before kissing her.

"Are you really happy about being a father?"

"I am elated. I never thought this day would come. No woman I have been with has ever conceived. How do you feel about the child?"

"Scared. Happy. Thankful I fell off a mountain, so they will know their father." Jillian loved the chuckle that filled her ears. She had missed hearing it.

Rouen's thumb caressed her cheek. "I wanted to go straight to Texas once I found myself revived, but then I overheard Brian and William speaking about you and Kieran. Even though it hurt, I didn't want to interfere after William said the two of you seemed happy together. The last thing I wanted was to cause you any more hardship. How did you know where to find me?"

"Someone sent me an airline ticket and a letter hinting I would find something related to you here. It is in my book bag, if it isn't buried under snow, still out on the trail."

Rouen saw the mauve bag sitting on a nearby chair. "Lars made sure it stayed with you. It is in a chair on the right side of the room. We can talk about the letter later. Let us ensure our son or daughter has proper nourishment after an undoubtedly traumatizing day."

Jillian laughed as Rouen held a forkful of food up to her mouth. "I can feed myself, Rouen."

"Stubborn woman. Allow me to assist you. You have done a great deal to help me. I am simply returning the favor."

CHAPTER THIRTY-FOUR

Curious about the letter Jillian received, Rouen unzipped the large pocket of her book bag. He glanced over at her to ensure the noise didn't wake her. It took some time for her to fall asleep between the excitement of being back with him and the soreness from her fall. The yellow parchment envelope might as well have been bright neon green with how vividly it stood out amongst her bag's contents.

He unfolded the stiff, cream-colored paper. By the varying ink thickness and the curves of the letters, someone drafted it with a quill. Medieval English flowed across the page instructing Jillian to board the flight to Salzburg then take the bus to Grossglockner National Park to learn more about what happened to Rouen. If she did not get on the flight booked for her, she would miss the opportunity to obtain the information she sought.

He shuffled the first page behind the second. The later explained how she found the closed trail and was out on it. An order member made up some bogus clues to a relic hidden on the trail that would help her find a supposed lost journal of his. The directions led her directly to him.

Who, besides Jordan, knew his whereabouts? And who in the order knew he would be hiking this weekend instead of working?

Part of him felt grateful to whoever sent Jillian the note. The other part of him wanted to find the author and berate him for endangering her and his child.

He refolded the letter and returned it to her backpack. A journal inside it caught his eye. He pulled the purple leather planner out to find it filled with research notes about him. A pocket in the front cover held photos of the paintings of him. He had never sat for either painting. Their existence further surprised him. Someone captured him from memory in England and Urbino. He smiled, looking at the photograph Jillian took of him on the balcony of the Palazzo Ducale. Little did he know the photographer who annoyed him that evening would be the person to set him free from Giselle's dark magic.

Rouen skimmed Jillian's handwritten notes. She worried about what happened to him after his arrest. She actually found snippets of information detailing his being framed then released by the king; that he died three years later protecting Henry and Charles Brandon from an assassination attempt. She found his grave in Westminster. He almost dropped the notebook reading William himself confirmed it was indeed Rouen's resting place.

William never randomly made public appearances.

The entry ended with William's statement, "That it was a shame they wouldn't know whether those that followed would have their father's eye color or their mother's."

Rouen closed the notebook, not wanting to read any more.

He fished Jillian's cell phone out of the bag. He stared at

the locked screen, unsure of what her passcode could be. Taking a wild guess, he entered 1535. Surprisingly, the phone unlocked for him. Her using the year he was in Urbino made him smile. He scrolled through her contacts until he found Kieran's number then hit the call icon.

"Kind of late on this side of the pond, but I am glad you called as you were on my mind, beautiful."

The term of endearment annoyed Rouen. "I highly doubt *I* was on your mind, nor should the woman you are calling beautiful be from this point forward."

"Who is this? Where is Jillian?" Kieran's voice mirrored the irritation in Rouen's.

"If the guardian responsible for protecting the Durrant line was executing his directive properly, you would know where the woman carrying my heir is at the moment."

"Your heir? I am not sure who this is, but if you've done anything..."

"As if I would ever harm Jillian. Do not try my patience any further by uttering threats you will regret making, Moreland. I am already contemplating the various ways to end you for what you've done. I trusted you to look out for her, which was obviously a grave mistake."

The gruff tone and comment clued Kieran in to who the man on the other end was. "Rouen? You're alive?"

Rouen walked into the hallway to finish his conversation with Kieran. "Very much so, but you won't be if you don't have a damn good explanation for sending Jillian to Vienna."

"Vienna?" Kieran's voice changed octaves. "I don't know anything about her being in Vienna. When we spoke a day ago, she was in Texas. And how in the hell are you living in modern-day Vienna?"

"For some reason, I find it hard to believe you don't know her whereabouts or mine. You are damn lucky she and the child survived today. If she had died or I learned she miscarried due to the fall, we would be having this conversation face to face as I disemboweled you."

"Rouen, the thought of anything happening to Jillian is as equally horrifying as being disemboweled. I hope neither ever occurs. Now what is this about a fall? You are certain she and the baby are okay?"

"They are fine. Clearly, you knew about the child, even though you deny having anything to do with why she is here."

"I knew nothing about you or her being in Vienna. I did know about the baby. She told me last week."

"You didn't send the plane ticket and the letter directing her here?" Rouen still found that hard to believe.

"For the last time, I have no idea what you are talking about. I swear on my ancestor's soul and the stone of the order, I never sent anything pertaining to your reincarnated self or Vienna to Jillian. In all honesty, I am a little disappointed to learn you are back in the picture as you just killed any chance I may have had left with her. Where in Vienna are you two? I'll be on the next flight out, so we can resolve this mess."

Finally believing Kieran, Rouen frowned and leaned back against the hall wall. "Don't come here. Jillian and I have enough to deal with at the moment. Find out what reckless bastard in the order sent her instructions to undertake a perilous hike to find me. When she is well enough to be up and around, I will return to England to strangle the son of a bitch responsible for everything myself."

"You know if it is someone from the higher echelons, I

won't be able to find much."

"Just send me whatever you can, and I will handle it from there." Rouen hung up, plotting all the ways he'd torture the man responsible for Jillian's current state.

D r. Leitner knocked on the room door before cautiously opening it after Rouen invited him in. Dark circles under Rouen's eyes gave away the ranger hadn't slept.

Jillian yawned, just waking herself.

"How are we feeling this morning, Miss Fitzalan?"

"Sore."

The doctor chuckled at her response. "Is your vision any better?"

"A little bit. I can see things with a little more definition."

"I am going to take another look at your eyes later today. The snow stopped during the night. Hopefully, they clear the roads soon and we can get an MRI done before the day ends." Dr. Leitner pulled out a penlight and scope. "We will need a designated party to sign paperwork on your behalf. Is there someone we should contact to do so?"

"I will sign any paperwork that is needed and will pay for whatever bills she incurs as well. Her family is in the US. It would take two days for one of them to get here."

Rouen felt responsible for her injuries with the order sending her to find him.

"Do you consent to letting Henry act as your representative, Jillian?" The law required the doctor to ask the question.

"I do."

"I will ask Annika to bring you your breakfast. Henry, if I could speak with you in the hall." Dr. Leitner patted Jillian's leg before standing.

Rouen kissed Jillian's forehead then followed Dr. Leitner into the hall.

"Two things for you, Ranger Strauss. One, you should get some sleep yourself this morning before we transport her. You cannot make good decisions when exhausted. Two, the MRI and her care will not be free as she is not a citizen. The costs may be on the high side."

"I will pay for whatever is necessary. And I will sleep later after Jillian is evaluated."

Lars raised a brow at his peer, coming down the hall with food for Jillian. "Henry, follow doctor's orders. I will keep an eye on her while you get a couple hours of sleep."

"I am in room 337. Wake me if she asks for me or if anything happens."

"Hey! Paramedic here. I can do more for her than you can if anything happens. I'll also remind her you aren't Superman and need sleep too." Lars continued past the new ranger to ensure the woman, who caused all the havoc over the past twenty-four hours, ate breakfast.

***

Shortly after lunch, the ambulance arrived. The ride to the hospital went smoothly. Dr. Leitner took Jillian straight to the MRI room.

Rouen and Lars waited patiently for the MRI to complete.

Lars didn't want to leave Rouen alone to deal with any more shocking news. Considering the ranger watched the woman he loved take one hell of a fall, learned he'd be a father in six months, and may have to care for a vision-impaired woman who flew across the Atlantic to find him again, the man seemed to be managing things well. But Lars knew that outward appearances could be deceptive. He liked Henry and didn't want to lose him from the team.

Once Jillian settled into a hospital room, Lars bid the two farewell.

"I have lots of good news for you, Miss Fitzalan." Dr. Leitner walked in with her charts in his hand.

"Let's hear it, doc." Jillian heard him sit down and felt his hand on her arm.

"As we guessed, you have a concussion. That is causing the blurred vision. We believe your sight should return to normal in another day or so. If it doesn't, we will run some more tests. Other than the minor swelling, the brain appears to be fine and functioning as it should. You are a very lucky lady." The doctor paused as she whispered "thank you" relieved that her sight should clear up and everything else appeared okay. "We need to keep you overnight for observation. It is strictly a precaution to ensure there's nothing we've missed."

"Thank you, Dr. Lietner. We are appreciative of everything you and your team have done." Rouen was thrilled by the report.

"The midwife is on her way up to check on the baby. You two will want to schedule regular neonatal appointments if Jillian plans to stay in Austria. We can set the first one up

Tale of Rouen ❦ 315

today if you would like."

Rouen listened to his child's heartbeat coming from the ultrasound machine. Based on everything she could see, the midwife declared the baby perfectly healthy.

"Come back in another month and a half and we will see if he or she will cooperate, so we can see the little bean's gender. You do need to start seeing your doctor monthly to ensure a healthy delivery, especially with your age, Miss Fitzalan."

Rouen liked the midwife's bedside manner and thoroughness. "May we continue her care with you?"

"You can. Here's my card. Call the office next week and we'll get her monthly visits squared away. You have enough on your plate today, Ranger Strauss." The nurse handed him her card then left.

"We need to talk about the new name. I'm not sure I like it. You will always be Rouen Durrant to me." Jillian looked in the direction of his voice.

"I prefer Rouen as well. I chose Henry as it is the most modern name I have. Additionally, people don't ask me to spell it all the time like they did Rouen or Droyn when I first tried using them here." He made her laugh with his explanation.

***

The next morning, she looked across the room at Rouen sleeping in the chair next to her bed. Someone brought him a blanket during the night. He woke as she gently touched the side of his face.

"I am still here, sweeting."

Jillian loved the husky rasp to his voice. "I can see that."

"Can you truly see me, mon coeur?"

"I can, and I can still hear you really well if you are

wondering about that." She said one of the first things she ever told him on that frosty morning they met in Urbino.

Rouen laughed as he sat up, then kissed her good morning.

"Hit the call button, Rouen. I want out of this bed. I've got a million questions for you and I know you can't answer half of them as long as I am in the hospital. The most important one being where do we go from here?"

Rouen pressed his lips to her forehead, thankful to have her back in his life. "All in due course, sweeting. We'll see what Dr. Leitner has to say first."

Dr. Leitner felt comfortable letting Jillian go home now that her vision returned, on the condition that she came back in a week as he wasn't sure flying back to the US was a good idea yet.

"I will make certain she doesn't go off on any more adventures and gets her rest, Doctor." Rouen winked at Jillian as the doctor signed her discharge forms.

"See you in a week, Ms. Fitzalan."

Rouen swung her backpack over his shoulder then offered her his free hand. Jillian clasped it, eager to spend time alone with Rouen. They walked over to the elevator, took it down to the first floor, then headed towards the exit.

"Ranger Strauss!" Dr. Leitner's nurse shouted from across the lobby, waving a bag at them. "Her medications!"

"Sit here." Rouen guided Jillian to a nearby chair and set her bag down next to her. "I will be right back."

After Rouen walked over to the nurse, a man passing by handed Jillian a legal-sized envelope. "You dropped this."

Thinking it might be her discharge paperwork after seeing the zipper of the main pocket partially open on her book bag, Jillian started to push the envelope into the large compartment. Noticing the dark yellow top of a similar packet with her name in the right-hand corner peeking out above her notebook, whatever the man gave her couldn't be her paperwork.

"Wait a minute, this isn't mine!" Jillian turned in her chair to find the gentleman was gone.

She opened the envelope to see if she could find its owner. Inside was the deed to the Stafford property and a note.

Your bills are paid in full.

The lands are still yours.

Tell Rouen when you see fit.

B.

"Brian?" Jillian knew who handed her the papers. *What was going on? Why give her the deed and not Rouen?*

Rouen returned from speaking with the nurse and noted the confusion on Jillian's face. "Everything all right?"

"Yes. I think so anyway." Jillian slid the deed into her bag.

"Any particular reason you pulled the discharge paperwork out?" Rouen didn't like the way Jillian hesitated before she answered him.

"I wanted to double check my restrictions again."

Rouen doubted that was the case. "I will find a way to cover the bills, Jillian. Do not worry yourself about those."

Jillian zipped her bag shut and held it out to him since she wasn't supposed to lift anything over ten pounds for a few days. "I know you will. I love you, Rouen."

Rouen grinned, taking the backpack. "I love you too."

***

The cab driver politely held open a door for them.

Her phone vibrated in her pocket as the cab pulled out of the parking lot. Jillian smiled seeing Kieran called her.

"Kieran! You won't believe what has happened the past few days!" She paused as Kieran asked if she was okay. "I'm fine."

"That's good to hear, Jillie. Is Rouen with you?"

The inquiry caught her off guard. "How did you know about Rouen?"

"He called me two days ago and told me about your fall; along with your impromptu trip to Vienna."

"Did you know he was back?" Jillian wondered if Kieran hid Rouen's being alive.

"No, I had no idea until he called. I was quite surprised to learn of his return myself. He asked me to look into something for him. May I speak with him?"

"Sure." Jillian handed the phone to Rouen.

Rouen didn't bother with any polite greetings. "Find anything?"

"Nothing definite yet. Jordan and William both traveled recently and have several large travel expenses on the books. I've requested their card statements. There is one other order member that flew to some conference in New Orleans. I am not familiar with him, but thought I'd see if you recognized the name, its Bernard Lefebvre Chastain."

Rouen knew exactly who Bernard was. "Brian? How is he..." Rouen knew better than to finish the question.

"So you two know one another?"

"Yes. He was my steward back when I..." Rouen noticed the cab driver looking at him through the rearview mirror. "We worked together in Stafford. He was the Director of Accounting. When did he get back from his conference?"

"According to the travel plans, he left for New Orleans a

week ago, and isn't coming back to London until Friday."

"Hmm... well, this call has been enlightening. Let me know what you find on the other two. And, um, well, thank you for your assistance." Rouen didn't know what to think.

"Am I to assume a potential disemboweling is off the table now?"

Rouen laughed. "For you anyway. I am sorry about the threats the other night."

"We're good, Rouen. I wouldn't react too well if someone hurt my loved ones either. Give Jillie a hug for me and enjoy the rest of your day." Kieran ended the call.

"Everything okay?" Jillian eyed Rouen, worried about the half of the conversation she could hear.

"Nothing for you to fret about. Just getting some updates on things at the office with being out the past few days."

CHAPTER THIRTY-SIX

J illian laughed, putting away the plates they had just washed. Rouen's small apartment gave them the perfect place to start over.

"How much stuff do you need to retrieve from Texas?" Rouen looked around his meager home, debating if it could handle her things along with his.

"More than this place will hold."

Rouen groaned. "Women and all their shopping. I suppose we will need more room with the little one joining us anyhow. I have no idea how I will afford a larger flat on a park ranger's salary."

"Why is it men think they need to be the breadwinner of the household?"

Rouen scoffed, sitting down at the table.

How she missed hearing him do that!

"If God intended women to do more than raise children, he would have given them a man's strength. Men are destined to be the patriarchs in this world. We are rational and able-bodied while women are emotional, irrational, and the weaker of the species. We would all be lost if men were not there to guide their wives."

Jillian knew he was enjoying trying to rile her with the grin on his face. "Why, my dearest Petruccio, I believe you are mistaken. The moon, you say? The sun! It is not moonlight."

"I say it is the moon that shines so bright." Rouen recited the actual line from Shakespeare's *Taming of the Shrew* as Jillian strolled towards him.

"Unlike Kate, I won't agree that it is the moon. Times have changed. We women have something greater than all those qualities you attribute to men: wisdom, my handsome knight." Jillian sat in his lap.

"Wisdom only grows when a man allows his wife or daughter to study." Rouen chuckled before kissing her.

"Well, it's a good thing for both of us the men in my life support me being learned. Stop worrying about money, Rouen. You have a financially sound betrothed who is anxious to become your wife." Jillian's statement caught him off guard.

"I would legally make you my wife this very moment if I had the means to do so. Know that I already think of you as such. I cannot yet afford the ring women in modern times expect." Rouen frowned, wanting nothing more than to give her his name.

"Is a ring all that is stopping our marriage?" Jillian knew his desire to provide for her prevented them from wedding. "Most people marry for love these days, not wealth or titles."

"You know it is more than a ring, Jillian. If you truly desire to marry, I will take you to the court to do so. I just figured you wanted a ring and a formal ceremony."

"When does the court close?" Jillian brought a smile to

his face.

"Seven for civil matters." Rouen looked at his watch. "We have two hours if you wish to marry today."

"Get your coat, Rouen. Big weddings are overrated. I want our child to have their father's last name."

Neither he nor Jillian could stop smiling as the magistrate married them.

Rouen looked sheepishly at the official when they reached the point of the ceremony to exchange rings. "We don't..."

"I have them right here." Jillian pulled the wooden box Brian gave her from her pocket. She set it in Rouen's hand.

Rouen gave her a puzzled look, opening the box.

"So you do." Rouen pulled out the ring he designed for her, shocked she had it and created a virtually identical one for him. "How did..." Not sure he wanted to know the answer, he didn't finish his question and handed the rings to the judge.

"I also have some land in England willed to me by some low-ranking gentleman five hundred years ago."

"Low-ranking?" Rouen raised a brow, playfully disagreeing with her statement.

Jillian nodded at the magistrate. "Can we finish getting married instead of debating the status of some dead aristocrat?"

Rouen took the ring the justice offered him. He smiled, remembering the first time he held it in 1537. The jeweler had stared at him, worried that he hadn't properly brought the earl's vision to life. The anxiety disappeared from the jeweler's face as Rouen praised the man's skill in creating the perfect piece for his betrothed. Like the jeweler's anxiety, the fears Rouen had of providing for them vanished as he slid the ring onto Jillian's finger.

Once the rings were exchanged and the marriage certificate signed, the magistrate wished them a good night.

Rouen happily escorted his new wife to the cab waiting for them.

"When do you want to return home, my lord?" Jillian noticed how Rouen's lips twitched into a slight smile.

"Do not say that too loud. You will garner more attention than we can deal with tonight. As far as returning to Stafford, we will be on the first flight after our daughter is born, Jillian Durrant."

"How do you know we are having a girl?"

"I saw Nurse Ferguson after your appointment the other day. I had planned on paying the bill only to find someone else already had. She saw me in the hall and shared that she believes we are having a little girl. We will confirm that next week." Rouen opened the cab door for her.

"Will you be disappointed if you have a daughter instead of a son?" Jillian knew how nobles prized sons in the past.

"No, not at all. I will treasure her as I treasure her mother." Rouen never expected Jillian to ask him a question like that with as much as he longed for a family.

Giselle's words rang true. A woman of his time would not provide him with heirs or a happy marriage. The woman meant to do so was from a different age.

He couldn't care less if he had a son or daughter as long as they were born healthy. "The news of a daughter gives me additional incentive to take my wife to my bed each night. Her conception proves that I can be blessed with children of my own. I hope the future holds a son for me. If not, I look forward to raising a house full of daughters."

"A house full? How many children do you plan on having, Mister Durrant? I am not exactly a young woman." Jillian could barely imagine one child at the moment, much less a house full.

"I will be satisfied with one if that is all you wish, but don't expect me to abstain from my conjugal rights now that you are my wife." Rouen muttered in her ear.

"I wouldn't dream of asking you to do such a thing, husband. We have other methods of birth control in the twenty-first-century. I enjoy your rights as much as you do." Jillian laughed before she kissed him.

"That's good to hear, Mrs. Durrant, as I intend to spend the rest of the evening exercising those rights."

**

Jillian expected to wake up beside a smiling Rouen. Instead, she woke to him not sounding happy on a phone call. Seeing she was awake, Rouen ended the call.

"What was that about?"

"Work." Rouen smiled then softly placed his lips against hers, giving her a lingering good morning kiss. "There is no higher honor I have than being your husband, mon coeur. I am a blessed man to be given this lifetime with you."

"You flatter me, Rouen of Normandy." Jillian mimicked the old formal manner of speech he used, making him laugh.

"Sadly, my love, I have to go out of town for a few days. I need to attend a training seminar in London. Are you okay being here alone or should I find someone to stay with you?"

"I'll be fine. It will give me a chance to go sight-seeing."

"Promise me that means visiting places around town

and no mountainside hikes. Also, no activities that will cause your husband to worry about what you may be doing in his absence, especially since you are with child."

"So, no base jumping or hang gliding?" Jillian innocently stared up at him.

"Good god, woman! Are you trying to give me a heart attack?"

Jillian laughed. "I wouldn't dream of it, Lord Hurrey. We better grow old and gray together this time around. You're not allowed to die anytime soon." Jillian kissed him. "Or get arrested for something like treason while you are back in England."

"I will do my best to avoid the Tower." Rouen chuckled, enjoying how Jillian drew him back into the pillows and draped her leg over his.

Her arms settled around his shoulders. "You'd better. You'll have a very unhappy spouse if you don't."

His hand traveled down her back and over the curve of her hip, pulling her closer against him. "I definitely can't have that, not with being a newlywed."

"No more Tower talk, make love to me instead, mon prince.

CHAPTER THIRTY-SEVEN

Kieran and Rouen entered the private conference room reserved for the order. William, Jordan, and Brian sat at the large table awaiting the two of them.

"Rouen, we understand you intend to return to England." William extended a hand to the man.

Rouen clasped it and flashed a friendly smile. "With Jillian inheriting the land in Stafford, I thought it only made sense for us to settle there."

"Sit down. Let's discuss some potential employment opportunities for you and how the order can help with the move."

The calm demeanor Rouen maintained throughout the conversation surprised Kieran. He knew there was nothing cordial about this visit. The former Norman knight was in the order's offices to learn who sent Jillian to Vienna.

Kieran sat beside Rouen, not detecting any hint of the three men knowing a thing about the events that transpired.

As the meeting wrapped, William raised his hands. The

colorful, enameled cuff links he wore caught Kieran's attention. Only one jeweler in Europe made that style of cufflink.

Kieran nudged Rouen and nodded towards William.

Rouen studied William, but didn't see whatever Kieran did.

William reached to shake Rouen's hand again, giving Kieran a good view of the cufflinks.

"His cufflinks." Kieran coughed the statement then picked up a glass, pretending to have something caught in his throat.

Rouen tightened his grasp on William's hand and turned the man's wrist, now noticing the green, gold, and gray enameled round pins keeping the white starched sleeve shut. "Interesting design. The gold trim makes the greens stand out. They go nicely with your tie."

William gave Rouen a big smile and pulled his jacket sleeve back to better show them off. "They are unique. I bought them in Vienna before flying to New York last month."

The speed at which Rouen pinned William to the wall stunned even the seasoned fighters in the room. "She could have been killed by your scheming, you miscreant bastard! Do you have the slightest clue what I would do to a man who caused the death of my wife and child, William?"

William choked from how tightly Rouen's hand clasped his throat. He squirmed against the pressure. "You refused to go to her. What else was I supposed to do to reunite the two of you?"

"Pick a safer location. Tell me things were not serious between her and Kieran, along with a thousand other things I can think of."

"Let him go, Rouen!" Jordan slowly approached the two men.

Rouen glanced over at Jordan. "Stay out of this, D'Aberon."

"You're threatening our grandmaster!"

Rouen shifted his gaze back to William. "This pathetic, lubberwart eating bobolyne and child endangerer doesn't deserve that position."

"I didn't know about the baby." William sputtered.

"What was that? I don't think I heard it clearly." Rouen lifted William slightly off the ground.

"I swear, Uncle, I didn't know about the baby!"

"He's telling the truth, Rouen. I never reported Jillian's pregnancy." Kieran wondered if Rouen would actually strangle Willian.

Rouen released his grip on William then shoved him away from the wall. "If the order ever does anything that even remotely harms my wife or children in the future, I will hunt down everyone who swore an oath, family or not, William. Do you understand me?"

Catching his breath, William stared over at Rouen. "Jesus, you're as foul tempered as your father. You can't go around choking and threatening people in this day and age, Rouen."

"Since you failed to understand my earlier request to look after Jillian's best interests and keep her safe, I want to ensure you understand what will happen if you ever do something so reckless again."

"I was looking after her best interest and yours, you bloody, ungrateful wanker! I am also fulfilling your father's last request with saving you from your wounds and sending you to the twenty-first century. Had I known this would be my thanks for doing so, I would have let you die from the assassin's blade."

"My father's last request? I fulfilled my father's wishes by killing Giselle."

"That wasn't his last request. Now, can we put the whole Jillian fell from a cliff thing behind us since the woman lived, and you two are finally married as you should be? I'd much rather get along with my family members than fight with them." William poured himself a glass of water, surprised Rouen behaved as he did.

"Wait. You saved him in 1540 to fulfill William's last wish?" Kieran wanted to make sure he heard everything correctly.

"Yes. After Rouen passed out from shock, Brian and Jordan told Charles to inform the king of his death. They took Rouen to modern-day Vienna, so no sixteenth-century acquaintances would find him as he recovered. I planned to bring Jillian to see Rouen the night we met in Westminster, but the woman declined a second chance with him, and foolishly threatened to expose the order if we did anything to disgrace his memory."

"What?" Rouen couldn't believe Jillian would do such a thing.

Brian now interjected into the discussion. "In Lady Jillian's defense, William neglected to tell her you were alive. She was worried we'd fish you out of the afterlife and didn't want to destroy any chance of peace your soul may have found. Jordan also wasn't very cordial to her that night." Brian caught the glare Rouen shot Jordan. "He did not behave in a manner that requires your intercession, Rouen. If he had, I would have boxed his ears, as I was present."

Kieran grasped why William threatened to discredit

Jillian's work. He was protecting the order as much as he was Rouen. "You didn't want her to publish the book as you knew the second she did the abbey would learn no one was in the tomb, and a records search would draw direct attention to the order."

"Yes." William looked over at Rouen. "I was also ensuring Droyn Hurrey remained a hero in the eyes of history since Cromwell tarnished his name with the conspiracy crap he made up. You should have let them take Croxden. Jordan could have relocated the monks to France."

"There is no way I was allowing Cromwell to dissolve Croxden. Not with what was hidden there at the time." Rouen grinned at his nephew.

The familiarity between the four men confused Kieran. "Are all of you from the Middle Ages?"

"No." William shook his head. "The only men from another age are Rouen, Brian, and Jordan. These three unlucky blackguards fell under the dominion of Giselle's magic. Once the founding members of the order figured out who Giselle picked to tempt as her main champion, they provoked the witch, causing her to curse two additional knights, the ones supposedly found dead in the old tale, to look after the apparent Prince of Surliness."

Rouen rolled his eyes at the title. "I am only surly when provoked."

"But, you called him uncle?" Kieran still worked to put the pieces of the puzzle together.

William laughed. "He is my however-many-greats uncle. I am descended from his half-sister Adela of Normandy. If his name or legacy gets slandered, so does mine. What say you, Rouen, are Normandy and England once again allies?"

Rouen grinned, offering William his hand. "We are,

William of England."

The two men hugged one another, letting the past be in the past.

William looked over at the knight who posed as Rouen's steward. "Brian, when can Rouen return to Stafford?"

"The renovations on the property should be complete in another month. If everything stays on track, he and Jillian can reclaim their home after that."

"They will stay on track or a certain steward will be fired." William grinned, sharing he only joked with Brian then turned back to Rouen. "Shall we expect our new Vice President of Government Affairs in the office, say, two months from today? Is that enough time for the move?"

"Sixty days is more than adequate to arrange for everything from Vienna to be brought to England. We will probably need longer to relocate Jillian's possessions from the US."

"I will see to storing and moving everything from Jillian's residence. I assume you do not want her traveling extensively until after the child is born." Brian was already used to handling logistics for the order and Rouen.

"It is perfectly safe for a woman to travel while pregnant this day and age. You two need to get with the times or Jillian's going to end up upbraiding the both of you." Kieran made Rouen chuckle.

"Leave me to worry about my wife, Kieran."

Kieran clapped Rouen on the shoulder. "As much as it pains me to say it, I am happy for you both, Rouen. She was devastated when we first got back. She really loves you."

William felt a little bit guilty for causing Jillian's injuries. "I wish we had known about the child. I would have left directions to your apartment instead of sending her out on the trail."

"Another option you had besides doing what you did." Rouen scowled once more at his nephew.

William rolled his eyes. "I need scotch, not water with you back in England. You are the biggest pain in the arse I've ever had to deal with, Durrant."

Rouen ignored the comment, looking back at Kieran. "Why didn't you tell William?"

"Jillian didn't want anyone to know. After all you went through, she was afraid of word getting out about a new Durrant. I only knew because she felt I should since we were dating. She didn't want any misunderstandings between us about who the baby's father was."

Brian gave Kieran a reprimanding stare. "Those are not valid reasons for a knight to withhold information from his superiors. What made you think you had the right to make such a decision?"

"I promised Charles Brandon I would protect Jillian. We both know the duke would have relayed that to Rouen if Cromwell lied about his execution. Additionally, from my perspective, her welfare and the child's should come before the order's agendas."

"You exercised excellent judgement and the highest loyalty to the Durrant family, Sir Moreland. Far exceeding that of your three superiors combined." Rouen complimented his former romantic rival.

"Especially this one." Rouen lightly smacked Brian on the backside of the head. "I know you put the plane ticket in her bag along with sending the texts the night prior to her flight. I half-wonder if the blame for all of this should fall on you, and not William. You, of all people, Chastain, should have known better."

Brian punched Rouen in the arm. "I brought her the deed to Stafford and covered the medical bills to make up for that. And who do you think gave her the wedding rings you both wear? It wasn't exactly easy stealing the ring back once Cromwell's greedy flunkies confiscated it from your room, not to mention having to worry about being mugged carrying it, along with the new one for you, on my person in present-day London. Churlish pillock."

CHAPTER THIRTY-EIGHT

Jillian sat at the table feeding Aveline. The little girl just started eating baby food. They named her after Rouen's mother. Aveline had his and her grandmother's gray eyes, but her mother's brown hair.

"I am afraid you will never be able to describe your family as normal, Avie." Jillian caught some food from the baby's lip with the spoon.

The little girl touched her mother's face and cooed.

Jillian smiled, thinking about how crazy the past two years or so had been: traveling to Urbino, meeting Rouen, finding herself in Tudor England, learning she was pregnant after returning to modern day, and finding Rouen once more in Vienna. When she and Nathan divorced, never would she have imagined she would be remarried with a child of her own and living in England, especially with how quickly everything happened. The move back to Stafford only experienced a few minor hiccups. She talked Rouen into legally changing his name back to an Anglicized version of his real one. He was now Rowan Durrant-Hurrey instead of Henry Strauss. Once they settled into their new lives, the days passed relatively smoothly with only the routine issues life brings.

Jillian's cell phone rang, making Aveline jump. The toddler reached for the phone as Jillian picked it up from the table.

"You think it's daddy, don't you? He won't be off work for another hour." Jillian looked at the phone to see who was calling, "It's Uncle Kieran. I bet he finally mustered the courage to ask Catherine out. Hel..."

"Jillian, turn on the television now!" Kieran didn't even let her get the word hello completely out. "Have you got it on?"

"Hang on a second. What channel?" Jillian turned on the TV, concerned by how excited he was. *What was going on?*

"Ten. They're just replaying the story."

Jillian increased the volume. A reporter standing outside Westminster held a book up to the camera.

"Oh my god! How did they get that?" Jillian recognized *The Tale of Rouen* in the reporter's hand. The book was supposed to stay within the family.

"A second book by the same author about Droyn Hurrey, the sixteenth-century Earl of Stafford, hit the shelves as well today. The book is a detailed account of a relatively unknown magnate responsible for Stafford County under Henry VIII. The only thing previously published about the man was that he stopped an assassination attempt on the king by a French Catholic ambassador. Both books have created quite a stir. The first is the revival of an old fairy tale. It suggests that William the Conqueror had a son with a woman other than Mathilda. There is no evidence to support this as accurate, but it certainly has England's leading historical minds talking with the two books being released simultaneously. The author's pen name Lady Di Rouen has the publishing world searching for her."

Jillian couldn't believe the both manuscripts hit the market, and the media picked them up.

"Kieran, I gave my word to bury my research, so no one else could find it. I turned everything over to the order. Any idea who sold them to a publisher?"

Kieran sighed, as frustrated as she was. "No clue. They were locked in the order's vaults. There is only one other copy of *Tale of Rouen*, which you have in your home safe. The printing of that copy was done in-house so that is not how these got out. I have reporters knocking on my door and requesting commentary on William's son. What do you want me to tell them?"

"I don't know. I need to speak with Rouen. Has he seen this mess?"

Rouen appeared on the flat screen. He walked towards a car waiting for him.

"Oh, no!" Jillian mumbled. In his new role as VP of Government Affairs, Rouen had learned to manage the press well, but the reporters were about to jump on him about a personal matter, which was a drastically different thing than the orders' programs and initiatives. Rouen didn't like any personal questions a reporter or two dared to ask at previous press events.

"He handles it all very well. They caught him on his way to lunch." Kieran reassured her as she watched the clip.

Rouen looked startled by the cameras and the questions, but was polite and collected. She laughed when he told one reporter he needed to expand his reading list as he hadn't read either book.

"Isn't the earl your ancestor with the two of you sharing

the last name Hurrey? And do you have ties to William's illegitimate son, Rouen Durrant? It's odd your name is similar to the two main characters of these books."

The questions threw Rouen by the way his brows raised. Jillian half thought Rouen might tell the man off. Instead, Rouen recovered with a brilliant smile and a nod of his head.

"I can confirm being related to the Earl of Stafford, but until we know more about the first man, I have no clue. It is a fairy tale. A work of fiction. There's no evidence to suggest William had an illegitimate son. Aren't we all related to William anyhow? I recently read that something like 1.5 million people have him in their family tree."

The reporters laughed. A second journalist stepped closer to Rouen. "They often say there is a bit of truth to tales of the period."

Rouen once again smiled. "My wife would call that phenomena origin myth. I am no literary expert or historian, but I believe fairytales and origin myths are two entirely separate things. Now, if you'll excuse me, I have an important meeting to get to."

The front door of the house opened then loudly shut. "Jillian?"

Rouen hoped to speak with Jillian before she learned of what transpired via the news or someone else.

"In the dining room." Jillian answered, still watching the news from where she sat.

Rouen came down the foyer to the family room that transitioned into a large open kitchen and dining room. "Jillian, we need to talk."

"I already know." Jillian gestured to the TV.

He cursed, seeing himself on the television screen.

"Kieran, I will call you back."

"Wait! Don't hang up!" Both men shouted before she could hit end call.

Rouen took the phone from Jillian. "Kieran?"

By the way Rouen looked at Jillian, she knew Kieran filled him in on the reporters outside his flat. "Tell them you need to research the issue further. The Society will issue an initial response in the next few days... The author?" Rouen studied Jillian. "You spoke with her management a few moments ago. She will join the Society in making the official statement if her schedule permits. All further press or publishing inquiries should be directed to Jordan or myself. Call me back after you take care of the reporters."

Rouen worried about his wife with the breaking news. "Are you all right?"

"I am fine; though, I am wondering who published the pieces. I only wrote them for the order's archives. How are you holding up with your various lives being made public?"

"Trying to figure out what to do next. I came home as soon as I could after the news crews showed up at the office."

Rouen kissed Jillian, relieved she seemed unbothered by the books being released.

Aveline squealed loudly, noticing her father after Jillian shut off the TV. The squeal was followed by spoon banging against the high chair and excited babbling.

He picked her up as he always did when he came home. "Hello, little one. What are we eating for an afternoon snack?"

Aveline swiped her spoon across Rouen's mouth, making him grimace.

"How you think this tastes good, Avie, is beyond my

comprehension. No wonder you spit it out everywhere."

As if disagreeing with him, she stuck her spoon back in her mouth and chewed on it. He grinned as she stared up at him, reminding him of her mother.

"You are going to cause me a great deal of anxiety when you are older. I can already see the independent, stubborn streak in you. What do you want to do about the books, Lady Di Rouen?"

Jillian wasn't sure what to say. "I don't know. Why would anyone release them?"

"Because the world should know my however-many-greats uncle's qualities and stories as well as they do William's other sons." William walked into the house. "You are parents. You should understand having pride in your family."

"You released the books?" Jillian couldn't believe what he admitted. The same man, who threatened to destroy her if she published any of her research, now opened Pandora's box to brag about his lost uncle to the modern world.

"I did."

"You promised me you would not ever do anything that would harm or disgrace Rouen." Jillian snapped, furious.

"And I have kept my word. Those books honor him with his wife writing them. My uncle deserves to be remembered with all that he has done. The proceeds from the two works provide income for him and his family."

"While they honor his past, they threaten his present and future. What if someone exhumes the grave and finds no one in it as you once pointed out to me? Or worse yet, puts two and two together and figures out Rouen lived three lifetimes?" Jillian almost shouted, making Aveline whimper.

"Lower your voice, sweetheart. You are upsetting Avie." Rouen calmed the toddler in his arms. It always baffled him how sensitive she was to any sort of raised voice around her. He kept his voice steady and low, so he did not spook her again. "While I appreciate what you are trying to do, William, I agree with Jillian. I do not need to be more than legend and don't want my family hounded. There is no point in a second chance here if I cannot live it with my wife."

"I have taken steps to prevent too much of an invasion into your personal life. Rouen, this could potentially pay for Avie's education or free you up to spend more time at home as you want. I have four publishers in a bidding war over both books. BBC is interested in making a miniseries on the earl since his story is unknown, and a film studio is interested in exploring making *Tale of Rouen* into a movie."

"How is that possible? You just released the books today." Jillian knew how hard authors worked to make things like that happen. Successful marketing of a work to lead to movie deals or a miniseries took months.

"I pre-marketed the works and got them into the right hands before they went public. All Lady Di Rouen needs to do is come forward to negotiate the sale of the rights to the books. What say you, Lady Durrant?"

"I defer to my husband on the matter. The books are *his* story. He is the only one with the right to make his history public. I merely put words on a page." Jillian took Avie from Rouen so that Rouen could discuss the situation further with William.

Rouen stopped her from leaving the kitchen. "It is our story when it comes to the Earl of Stafford. I want your voice heard in this decision."

Jillian sat down in the chair he gestured to. Rouen stood behind her and placed his hands on her shoulders. They were going to be a unified front.

"What assurances do we have that the press won't show up on our doorstep or any ill will come from the release of the books?" Rouen questioned William.

"You know I cannot promise you a hundred percent privacy, but I can help you manage the mayhem until it dies down. I will do what I can to prevent the press from parking outside your home. I already thought about what historians or archaeologists might be tempted to do. Another corpse is laid in your tomb. Honestly, the harm that could come from this is mild. You have a great story that the world wants to know, Rouen. Make your family proud and share it."

"Jillian, what do you want me to do, love? Do you want to move ahead with this new plan my impetuous nephew set in motion? The media attention will focus on you as the historian and author more than the rest of us." Rouen looked down at his wife and daughter.

"I will do whatever you believe is best. There was a time you wanted your secrets kept. If we agree to sell the rights, the whole world will know them."

Rouen squeezed her shoulders as he debated what to do. "The earl and prince took those secrets to the grave with them. Rowan Durrant-Hurrey has no secrets. The only things I have to protect now are you and Avie."

"You do have an incredible story worthy of a book or movie." Jillian admired her husband before looking at William. "And I guess the world can always use another hero."

"There are never enough heroes for us to look up to." William hoped they would allow the mass distribution plan to move ahead.

Rouen wanted to ensure his nephew understood that he was not happy for being placed in a precarious position. "You are reckless, self-serving, and avaricious to do what you have without discussing it with Jillian and I before now. We both know those aren't my father's most admirable traits. Actions like this provide fodder for those that enjoy highlighting the negative depictions of William I; they do not enhance our family's reputation, nor that of the order."

Jillian knew Rouen struck a nerve with how red William's face turned. William hated negative depictions of his ancestors.

Before William could snarl anything back, Rouen continued. "Even with all of that said, I realize your intent holds some good. Set up the meetings to hear the offers. Both the author and myself are to be given full knowledge of everything being done with the two pieces of literature."

Jillian wasn't sure they were ready for the changes headed their way. Hopefully, the spectacle around the books would fade as quickly as it came on. "Who came up with the pen name?"

"I did. You are the Lady of Rouen, are you not?" William owned Jillian's new alter-ego.

"Next time, I get to make up my pen name or use my own. I am not fond of Lady for a first name."

CHAPTER THIRTY-NINE

Rouen and William watched from the sides of the stage as Jillian and Kieran issued a formal statement from the historical society on *Tale of Rouen*.

A low murmur swept through the crowd as Kieran announced that newly discovered evidence suggested William indeed had a son out of wedlock with a woman named Aveline, who died giving birth to Rouen. While the new book certainly had some fantasy and fiction to it, the society was thrilled with the possibility that the main character actually lived in the Middle Ages. An ongoing dig in York produced well-preserved church records on Rouen. The Society was working with French partners to determine what might be in their archives to corroborate the records found in York.

The two of them fielded questions on the historical findings and elements of the story. After twenty minutes, Jordan announced there was no time left for further questions and ended the press conference. He escorted Jillian over to Rouen.

Rouen placed his arm around Jillian's waist, noting the

concern on her face as she stared at the mass of people they needed to pass through. "Stay beside me. Jordan and I will clear the way."

***

"Mrs. Hurrey, I have one last question for you." A reporter jogged up to them.

Rouen kept Jillian moving forward. "I am sorry, sir, but the conference is over. You can email or call my office with whatever question you have about Rouen or William and we will get an answer to you."

"My question is about the Earl of Stafford, not the Norman knight. Droyn's story is quite incredible with two very passionate love affairs. While we know what happened to Vivian, not much is known about what becomes of Jillian. It is kind of ironic that the woman bears your name and you end up marrying a Hurrey from Stafford five hundred years later, then write a book on the family. Do you believe in kismet?"

Jillian halted Rouen and thought about her answer as a few more news crews joined them.

"The similarity in names is an odd, but an explainable coincidence. The first-born female in each generation of my family has Jillian as a first or middle name going back centuries. Rouen's family regularly recycled names over time, just as many others have. Isn't that a European naming convention and tradition? Just look at how many Elizabeths, Annes, James, and Henrys there are in England. As to kismet, call me an old-fashioned romantic, but I firmly believe in it. How else could an American and a Brit randomly meet and fall in love?

Rouen grinned, gently pressing his hand into the small of Jillian's back, prompting her to start walking again.

The same insistent reporter followed them.

Rouen protectively pulled Jillian closer, not liking how the journalist continued on when the others respectfully fell back. He unlocked and opened the car door for Jillian then directed her to get inside. The relief in her expression that they would escape the media and curiosity seekers conveyed Jillian's thoughts on the press conference.

The reporter grabbed the car door, sorely testing Rouen's patience.

"Mrs. Hurrey, your book reads like you were in Jillian and Rouen's head at the time. I would really love to know how you were able to develop Rouen's perspective as a woman."

Jillian set her hand on Rouen's arm, seeing her husband's temper start surfacing with the glare he shot the man. If only the correspondent realized the danger he placed himself in.

"This is the last answer for today. Any more questions or statements need to come through Jordan or Rouen's offices. As you might have noticed, I have an amazingly supportive husband. He encouraged my research into Droyn Hurrey and assisted in the publishing of the books. Without him, there would be no story. The manuscripts would have stayed on the computer, and the world would never know the Earl of Stafford or Rouen of Normandy. Please keep in mind that both books contain a mix of fact and fiction. That is what makes historical fiction fun to write. When I needed Rouen or Droyn's perspective, my husband helped provide it after reviewing the research and documents I had. Ultimately, my husband is the inspiration for both works. Have a good day." Jillian climbed into the car and smiled up at Rouen.

Rouen intentionally bumped into the newsperson when he shut Jillian's door to send a clear warning that the man overstepped his boundaries.

The physical contact forced the reporter away from the car. He stared at Rouen in disbelief as the knight turned executive climbed into the driver's seat.

"You don't want to cross the man when it comes to his wife." William stepped off the sidewalk with a smile, gently grasped the correspondent's arm, and moved the man out of the way, so Rouen could pull out.

The journalist recognized the CEO of Alencon-Deveroux Industries. "Hurrey's never been ill-tempered to a member of the press before."

William laughed. "He's never represented his wife until now. Being the media liaison for a business is far different from acting as such for a family member. Next time, back off when the man tells you to."

After a few months, the commotion around the books died down.

Rouen and Jillian enjoyed the quiet of the evening. Avie slept soundly in her room. Jillian read a new book released on Charlemagne to use in a lecture the university invited her to give.

Rouen pulled it out of her hands. "Avie is almost a year old."

"I know." Jillian wondered what he was up to with the intent look on his face.

"I think that it is time for us to start working on a brother or sister for her, Lady Durrant. If we were still in the fifteen-hundreds, your belly would already be swollen with my second child."

"I suppose we could do that. Most doctors would recommend waiting at least another year." Jillian wrapped her arms around his neck.

"Why don't we put it in fate's hands, mon coeur? That seems to work well for us."

Two years later to the day, Rouen proudly held the

future of the Durrant legacy. He cradled his newborn son in one arm, with his other around his daughter. Avie sat in his lap, looking down at her little brother, telling the newborn she loved him already.

Jillian napped on the couch across from them.

William couldn't help but smile at his uncle and new cousins. Half of the order's primary mission was now complete. At long last, William the Conqueror's actual final wish of Rouen being gifted the same legacy and honors as his recognized sons was beautifully carried out. The guilt of what Rouen gave up to protect others ate at the old king as time went on. Hopefully, the Norman ruler rested easy with Giselle dead and Rouen finally having the family and peace he long desired.

All the wrongs of the past were finally set right. Thus, truly ends the tale of Rouen of Normandy; he and his wife were destined to live...

Happily Ever After.

ABOUT THE AUTHOR

Caterina is passionate about history, music, romance, old languages, and travel. She regularly intertwines these subjects in her writing.

When not traveling or working, Caterina finds time to sing classical music, make soutache jewelry, write, paint, shoot archery, and fence. She is always up for trying something new so the list of hobbies is ever expanding.

If you would like to contact her or learn more about her and future works, you can find her on Twitter, Facebook, Instagram, and at her website, https://caterinanovelliere.com.

If you enjoyed *Tale of Rouen*, check out the first two books in Caterina's historical fantasy series about the Four Horsemen, *Mark of The Night* and *When The Moon Bleeds*.

www.ingramcontent.com/pod-product-compliance
Lightning Source LLC
Chambersburg PA
CBHW030249270626
47156CB00021B/281